TERRORS OF THE TOMB . . .

An Italian Prince is selling something more sinister than art objects in **View by Moonlight.**

The Sword of Damocles is put to murderous modern use in **There Hangs Death!**

An insane killer explains the method of his madness in **The Pattern.**

When Emma discovers the secret ingredient in her lover's tobacco, their romance goes up in smoke in **Pipe Dream.**

Mr. and Mrs. Duvec argue fiercely, but death has the last word in **The Sound of Murder.**

ALFRED HITCHCOCK PRESENTS:

I WANT MY MUMMY

(formerly titled *Stories to Be Read with the Door Locked*, Vol. II)

A DELL BOOK

Published by
DELL PUBLISHING CO., INC.
1 Dag Hammarskjold Plaza
New York, N.Y. 10017

Dell ® TM 681510, Dell Publishing Co., Inc.

ISBN: 0-440-13985-6

Reprinted by arrangement with
Random House, Inc.

Printed in the United States of America
Previous Dell Edition
One printing
New Dell Edition
First printing—February 1981

ACKNOWLEDGMENTS

"View by Moonlight" by Pat McGerr: Reprinted by permission of Curtis Brown, Ltd., New York. Copyright © 1964 by Patricia McGerr. Published in *This Week* (United Newspapers Magazines, Inc.), April 19, 1964.

"There Hangs Death!" by John D. MacDonald: Reprinted by permission of the author and the author's agent, Maxwell P. Wilkinson. Copyright © by United Newspapers Magazine Corp.

"Lincoln's Doctor's Son's Dog" by Warner Law: Reprinted by permission of the author's agent, H. N. Swanson, Inc. Copyright © 1970 by *Playboy*. First published in *Playboy* magazine, March 1970.

"Coyote Street" by Gary Brandner: Reprinted by permission of the author. Copyright © 1973 by Gary Brandner. First published in *Ellery Queen's Mystery Magazine*, September 1973.

The editor gratefully acknowledges the invaluable assistance of Harold Q. Masur in the preparation of this volume

CONTENTS

CONTENTS

VIEW
BY MOONLIGHT

Pat McGerr

Far below, the Bay of Naples was an iridescent jewel in the afternoon sun. Selena looked out on the white ships, the Mediterranean's deep blue. The ride was breathtaking—in both its scenic beauty and the perilous curves which her driver, like all Italians, rounded with equal pressure on gas and horn. He was a darkly handsome young man named Eduardo, nephew and secretary to the Prince whose cliffside villa they were approaching. He turned to smile at her, relishing her unease.

"Tomorrow," he said, "you will have a slower ride as my uncle will be himself your chauffeur."

"He is most kind."

"It is no trouble," he assured her. "He has a package to deliver personally to the shippers."

Selena knew about the package. A year earlier the Prince had begun selling parts of his ancestral art collection to an American dealer. Going out tomorrow was a silver vase by famed 16th-century artist Benvenuto Cellini. It would also contain, American agents suspected, a message for Red agents in the United States. That was why Selena had interrupted her European holiday to fly to Naples. She was again working for Security's Section Q.

"It's a neat dodge," her contact had conceded, "pass-

ing instructions and information inside art objects.
They use microdots—film reduced till a whole sheet of
paper is no bigger than the head of a pin. The Prince is
no Communist. But for most of the old aristocrats,
these are lean years and he evidently couldn't resist the
lure of the lire. Several of his bundles got through before our men tumbled. But now they're ready to arrest
the New York importer as soon as we lower the gate on
this side. The Prince's high connections make our
problem more delicate. The Italian authorities will make
a full inspection only if we guarantee they'll find contra-
band. Making sure of that is your job."

"Mine?" she protested. "I've never even seen a mi-
crodot."

"But you speak Italian, you can tell Raphael from da
Vinci and, as a diplomat's daughter, you know people
who can get you an invitation to see the Prince's
treasures. Arrange to be his guest next Tuesday night
and check the vase. What you're looking for is a small
piece of film—like transparent celluloid—with black
dots on it. If you find it, wrap a bright scarf round your
hair when you start down the mountain the next morning. If the vase is clean, ride bareheaded. Our man
will be watching, he'll get word to Naples, and we'll take
it from there."

At the villa the Prince welcomed her with such genuine pleasure that she felt a qualm at betraying the
warm hospitality. The Princess—his wife for less than
two years—was beautiful, gay, imperious and some
thirty years his junior. Seeing her clarified the Prince's
recent need for money. They dined formally, then
toured the gallery. Selena tried to show the proper enthusiasm for the magnificent paintings and tapestry
while she wondered about the Cellini vase. How could
she find it?

At the end of the gallery a shelf of small pieces
gave her the opening she wanted. She picked up a paper
cutter shaped like a dagger whose gold handle was in-
laid with intricate design of leaves, flowers and masks.

"What exquisite workmanship!" she exclaimed. "It must be Cellini."

"You're an admirer of the Florentine?"

"Indeed I am. It's a pity so much of his work has been destroyed."

"You should see our vase," said the Princess carelessly. "It's considered one of his finest."

"You have a silver vase?" she looked inquiringly at the Prince.

"No!" His answer was curt.

"But, Gino, since she loves Cellini—"

"I have no vase."

"Ah, well." The Princess threw her hands in the air. "It goes to your own country. Perhaps you will see it there, since my husband is so obstinate."

"It is packed," Eduardo conciliated. "If only the *signóra* had come yesterday—"

"What is packed can be unpacked." The Princess took the paper cutter, moved to a near-by corner and leaned over a square box. *"Ecco!"* The cutter's steel edge sliced the rope. "Don't look so glum, Eduardo. In the morning you will find another rope and tie it up again."

"The *signóra* must forgive me if I appear discourteous," the Prince said. "It is that I am ashamed. The vase is no longer mine. It is sold and I try to forget it exists. It is not, you understand, a thing of pride to part with beauty for money."

"I'm sorry, *Principe*." Selena moved impulsively forward. "Of course you must not unwrap the vase. You have shown me so much beauty tonight, I should not ask for more."

"No, no, you shall see it." He looked at the Princess, who was raising the box's lid, and his shrug was eloquent. "My wife rules here." He went to her side, tenderly lifted the urn from its nest of excelsior and listened with satisfaction to Selena's admiring exclamations.

The admiration was sincere, but it occupied only the

surface of her mind. Excelsior filled the vase, spilling
from its throat. If there was film, it was buried in this
stuffing. While she spoke she was formulating plans to
examine the interior.

Soon after that they retired. And when the household
was dark and silent Selena slipped cautiously out of her
bedroom. At the foot of the marble staircase she
stopped to listen, heard no movement and went on.
She eased open the gallery door, went inside. A sliver
of moonlight showed her the package, still in its corner,
still topped by the paper cutter with which the Princess
had severed the rope.

She opened the box, took out the vase. She put a
hand inside, moving her fingers slowly and carefully
through the excelsior till she felt a sharp edge and
smooth surface. What she was seeking she had found.
But she felt no triumph, only regret that the Prince's
love of beauty—both ancient and young—had caught
him in so ugly a trap. She drew out the tiny film strip,
hardly distinguishable from the excelsior that covered
it. Suddenly a light flashed in her eyes and the gallery
door clicked shut behind the new arrival.

"So," he said in a sibilant whisper, "we have a guest
who spies."

"Principe," she stammered, "forgive me. This vase—
it's so beautiful. I had to see it once more."

"To see in the dark?" He laughed harshly and she
realized it was not the Prince but his nephew. He
moved the light to focus on the strip and she could see
on it tiny dots like grains of pepper. "You have found
my little cache. You know what it is?"

"I know." She abandoned pretense. "Is it you who
hid it? Not your uncle?"

"The old man knows nothing. When the money runs
out he sells one of his pretty pieces. And I make my
fortune with what I put inside."

"For that you risk prison, disgrace?"

"I risk nothing. The danger, *signóra*, is to you. I have a gun and must now use it. I will explain that I heard sounds in the gallery and thought someone had come to rob us. I will be desolated to discover that it is not a robber I have killed but our American visitor."

"And how——" Selena thrust the strip back into the vase, then upended it and strewed excelsior on the floor around her "——will you explain this?"

"You make trouble for me, *signóra*, but you do not help yourself. After I shoot you, I will gather it up and put it back in the vase."

"In the short time it takes your uncle and the servants to hear the shot and come? Finding your strip will take more than a minute. So the excelsior will still be on the floor when your uncle gets here and, as a man of honor, he'll let nothing be moved till the police are summoned. If they sift it for evidence it will make your story of the killing a little unlikely."

"You are clever," he admitted. "It would be foolish to shoot you here. So I think we will take a walk. I shall show you our view by moonlight." He waved the flashlight toward French doors that opened onto a terrace. "Pray go ahead."

She walked before him through the doors. When they were well away from the house, she paused to point out that his story of shooting a burglar would make no sense if he killed her outside.

"So pretty to be so wise," he mocked. "I no longer intend to shoot you—unless you compel me by disobeying orders. Let us walk in this direction. It is romantic to see the moon on the water." The gun at her back urged her forward while he continued in conversational tone. "You Americans are rich. You do not know what it is like to have a great name and be too poor to support it. Before my uncle married, all this——"

A gesture took in the estate, "——was to some day belong to me. Now I have lost even the expectation. So when it was suggested that I help arrange the sale of some of my uncle's art and then put inside it certain small objects—well, I do what I must. Ah, here we are!"

They had reached the edge of the cliff—a sheer drop of hundreds of feet.

"Scream if you wish," Eduardo said. "No one will hear. At daybreak no doubt a fisherman will discover your body and it will be thought that you were unable to sleep and came for a walk in the dark."

"You—you intend to shoot me and throw me over the cliff?"

"Not to shoot. A bullet would confuse the police. I shall use the other end of the gun. A tap on the head will keep you from struggling and leave only a wound for which the sharp rocks below will account. Pardon, *signóra,* I do only what you make necessary."

Holding the gun by its nose, he lifted his arm, braced himself to bring the butt down with force on her head. As he did so Selena moved closer to him, bringing from the folds of her robe the Cellini paper cutter. Before he could strike she was holding the steel point against the hollow of his throat.

"Drop the gun," she ordered.

"No," he said thickly. With his free hand he tried to pull away the steel but only drove it deeper.

"You've cut me," he shrilled, moved back again, ready to lunge with the gun. But as he did so his foot slipped, he over-balanced and in an instant was himself off the cliff. His scream stopped abruptly as he hit the bottom. The sharp rocks—Selena shivered slightly as his words came back to her—will account for any wound.

She stood undecided for a moment, looking at the dark, silent house. More of Eduardo's words returned in a new context. The police would think he had gone for a walk, stumbled and fallen. Before the body was found there would be time to repack the vase, leave everything as it was before they went to bed. She'd take the tiny film with her, to deliver to Section Q along with her report.

She strengthened, made her decision. Tomorrow she'd ride to Naples bareheaded. With Eduardo dead there was no need to implicate the Prince or even for him to know what had happened. The case would be closed without further hurt to his family pride.

THERE HANGS DEATH!

John D. MacDonald

The dead man was face down on the dark hardwood floor. He was frail and old, and the house was sturdy and old, redolent of Victorian dignity. It was the house where he had been born.

The wide stairs climbed for two tall stories, with two landings for each floor. He lay in the center of the stair well, twenty-five feet below a dusty skylight. The gray daylight came down through the skylight and glinted on the heavy ornate hilt and pommel of the broadsword that pinned the man to the dark floor.

The hilt was of gold and silver, and there was a large red stone set into the pommel. The gold—and the red of stone and red of blood on the white shirt—were the only touches of color.

Riggs saw that when they brought him in. They let him look for a few moments. He knew he would not forget it, ever. The bright momentary light of a police flash bulb filled the hallway, and they turned him away, a hand pushing his shoulder.

There were many people in the book-lined study. He saw Angela at once, her face too white, her eyes shocked and enormous, sitting on a straight chair. He started toward her but they caught his arm; and the wide, bald, tired-eyed stranger who sat behind the old desk said, "Take the girl across the hall and put Riggs in that chair."

Angela gave him a frail smile and he tried to respond. They took her out. He sat where she had been.

The bald man looked at him for a long moment. "You'll answer questions willingly?"

"Of course." A doughy young man in the opposite corner took notes with a fountain pen.

"Name and occupation?"

"Howard Riggs. Research assistant at the University, Department of Psychology."

"How long have you known the deceased?"

"I've known Dr. Hilber for three years. I met him through his niece, Angela Manley, when I was in the Graduate School. I believe he'd retired two or three years before I met him. He was head of the Archeology—"

"We know his history. How much have you been told about this?"

"Not very much. Just that he was dead and I was wanted here. I didn't know he'd been . . ."

"What is your relationship to his niece?"

"We're to be married in June when the spring semester ends."

"Were you in this house today?"

"Yes, sir. I went to church with Angela. I picked her up here and brought her back here. We walked. We had some coffee here and then I went back to the lab. I'm running an experiment using laboratory animals. I have to . . ."

"What time did you leave the house?"

"I'd say it was eleven-thirty this morning. I've been in the lab ever since, until those men came and . . ."

"Were you alone at the lab?"

"Yes, sir."

"Did you see Dr. Hilber when you were here?"

"No, sir."

"Did Miss Manley inform you that she was going to stay here? Did she say anything about going out?"

"She wanted me to go for a walk. I couldn't. I had to get back. We sometimes walk up in the hills back of here."

"Did you know that Miss Manley is the sole heir?"

"I guess I did. I mean I remember him saying once that she was his only living relative. So I would assume . . ."

"Did you know he had substantial paid-up insurance policies?"

"No, sir."

"He opposed this marriage, did he not?"

"No, sir. He was in favor of it. He opposed it at first. He didn't want to be left alone. But after I agreed to move in here after we're married . . . you see, he wasn't well."

"You had many arguments with him, did you not?"

Riggs frowned. "Not like you mean. They were intellectual arguments. He thought my specialty is a sort of . . . pseudoscience. He was a stubborn man, sir."

"You became angry at him."

Riggs shrugged. "Many times. But not . . . importantly angry."

The study door opened and two men came in. The man in uniform who had come in said to the bald man, "Can't raise a print off that sword, Captain. It wouldn't have to be wiped. It's just a bad surface."

The bald captain nodded impatiently. He looked at the second man who had come in. "Doctor?" he said.

"Steve, it's pretty weird," the doctor said. He sat down and crossed long legs. "That sword is like a razor. It was sunk right into the wood."

"If it was shoved through him and he fell on his face, of course it would be stuck in the wood."

"Not like that, Steve. It's a two-edged sword. If he fell after it was through him it would be knocked back. Some of the shirt fibers were carried into the wound. No, Steve, the sword went into him after he was stretched out on his face."

"Knocked out?"

"No sign of it."

"Check stomach contents and so forth to see if he was doped."

"That'll be done. But does it make sense?"

"How do you mean?"

"If you're going to kill a man, do you dope him, stretch him out on the floor and chunk a knife down through him? Now here's something else. After we got him out of the way we found another hole in the floor. A fresh hole, about four inches from where the sword dug in. It's a deeper hole, but it looks to me as if it was made the same way, by the same sword. And there was only one hole in the professor."

The captain got up quickly and went out. Most of the men followed him. Howard Riggs got up and went out, too. He was not stopped. He saw Angela in the small room across the hall. He walked by the man outside her door and went to her. She stood up quickly as he approached. Her face was pale, her eyes enormous. He took her cold hands in his. "Darling," she said, "they act so . . ."

"I know. I know. Don't let it hurt. Please."

"But he's dead, and the way they look at me. As if . . ." She began to cry and he held the trembling slenderness of her in his arms, murmuring reassurances, trying to conceal from her how inept and confused he felt in the face of the obvious hostility of the police.

The hard voice behind him said, "You're not supposed to be in here." A hand rested heavily on his shoulder.

Riggs turned out from under the hand and released Angela. He looked back at her as he left the room. She stood and managed a smile. It was a frail, wan smile, but it was good to see. He hoped he had strengthened her.

Out in the hall the captain was on his knees examining the gouges in the dark wood. He craned his neck back and looked straight up. The men around him did the same. It was a curious tableau.

The captain gave an order and the sword was brought to him. The blade had been cleaned. He hefted it in his hand, took a half cut at the air.

"Heavy damn thing," he said. He glanced at Riggs. "Ever see it before?"

"It's from Dr. Hilber's collection of antique edged weapons. It dates from the twelfth century. He said he believed it was taken on one of the early crusades. The second, I think."

"You men move back down the hall," the captain said. He plodded up the stairs, the incongruous sword gleaming in his hairy fist. Soon he was out of sight, and they could hear him climbing the second flight. There was silence—and then a silvery shimmer in the gray light of the stair well. The sword flashed down, chunked deeply into the floor and stood there, vibrationless.

The captain came back down. He grasped the hilt with both hands, planted his feet, grunted as he wrenched it out of the floor. He smiled at Riggs. "I look at her and I say she could just about lift a sword like this. She couldn't stick it through the old man, but she could drop it through him."

"You're out of your mind!"

"The other hole is where she made a test run when he was out, to see if it would fall right. She says she came back from her walk and found him. But I find clumsy attempts to make it look like a prowler did it. The jade collection in his bedroom is all messed up. We got to check it against his inventory. Dirt tracked into that room where the weapons are. Silver dumped on the floor in the dining room. If Doc wasn't on the ball, that stage setting might have sold me. *Might* have. But now we know it was dropped through him, and it was no theft murder, even if she tried to make it look that way."

They took Angela in on suspicion of murder. They did not let Riggs speak to her. They told him not to leave town. He did not understand why they didn't arrest him also. He sensed that he was being carefully watched.

Though he was emotionally exhausted that night, it took him a long time to get to sleep. A nightmare awakened him before dawn. In his dream a shining sword had been suspended high over him, in utter blackness. He did not know when it would drop. He recognized the similarity to the legend of Damocles. He lay sweating in the predawn silence until his frightened heart slowed its beat. It seemed then that it was the first time he had been able to think logically of the death of Hilber. He thought carefully and for a long time, and when he knew what he would do, he went quickly to sleep.

He walked into the captain's office at two o'clock on Monday. It was raining heavily outside. The captain was in shirt sleeves. "Sit down," the captain said. "You asked to see me, but I'll tell you some things first. The girl is sticking to her story. I half believe her. Besides, that corpse was in the center of the room with the sword sticking straight up. I can't see anybody throwing it and making it land that way, so we're trying to uncover other angles."

"Hilber had a good academic mind, but not what you'd call a practical mind."

"Keep talking."

"If he wanted to kill himself and make it look like murder, he would try to clear Angela by such clumsy business as the dirt tracked in, the silver on the floor, the disorder in the jade case. He'd never stop to think of the next logical step, that the police would accuse Angela of doing all that to mislead them."

"You try to read a dead man's mind and he can't tell you if you're wrong. You've got more than that, haven't you?"

"This morning I talked to his lawyer and his doctor, Captain, and I went to the house and they wouldn't let me in."

"I know that."

"He had very little money. His illness used up most of it. He had forty-five thousand in insurance, in two policies, one of ten and one for thirty-five thousand. There is a suicide clause in the larger policy."

"So he heaved a sword up in the air and it came down and hit him in the back."

"He was operated on two years ago. The operation was not completely successful. The malignancy returned and this time it was widespread. He had six months to two years, and in either case it would not have been pleasant."

"So?"

"Did you ever hear of the Sword of Damocles?"

The captain frowned. "They hung it on a thread over some joker's head when he wanted to be king, didn't they? It would take a special kind of nerve. Some timing device. Candle maybe. Let's go take a look, Riggs."

They looked. The captain brought the sword along. They experimented. It would have had to drop from the top floor. The railing encircled three sides of the stairwell. Nothing was tied to the railing. Nothing had been fastened to the skylight. They searched for a long time. The captain thought of the possible use of rubber bands, so they would snap back into one of the bedrooms. They could find nothing. The captain rubbed his bald head. "No goods, Riggs. The sword had to be dead in the middle. Nothing could have held it. The girl didn't come upstairs. The house was searched after we got here. And who could have held the sword out that far—in the center of the room?"

"Let me look around some more, please."

"Go ahead."

Riggs finally wandered to the study. Dr. Hilber had spent most of his time there. He sat moodily in Hilber's chair and went back over every aspect of the previous day to see if he could remember anything that would help.

They had come back from church. Angela had opened the front door with her key, mildly surprised to find it locked. They had walked back through to the kitchen. He remembered that Angela had wondered if her uncle would put in his usual appearance for Sunday morning coffee, then thought that he was probably immersed in reading one of the many scholarly books that were so much a part of his life. She had decided not to disturb him.

The memory of the morning gave him no clue. The Sword of Damocles had hung over the stairwell. And it had fallen. And the means of suspension was utterly gone, as though it had never been. As though it had vanished. He sat very still for a long moment and then got up quickly.

Angela was released at six. Riggs was asked to perform the experiment again for the city District Attorney and two members of his staff. He and the captain had found the proper material after experimenting with various kinds of thread, and had purchased a sufficient supply of rayon tire cord yarn. Riggs took the sword to the top floor, knotted one end of the yarn around the metal railing, and cut off a piece long enough to reach to the opposite railing. To the middle of that piece he tied a length sufficient to reach to the floor far below. He then tied the sword to the middle of the strand, took the free end around and tied it to the opposite railing. The sword danced and shimmered in the air and grew still.

They all went back down to the main floor. Riggs lighted a match and touched it to the strand of yarn hanging down. It caught at once and a knot of flame raced up the piece of yarn with stunning speed. Soon the heavy sword fell and imbedded its point deeply into the hardwood of the hallway.

By the time they reached the top railing, all traces of the suspension method had disappeared. The heat generated had not been sufficient to leave any mark on the metal railings.

The District Attorney sighed. "It's half crazy, but I guess I've got to buy it."

The captain shook his head and said, "It's the only thing possible. Nobody could have thrown that sword and made it land at that angle—or rather without an angle. And that sfuff he used doesn't leave a trace. Without Riggs figuring it out, though, I don't know where we'd be."

The District Attorney stared curiously at Riggs. "How did you figure it out?"

"He was a classical scholar and with this setup—" Riggs indicated the open space above them and the railings. "It almost had to be based on the legend of the Sword of Damocles. That and the second hole in the floor. Those were the clues. He tested the method while we were out. That's why there were two holes in the floor. The Sword of Damocles gave him his idea. Modern technology gave him the method."

And then he was free to go to Angela.

LINCOLN'S DOCTOR'S
SON'S DOG

Warner Law

Among the local coterie of truly important writers, of which I am a leading member, it's legendary that Mark Twain once said that since books about Lincoln are proverbially best sellers, and since stories about doctors are always popular, and since Americans love to read about dogs, a story about Lincoln's doctor's dog must surely make a mint; and Twain said he was going to write it as soon as he could think of a story about the confounded dog.

After considerable research, I can't find that Mark Twain ever said this at all. But it's a widely printed anonymous witticism, and it sounds so much like Twain that if he didn't say it, he should have, so let's just accept it as a genuine Mark Twain quotation.

Since he never wrote the story, it's obvious that he had troubles with it. I can guess why. It wasn't the dog at all. There's a vital ingredient missing and, of all writers, Mark Twain should have spotted it. There is not a single freckle-faced American youngster with an engaging smile indicated in this story!

Once this sorry omission has been corrected, the story practically writes itself. And I have written it, in Mark Twain's honor. It's not that I want to make a mint —it's just that in this day of cynical literature, there's a crying need for old-fashioned stories that have true and heart-warming qualities and happy, upbeat endings, and here it is:

It was the fourth of March, in 1865. In Washington, Abraham Lincoln was being inaugurated for his second term.

Back in Springfield, Illinois, young Sam Haskins was alone in his parents' house on a quiet, tree-lined street.

Sam was the son of Dr. Amos Haskins, who was Abraham Lincoln's kindly family doctor and who had delivered all four of the Lincoln boys. The Lincolns loved Dr. Haskins, and so the President had invited him and Mrs. Haskins to come to Washington and be his guests at the Inauguration.

Sam was twelve and an only child. He was disappointed at not being asked to Washington; but since he was a freckle-faced boy with an engaging smile, he was happy because at least his mother and father would be having a fine time. His aunt Sally had come down from Chicago to look after Sam for the week his parents would be away.

Sam was a healthy, well-behaved boy, who seldom got into mischief. His only minor complaint was that his parents were strict vegetarians, so meat was never served in the Haskins family. But Sam was very fond of steaks and roasts and stews, and when he was nine, he'd stolen a meat pie from a neighbor woman's window ledge and his father had birched him for it. Sam knew he'd deserved the whipping and loved his parents just the same, for he was that kind of boy.

Next to his parents, Sam loved his dog, who was a lovable mongrel named Buddy. He was so lovable that everyone loved him—with the exception of Aunt Sally.

On this fourth of March, Aunt Sally had gone out to do some shopping and Sam was alone in the house. Suddenly, there was a banging on the front door. Sam went and opened it, to find Mr. Robbins standing there. He was their next-door neighbor and he was in an absolute fury.

"That damn dog of yours just chewed up my little baby boy!" he shouted at Sam. "He bit him in the calf!"

"Buddy?" Sam exclaimed in disbelief. "No! Not Buddy! He loves your little boy! He'd never hurt him!"

"I found my little boy bleeding from bites in his leg! And Buddy was standing over him and there was blood around his mouth! He could have killed my little boy! He's a vicious dog and I'm going to see that he's destroyed!" Mr. Robbins stormed off.

A little later, Buddy slunk in the back door, looking guilty. Sam saw that there was, indeed, blood around his mouth. But he was sure it wasn't the blood of the Robbins boy, for Buddy was simply not that kind of dog.

Later on, Aunt Sally came home and Sam told her all about this, with tears in his eyes.

"I never *did* like that vicious mongrel!" Aunt Sally said. "Mr. Robbins is right! He *should* be destroyed!"

"But he's *not* a vicious mongrel!" Sam protested.

"There's always a first time!" Aunt Sally said.

Sam realized that he was not going to get too much support from Aunt Sally. He didn't know what to do. He couldn't get in touch with his parents, because he didn't know where in Washington they were staying.

Late that afternoon, Constable Ferguson came to Sam's house. He was a kindly man and Sam knew him well. Reluctantly, he told Sam that Mr. Robbins was bound and determined to have Buddy destroyed and that a court hearing was scheduled before kindly old Judge Lockwood the following afternoon and that Sam would have to appear and bring Buddy.

Now, Sam was desperate. He didn't know to whom to turn. Then he remembered Abraham Lincoln, who had always been so kind to him and who had sat Sam on his knee and told him amusing stories full of wisdom.

Sam ran down to the local telegraph office. The only person on duty was a young telegrapher who was about six years older than Sam. His name was Tom Edison

and Sam knew that one day, Tom would amount to
something. Young Tom was kindly and sympathized
with Sam's problem and, between them, they composed a telegram:

PRESIDENT ABRAHAM LINCOLN. WASHINGTON. I AM
SON OF DR. AMOS HASKINS. THEY ARE TRYING TO PUT
MY DOG TO DEATH FOR SOMETHING HE DID NOT DO.
PLEASE HELP ME. SAM HASKINS.

Young Tom rattled off the message on his key at
lightning speed, but both boys wondered if Mr. Lincoln would ever actually see it himself. He would be a
very busy man now, with the Inauguration and all.

That night, Sam held Buddy in his arms and cried
himself to sleep. Early the next morning, there was a
banging on the Haskins front door. Sam ran down
and opened it, to find young Tom Edison with a telegram addressed to Sam. It read:

GO TO HERNDON'S OFFICE AND TELL THEM I WANT
THEM TO HELP YOU. A. LINCOLN.

Sam knew that William Henry Herndon had been
Lincoln's law partner for many years. As soon as he
had dressed and gulped down some breakfast, Sam ran
downtown to the law offices of Mr. Herndon. There,
he found that Herndon and almost all the others in the
fairly large firm had gone to Washington for the
Inauguration. The only man in the office was a kindly
gentleman named Mr. O'Reilly, who said he was a very
fine attorney. Sam showed him the telegram from
President Lincoln, and Mr. O'Reilly said he would be
in court that afternoon and that he was a crackerjack
orator and was sure he could talk the judge into spar-
ing Buddy's life.

That afternoon, dressed in his Sunday best and accompanied by Aunt Sally, and with Buddy on a long
rope, Sam set out for the Springfield courthouse. It

was a long walk and Sam had somehow injured his right leg and it became sore, and Sam was limping.

Outside the courthouse he took off his cap and saluted the American flag that flew over the building and then paid his respects to George Washington, whose statue stood in the courthouse square.

In the courtroom, Sam sat down at the defense table, next to Mr. O'Reilly. Buddy curled up at Sam's feet. Sam noticed that Mr. O'Reilly smelled of whiskey and seemed half asleep.

Then kindly old Judge Lockwood came in to preside over this informal hearing. Mr. Robbins told the judge what he'd seen with his own eyes and demanded that this vicious dog be destroyed before he bit any more innocent little children.

Mr. O'Reilly turned to Sam and whispered thickly: "I fear we don't have a chance, m'boy. This Robbins is the judge's brother-in-law."

"But that's not fair!" Sam cried.

"Quiet in the court!" the judge shouted, banging his gavel. Then he said, "Is there anyone here who has the effrontery to speak in defense of this miserable cur?"

At these words, Buddy got to his feet and growled and stared in the judge's direction, and his hair rose on his back.

Sam nudged Mr. O'Reilly. "Say something! Do something!" But Mr. O'Reilly's head had fallen forward onto his chest and he was snoring, in a drunken stupor.

"Well?" the judge demanded.

"*I* want to speak in defense of my dog, Buddy," Sam said bravely and rose to his feet. He addressed the judge, telling him how he had raised Buddy from a puppy and describing his gentle nature and assuring the judge that it was impossible for Buddy to have done this thing.

Judge Lockwood yawned and then said he was sorry but that the evidence indicated to him that the dog was guilty and should be destroyed. "Bailiff," the judge ordered, "take this dog away and put him to death!"

At that moment, Buddy leaped in the direction of the judge's bench with an angry growl, pulling his rope out of Sam's hand. As the dog mounted the steps leading up from the courtroom floor, Judge Lockwood rose in fear, his gavel in hand to protect himself.

But Buddy darted past the judge's seat and began to wrestle with something on the floor. No one but the judge could see what it was.

"Good Lord!" the judge exclaimed. "It's a copperhead!"

What had happened was that Buddy had sensed that a deadly copperhead had slithered in from an adjoining room and was making for the judge, and Buddy had rushed to attack the snake to protect him. In a few moments, Buddy had killed the copperhead and the snake had been taken away.

Buddy returned at once to Sam, who petted him and said, "Good dog, good dog!"

Tears were forming in the judge's eyes. "Well, I'll be . . ." he said. "That dog saved my life! Here I'd sentenced him to death and he saved my life."

"That just *proves* what a good dog he is!" Sam said happily.

"It proves nothing of the kind, you young idiot!" the judge snapped. "All it proves is that this damn dog will bite anything that moves! If an innocent little baby boy had crawled up behind me, he would have tried to kill him, too!"

"That's not true!" Sam shouted.

"Oh, shut up and sit down!" the judge barked. "My order still stands! Bailiff—take the dog!"

As the bailiff moved toward him, Sam rose. "Please, your Honor—I believe in American justice, and if you say Buddy has to die, you must be right, because you're a judge. But wouldn't you let me take care of Buddy myself? Please?"

"How do you propose to destroy him?" the judge asked.

"Well, I'll take him out into the north woods near

the old forked cottonwood on top of the hill," Sam
answered. "And I'll dig a little grave, and then I'll shoot
Buddy though the head with my father's Service pistol
from the Mexican War—which was a just war, no
matter what anyone says—and then I'll bury him."

"How do I know you'll actually do it?" the judge
snarled.

"Because I give you my word of honor that I will,
and I'm Abraham Lincoln's family doctor's son, and
when I say I'll do a thing, I'll do it."

"*When* will you do it?" the judge demanded.

"This very afternoon, sir," Sam answered.

After a moment of glowering thought, the judge said,
"Very well. But if you *don't* do it, I will hold you in
contempt of this court and you could go to prison for
thirty years."

And so it was that later that afternoon, Sam limped
miserably into the woods north of Springfield and up
the hill on which was the old forked cottonwood. Sam
carried his father's loaded pistol in a sack and had a
shovel over his shoulder. Buddy danced around him
at the end of his rope, for Buddy loved to go for walks
in the woods.

Sam tied Buddy to the tree and then dug a small
grave. Watching, Buddy wagged his tail eagerly, for he
was stupid enough to think that Sam was digging up a
bone for him.

The grave finished, Sam got out the pistol and then
called Buddy to him, and the dog came, waggling and
wriggling with happiness. He licked Sam's hand—the
same one that held the pistol.

Tears came once again to Sam's eyes and he felt he
couldn't go through with it. But he had no intention
of going to prison for thirty years, and so he cocked
the trigger and took careful aim, directly between
Buddy's soft and appealing eyes.

"Don't shoot that dog!" came a cry from the distance.

Sam turned to see Judge Lockwood running toward

him, and just behind the judge was Dr. Morton, Sam's dentist. He was also Abraham Lincoln's family dentist.

"There might have been a miscarriage of justice!" the judge shouted.

"That dog might be innocent," said Dr. Morton, as he ran up. "Let me see his teeth!" He reached down and opened Buddy's mouth and looked into it. "I was right!" Dr. Morton announced.

"I don't understand!" Sam said.

Judge Lockwood explained: "Dr. Morton, here, happened to examine the Robbins boy's leg, and he didn't think that a dog of Buddy's size could have made those wounds at all."

"If it *was* a dog," Dr. Morton said carefully, "it would have to have been a very small one. Buddy's canines are too far apart."

"Well," Sam said, overjoyed, "I just knew for *certain* that Buddy hadn't done it."

The reason that Sam knew this for certain was that it had been Sam himself who had been chewing the Robbins boy in the calf when Buddy had come along and tried to protect the child by biting Sam in *his* calf. It had been Sam's blood in Buddy's mouth. This was why Sam had been limping.

As it happened, Dr. Morton knew the truth, for he was quite familiar with Sam's occlusion and had recognized the tooth marks as being Sam's.

However, Dr. Morton was a wise and kindly man, and he was also a student of the occult and he knew an incipient werewolf when he saw one. But, also, Dr. Morton knew the cure.

When Dr. Haskins returned from Washington, Dr. Morton went to him and said that it was vital that Sam have lots of red meat in his diet. "Otherwise," said the dentist, "all his teeth are going to fall out. Also, he may well go blind."

"Is that a true medical fact?" asked Dr. Haskins.

"I assure you that it is," Dr. Morton said. "In addition, his fingers and toes might fall off."

"Good heavens!" Dr. Haskins exclaimed. Not only was he a badly educated doctor but he was also one of the most gullible men in Springfield. "Well, even though it's against my principles, Sam will have meat from now on."

From that day forward, Sam was given all the red meat he could eat—which was considerable. Dr. Morton was pleased to see that all of Sam's werewolf tendencies rapidly disappeared.

Buddy lived to a lovable old age.

As Sam grew up, his father pressed him to become a doctor or a lawyer, but Sam had other ideas. In later years, he was to become the most respected, successful, well-adjusted and sublimated retail butcher in all Springfield.

To me, this seems a perfectly straightforward and simple story, with touching human values and a happy, upbeat ending. In all modesty, I feel that the addition of young Tom Edison was a brilliant touch, verging on the profound.

I really don't know what kept Mark Twain from writing this story. But then, one of his great failings was that he wrote only what *he* wanted to write, rather than what people wanted to read.

This is, of course, why Mark Twain is not remembered as a writer today.

COYOTE STREET

Gary Brandner

She was a little bit of a thing. I could see her in silhouette reading *D. Stonebreaker—Private Investigator* on the frosted glass of my office door. She made a couple of half-hearted moves toward the doorknob, then drew a deep breath, straightened her shoulders, and marched in.

She didn't say anything right away, just stood inside the door looking at me. I have an unnerving effect on people sometimes. Partly because of my size. Even sitting down behind a desk I look big. Then there's my face. It's been compared to a granite head that a sculptor had quit on. To help the girl relax I tried to smile. Sometimes that scares people, too.

It worked this time, though. The girl unfroze and walked closer to my desk. She was tiny, all right, but the soft sweater and tight pants left no doubt that she was a full-grown woman.

"You are Stonebreaker?" Her English had the musical accents of Mexico.

"That's me."

She studied me with black-coffee eyes. "My name is Elena Valdez. My husband Ramon works here in your building with the sweepers."

That would be the once-a-week cleaning crew the

owner brought in to keep the L.A. Sanitation Department off his back.

I said, "Sit down, Mrs. Valdez, and tell me what I can do for you."

She perched on the edge of a wooden chair. "Will my husband have to know about this?"

"Not if you don't want him to."

"I can't pay you very much."

"I don't charge very much. What's the problem?"

"It's my brother, Carlos. He is—" She chewed on her lip as if she were having seconds thoughts about trusting me. "He is in the country illegally," she finished with a rush.

I waited for her to go on. Illegal Mexican immigrants are not a real hot item in Los Angeles. You can hardly throw a rock down Whittier Boulevard without hitting one.

"My husband and I paid two hundred dollars to have him smuggled across the border at Tecate. Carlos will pay us back when he can. Already he has a job, and soon he hopes to become a citizen."

"Good for him. Why do you need a detective?"

"Because of the coyotes."

"Coyotes?" I repeated.

"The streets are full of people who prey on the Mexican aliens. People like my brother are confused and afraid. They do not want to break the law, but also they do not want to be taken back to Mexico. The coyotes pose as friends. 'I will help you,' they say. Then they take the little money such people earn and do nothing for them. If one complains he finds one day he has been reported to the *migras,* the immigration people."

"How do you know your brother's in trouble with the coyotes?"

Her eyes flashed with a hint of Latin temper. *"Ai,* that Carlos can be such a *burro!* I know someone is taking from him the money he makes at his job, but he will not talk to me about it. He says a man must learn to make his way without the help of a woman."

"He has a point there."

"But I know he must be in some kind of trouble. You could find out, couldn't you?"

"Maybe. Tell me, Mrs. Valdez, why don't you want your husband in on this?"

"Ramon has done enough for my brother. I cannot ask any more of him." Elena held up her fine little head and looked me in the eye. "I will pay you with my own money that I earn from housekeeping."

She dipped into a woven handbag and pulled out several bills. She laid them on my desk, smoothing out the wrinkles.

"Is this enough?"

I pushed one of the bills back to her and pocketed the rest. "This is enough. I'll want to talk to Carlos first. How's his English?"

"He has a little. I will go with you and help. Will tomorrow morning be all right?"

"Yeah. I'll be here about ten."

"I will meet you then," she said.

I had a feeling she wasn't giving me the whole story, but I didn't get a chance to ask. The door opened behind her and a dark heavy-bodied man in coveralls came in.

"Elena," he said, "I thought I heard your voice."

"Ah, Ramon," she said quickly, "I was just asking this man if you had been on this floor yet. I thought we could go home together."

"Didn't I tell you I work till midnight tonight?"

"I must have forgotten," Elena said. "I could wait for you."

"No, that will be two more hours. You go home and I'll see you later."

"Yes, Ramon," she said, lowering her eyes, and the two of them walked out of my office together.

I spent another hour finishing the report I was work-

ing on, then left the building, tromping down four
fights of stairs since the elevator is shut down when
the cleanup crew leaves. I went home and fell asleep
watching the late late movie.

When I showed up the next morning at a quarter after
ten Elena Valdez was waiting for me. The boys who
ran the tout service across the hall had their door open
and were eyeballing the girl and making loud remarks.
I gave them a scowl and they got busy with something
else.

We went downstairs and got into my jalopy. Elena
was bright and talkative as I tooled over to East Los
Angeles. As we drove she told me how a year ago she
herself had slipped illegally across the border. She
married Ramon, a U.S. citizen, giving her legal status
here. Now she hoped her brother could make it, too.

The street where Carlos lived could have used a good
rain to wash it down. The people who moved along the
gritty sidewalk made a point of not looking at Elena
and me as we got out of the car.

We climbed a flight of stairs between a pawnshop
and a four-stool café. Recorded mariachi music followed us up from the open door of a tavern across the
street.

Elena led me down a hallway on the second floor
to a door with a white card thumbtacked to the panel.
On the card in penciled letters was printed: *C. Guerra.*

She knocked lightly, waited, then knocked again.

"Carlos must be asleep," Elena said. "He works the
night shift."

She called his name, but there was no response from
inside. I didn't like it and neither did the girl. The little
smile faded from her lips.

I tried the knob. The door swung open and we
walked into the room.

It was a room to make you want to be out on the
street. The wallpaper was blotched with squashed bugs,
and there were old foul-looking stains on the rug. Not a

piece of furniture in the place stood solidly on four legs.

On the other side of the unmade bed I found Carlos. He was a slim good-looking kid lying on his back with his eyes open and empty. The front of his blue work shirt was crusted with dried blood.

Elena gave a little cry and started for the body. I grabbed her and held her away.

"Madre Dios," she said, "who could have done this?"

I put her in a chair and went over to take a look. The body was stiff and cold, so he'd been dead for some hours. I counted at least four wounds in the chest. Under the bureau was a black-handled knife with dark stains on the blade.

Leaving the knife and the body where they were, I took Elena back down the stairs. She didn't sob, but the tears ran out of her big dark eyes and made shiny tracks down her face. We went into the café next door and I called the police. Then I bought Elena a cup of coffee and asked for her home phone number.

I dropped a dime in the slot and dialed. The receiver buzzed six times in my ear before a sleepy voice came on the line.

"Ramon Valdez?" I asked.

"Yes. Who is this?"

"Stonebreaker. You were in my office yesterday. I've just come from your brother-in-law's place. Elena's with me and she needs somebody. You'd better get over here."

"What's the matter? What happened?"

"Carlos is dead."

Ramon caught his breath on the other end, then he said, "I'll be there as soon as I can."

As I hung up, the first police car pulled to the curb. A small crowd began to gather in the street. They stared silently at the officers with cold impersonal dislike.

The patrolmen in the car were both youngsters, and I didn't recognize them, but the head of the homicide team was Dave Pike. We'd been partners once. I filled him in on what little I knew, then hung around while the police went over the room and questioned the neighbors. After a while Pike lit a cigarette and walked down to the street, motioning for me to join him.

"How you doing?" I asked.

Pike made a sour face. "Nobody heard anything, nobody saw anything, nobody knows the dead man. All I know for sure is that it wasn't robbery. He had eight dollars on him, and that's a good haul in this neighborhood. Are you going to keep on working for the girl?"

"Sure. I haven't earned my fee yet."

"If you run onto anything you'll pass it along? You can operate without all the rules that hold us back." Pike chuckled. "In fact, you operated that way when you were with the Department."

"Yeah, that's why I'm a civilian now," I reminded him. "Don't worry, I'll give you anything I get that you can use. What about the knife?"

"A three-dollar switchblade. Every other kid on the street carries one."

Elena Valdez came down the stairs leaning on the arm of her husband.

"How is she?" I asked Ramon.

"Not so good. This is a terrible shock. When last I heard from Carlos just a week ago he seemed so happy. He had a job and he said he would soon get his permanent resident card."

"Where did he work?" I asked.

"At the Eastside Furniture Company. It's just a few blocks from here."

"Take care of the lady," I said. "I'll be in touch."

Eastside Furniture had a showroom on Atlantic Boulevard next to an auto salvage yard. The windows were plastered with bright posters advertising the incredible bargains inside. I went in and picked my way through the bright cheap furniture to the manufacturing area in the rear of the building.

Some two dozen men and women, all apparently Latins, were busy there hammering, sewing, and glueing the stuff together. Watching them work was a tall balding man with a buzzard-beak nose. I walked over and introduced myself. He told me his name was Bert Kettleman, he owned Eastside Furniture, and he was too busy to talk to me.

"Let's go into your office," I said, pretending I didn't hear the last part.

He started to brush me off, then he took another look at my size and my face and decided he could spare a couple of minutes.

"Did you have a Carlos Guerra working here?" I asked.

" 'Did have' is right," Kettleman said. "He didn't show up last night, and that's it as far as I'm concerned. I can't keep people on the payroll who don't show up every day."

"He didn't show up because he's dead."

"Oh. Well. Sorry to hear that." Kettleman made a try at looking sorry.

"How did he get along here?"

"Fine, as far as I know. Did his work, didn't say much, had no beefs with anybody."

"Did you know he was in the country illegally?"

"Sure I knew. Ninety percent of the people who work here are wetbacks. What of it? There's no law against hiring them."

"And they work cheap," I added.

"So what? It's still better than they could make in Mexico. If it wasn't for guys like me they'd all starve to death. Or be out holding up liquor stores."

"You're just an all-around good guy."

"Listen, I help these people when I can. Didn't I find your boy Guerra a room close to the factory just three days ago? Saved him a couple of bucks a week in bus fare."

"I don't suppose you got a kickback from the landlord."

"We do each other a favor when we can. What's your hustle, anyway, Stonebreaker?"

"I want to know where you get your workers."

"What do you mean?"

"I mean who steers them to you, Kettleman? These Mexicans don't just walk in off the street on the chance you might have a job for them."

I could see Kettleman was searching for a reason not to give me the information. I scowled at him and he shrugged as if it really didn't make any difference anyway.

"Joe Figueroa sends most of 'em over."

"Who's he?"

Kettleman dug through his wallet for a business card and handed it to me. It read: *J. L. "Joe" Figueroa, Immigration Services. Se habla español.* The address was not far away, on Brook Avenue.

I tucked the card into my pocket and walked out. Before I was out of the manufacturing area I heard Kettleman pick up the phone and start dialing.

On Brook Avenue I stopped at a *burrito* stand across from Figueroa's address and ordered a *chile relleno*. I took a seat at the end of the outdoor counter where I could keep my back to the wall.

They came sauntering across the street looking almost like twins—long black hair, fleshy mouths, tight low-riding pants. One of them had a scar that pulled down the corner of his right eye, and he was a couple of inches taller than his pal. They slouched up and stood in front of me with their hips canted to one side, old Marlon Brando style.

"You got a match, man?" the taller one asked me.

"No."

"Hey, what you mean 'no'? I see you smokin' a cigarette. You don't like chicanos or somethin'?"

"I don't like *you*. Get lost."

He turned to the other in mock astonishment. "Did you hear that, Chongo? Here's this Anglo comes into our neighborhood and tells us to get lost. I think we better give him something to take back to his own part of town to remember us by."

They were amateurs. Pros move in and do their job without wasting time talking about it. These two sounded like characters in an old Bowery Boys movie.

They were still doing their act when I hit the tall one on the side of the head with the sugar container. He hit the concrete face first in a shower of sugar and broken glass.

The one called Chongo dived a hand into his pocket and came up with a knife that was brother to the one that killed Carlos. He feinted twice, then lunged at me as I came off the stool.

Before I got completely out of the way the blade sliced through the sleeve of my jacket and up my forearm. While Chongo was off balance I drove my fist into his belly. He sat down hard, looked at me as if I'd cheated. To discourage him from getting back up I kicked him in the jaw.

I scooped up the fallen knife, dropped it into a pocket, and headed across the street to the office of Immigration Services. The cut on my arm was not deep, but it was bleeding on my clothes, and that made me mad.

The waiting room was full of Mexicans who looked ready to bolt out of the door at the sight of a badge. I ignored them and strode up to the lacquered blonde who sat at a desk at the far end.

"Where's Figueroa?" I said.

She glanced at my bloody hand, then at a closed door behind her. "I think he's busy with a client. Let me buzz him for you."

"Don't bother." I stumped past her and pushed in through the door. Behind the desk sat a soft-bodied man with thick black eyebrows and a matching mustache. He looked surprised to see me.

I put the knife on his desk blotter. "One of your boys dropped this."

His eyebrows formed into a V. "What happened?"

"They fell down and hurt themselves."

"That has nothing to do with me, mister. What do you want here, anyway? I'm not breaking any laws."

I said, "Maybe sending those punks to carve me up is not illegal, but I find it mighty irritating. Now I want some straight answers from you, Joe."

"I don't have to answer anything for you. This is my office and you have no right to come in here and threaten me."

As he talked, Figueroa's hand crept toward the top desk drawer on his right. I let him get four fingers inside, then I reached across and slammed the drawer. He sucked in a couple of quarts of air, but with a great effort he kept from screaming. I reached into the drawer and pulled out the pistol he was after.

"Tell me about Carlos Guerra, Joe," I said.

He looked at me through eyes that glittered with pain and hatred. "I don't know the name."

"Joe, you've got one good hand left. If you want to keep it, don't play games with me."

It took him two seconds to decide to cooperate. "What do you want to know about Guerra?"

"Who put the blade in him last night?"

Figueroa managed to look surprised through his pain. "I don't know anything about it. So help me. Is he dead?"

"He's dead."

"Hell, I liked the kid. I wouldn't have any reason to want him dead. I got him his job, did you know that? I was tryin' to get him a resident card."

"How much of his wages were you taking for that little service?"

"Look, I gotta live, too. Don't you think it costs anything to get these people straightened out? Guerra didn't have no papers at all, and when they got no relatives who are citizens that makes for a lot of trouble. You gotta get notarized statements from people who'll swear he is who he says he is. And believe me, these chicanos don't like to put their names on anything. Sure, Guerra paid me to get a card for him. I can't work on credit. These wetbacks can be picked up any time and packed into a bus back to Mexico next day."

So I'd found at least two of the coyotes who were feeding off Carlos Guerra, now that it was too late to do him any good. Also, I had a pretty good idea now who killed him. And why.

I left Joe Figueroa sucking on his injured fingers and drove out to see Ramon and Elena Valdez. They lived in the rear half of a stucco duplex. The neighborhood was old but clean, with tiny green lawns in front of every house.

Elena came to the door. Her eyes were red and her face puffy. "What is it?"

"Is Ramon here?"

"He is sleeping."

"Get him up."

She moved aside and let me come in, then walked through a door into the bedroom. In a couple of minutes she was back with Ramon. He was unshaved and wearing a bathrobe too big for him.

I said, "Ramon, did you tell me you hadn't heard from Carlos for a week?"

"That's right."

"Then how did you know where to find his place this morning? He only moved in there three days ago."

"You told me the address on the phone."

"No, I didn't. I just told you to come over to your brother-in-law's place."

"What are you saying?" Elena asked, moving a step closer to me.

I ignored her and went on. "And you didn't work until midnight last night either. The building was empty when I left at eleven o'clock. You killed Carlos, Ramon."

"You're crazy!" he snapped. "Why would I kill my wife's brother?"

Elena stared at her husband in growing horror. She said, "You *knew*, didn't you!"

"He knew," I said. "He probably found out from Joe Figueroa that Carlos had no relatives in the States. No mother, no father, no sister."

Ramon sagged into a chair. "Okay, Stonebreaker, you called it. I found out that Carlos was no brother to Elena when Figueroa wanted me to sign a paper for him. I guess they must have had a lot of laughs at me. Imagine a guy spending his own money to bring his wife's boy friend into the country. Real funny.

"I followed Elena when she left your building last night. I saw her go up the stairs at the crummy room-inghouse and I saw what room she went into. Then I waited in the bar across the street and drank beer until she came out an hour later. I went up then and found Carlos getting ready to go to work. The smell of her was still in his bed."

Ramon looked to his wife as though for some sort of forgiveness. He found none and dropped his eyes to the floor. "Then I killed him."

In a little while the police came and took him away.

As I headed down the walk to my car Elena asked, "What am I going to do now?"

I looked back at the slim little body and the oval face with the huge dark eyes. I thought about what happened to two men because of her.

"You'll survive," I said, and left her standing there.

ZOMBIQUE

Joseph Payne Brennan

You may have heard of the Tyler Marinsons. He'd made a fortune on "the street" before he was thirty. Finally he tired of the stock market shuffle, bought a superb country house, with fifty acres, in Barsted, Connecticut, closed his New York office and began leading the life of a country gentleman.

He still had investments, of course, and he watched them closely, but his market maneuvers became little more than a hobby. If all of his remaining stock investments had been wiped out, it wouldn't have mattered much. He had enough real estate, municipal bonds, notes, trust funds, cash and personal property to survive almost anything except revolution or a nuclear attack.

He stayed on several boards of directors to "keep a hand in," as he expressed it.

His wife, Maria, was delighted with her new life. She'd hated New York and she loved the country. For nearly a year the Marinsons lived almost like recluses. They seldom entertained; they went to New York only twice in ten months.

At length, however, Maria felt that her husband was getting restless. She began having house parties and frequent week-end guests. Tyler, off the tightrope of tension which he had walked in New York, slipped easily into the new scheme of things. The Marinson house parties became "musts" and Tyler himself turned into something of a raconteur.

They were a handsome couple, mid-thirties and childless but not a bit maladjusted. Tyler, tall and dark with fine chiselled features; Maria, small and blond with the kind of arresting blue eyes that look unreal.

They met Kemley through the Paulmanns. Kemley had made it in oils. He spent most of his time poking around the Caribbean. He became the Marinsons' "pet." He was a bachelor nearing fifty and Maria, with a persistence which amused him, kept steering various women friends—widows mostly—in his direction. It became a standing joke between them. Kemley adored her and respected Tyler. He never returned from one of his jaunts without bringing back some souvenir for the two of them.

It wasn't easy. You don't buy typical tourist baubles for people like the Marinsons. Kemley concentrated on curios which, while not always expensive, were hard to get. Tyler appreciated them and Maria always received them with the wide-eyed enthusiasm of a child.

It was one of Kemley's curio gifts which precipitated the business. Or maybe it was all coincidence. You'll have to judge for yourself.

Shortly after a trip to Haiti, Kemley brought the Marinsons a Haitian "voodoo" doll. About four inches high, it was carved out of hard native wood, tufted with feathers and mounted on a thick wooden base. Branching from each side of it were narrow metal rods ending in carved wooden cylinders which resembled drums. The figure was so attached to the base that when you gave one of the rods or drums a push, the doll would execute a grotesque dance atop the base, twirling, bobbing and swaying as if suddenly animated with a life of its own.

Kemley told the Marinsons that if you wanted to bring bad luck to an enemy, someone you hated, you twirled the doll, spoke its name—*Zombique*—and told it what you wanted.

Tyler was fascinated by it but, for once, Maria's enthusiasm seemed forced. After Kemley had left, she admitted to her husband that she didn't like the figure. She confessed, in fact, that she was afraid of it.

Tyler joshed her about it, twirled the doll, spoke its name and asked that old Harrington's steel stocks drop twenty points.

The next day Harrington's steel stocks moved up two points. Tyler brought this to Maria's attention.

She frowned. "You didn't actually fulfill the conditions," she pointed out. "Harrington was never your enemy; you were just rivals. You never *hated* him. And you didn't *really* want his steel to drop twenty points."

Tyler laughed. "Maybe you're right at that. Anyhow it's all a bag of nonsense."

The Haitian doll remained on the mantel and Maria gradually forgot about it.

And then Tyler had a furious row with Jake Seff, owner of the local Atlas Garage. What it amounted to, in brief, was that the Atlas had done a shoddy repair job on Tyler's favorite sports car and then had grossly overcharged him for the inferior work. Jake Seff stubbornly refused to do the work over and just as stubbornly refused to reduce his bill.

Tyler came home swearing like a whole platoon of troopers. Maria tried to placate him, but he sulked and brooded the entire evening.

"But darling," she pleaded as they prepared for bed, "it's only a few hundred dollars!"

Tyler scowled. "That's not the point. I don't like being made a fool of because I have money. I accumulated that money by my wits and it wasn't easy. I took some pretty risks. Seff thinks he can clip me and get away with it. Thinks I'll just shrug it off. Well—I won't!"

The next day he made telephone calls during the

morning and left after lunch. He returned in time for cocktails, still furious but more self-contained than on the previous day.

Over drinks he told Maria that he had checked into the financial status of the Atlas Garage. Jake Seff, he revealed, was nearing the brink of bankruptcy. He was so desperate for cash he had even allowed his insurance on the garage to lapse.

Tyler refilled his glass. "He's not only unscrupulous —he's plain stupid. That insurance should get priority over everything. He wouldn't get a dime if the garage burned down; he'd be finished."

Maria tried to change the subject, but Tyler wasn't listening. He paced around the room. By chance he stopped near the mantel, feet away from Kemley's Haitian voodoo doll.

He set down his glass. "By God, I'm going to try it!"

Maria came over. "Tyler! That's childish!"

He ignored her. Flicking a finger against one of the drums, he triggered the feathered doll into its twirling, bobbing dance.

"Zombique!" he commanded, "burn down Jackie Seff's Atlas Garage!"

Maria sighed and sat down. "Tyler, I don't *like* this. You shouldn't hate anyone like that. Let's get rid of that horrid thing!"

Tyler picked up his glass. "What? Get rid of it? Old Kemley would never forgive us. He looks to see if it's still on the mantelpiece every time he comes."

The next morning when Maria came down to breakfast, Tyler was already reading an area newspaper as he sipped his orange juice.

Pointing to a brief paragraph, he handed her the paper without a word.

She read the caption—*Seff's Garage Burns; Total Ruin*—and turned white.

"Tyler! You didn't—?"

"What? Set fire to Seff's junkyard garage? Don't be a

silly goose! And that doll had nothing to do with it either. It's all just a crazy coincidence."

Ignoring her orange juice, Maria poured a cup of coffee. She sipped it black. "Tyler, please take that voodoo thing out of the house and burn it—or throw it in the woods."

Tyler looked across at her. "You're talking like a ten-year-old. These things happen once in a while. Pity you can't see the humor in it! We could both have a good laugh!"

Maria shook her head. "Somebody's bankruptcy is nothing to laugh about—even if he is dishonest. And now I'm *really* afraid of that nasty little puppet."

Tyler finished his coffee and stood up. "Well, I think I'll take a spin to the village. Need a few things from Carson's store."

Maria watched as he slipped on his coat. "You just want to drive past Seff's and look at the smoking ruins!" she commented, with a vehemence which surprised him.

He shrugged and went out the door.

The voodoo doll remained on the mantel shelf but it was weeks before Maria appeared to throw off her uneasiness concerning it. On several occasions Tyler almost yielded to an impulse to destroy the doll, but each time, a certain implacable element in his nature, grounded, it seemed, in the very bedrock of his being, asserted itself. The Haitian doll stayed on the mantel.

And then Tyler got arrested by Sergeant Skepley. Maria was home, bedded down with the flu, and Tyler had to make one of his infrequent trips to New York. The directors' meeting was late; it was already dusk by the time he reached the parkway.

He traveled well over the limit all the way up to Hartford and nobody bothered him. He slowed down for the cutoff but by the time he reached the outskirts of Barsted he was way over the posted limit again. The roads in Barsted were narrow and winding. You were reasonably safe at thirty-five, but definitely not at fifty-five.

Tyler was fretting about Maria and inwardly cursing Templeton, whose long tedious spiel had held up the directors' meeting, when he saw the flashing red lights in his rear-view mirror.

Momentarily he pressed the accelerator a bit further toward the floor. He thought better of it, however, slowed up and finally braked to a stop.

The police car pulled up behind him, red signal lights still flashing. He had his license and registration cards ready by the time the sergeant came abreast of his own car window.

As the sergeant studied the documents, he studied the sergeant. Young. Officious-looking. Already a sergeant. No sense telling him he had a sick wife at home alone.

The sergeant pulled a printed form out of his pocket. "I'm placing charges, Mr. Marinson, for reckless driving, for exceeding the speed limit and for attempting to evade arrest."

Marinson felt the blood rush to his face. 'Now wait a minute! Maybe I was over the limit, but you can't throw the whole book at me! What's this about evading?"

The sergeant's humorless eyes stared back at him. "When you first noticed my lights, Mr. Marinson, you hit your gas pedal. That's 'attempting to evade.' "

He turned toward the patrol car. "I'll need about ten minutes to fill out this arrest form, Mr. Marinson."

Marinson sat waiting, flushed with rage. Twenty minutes passed before the sergeant returned with the completed form.

He started to explain something about Circuit Court in Meriden but Marinson snatched the form out of his hand, threw it on the car seat and turned the ignition key.

"It's on the form, isn't it?" he asked furiously. "I can read!"

When he got around the next curve in the road, he experienced an impulse to press the gas pedal down to the floor. He glanced in the rear-view mirror. The sergeant's prowl car was already coming around the curve.

When he reached home, he was trembling with fury. He drove into the garage and sat for a few minutes before going inside.

Maria said she felt better but she hadn't eaten and she still looked feverish. He wanted to call Doctor Clane again but she shook her head.

"I called him this afternoon. He said to go on with the medication, stay in bed and drink a lot of fluids. He said it runs its course and I'll be better in a few days."

Tyler sat with her for an hour before going down to get an improvised dinner snack. He had told her about the tedious directors' meeting but not about his arrest.

The kitchen looked uninviting. He decided he wasn't hungry and went into the living room. Pouring a stiff Scotch and soda, he took out the arrest form.

The form indicated that he had to appear in Circuit Court in Meriden on a specified date, unless he chose to plead not guilty. In that case, he had to so notify the court and he would be informed of a subsequent date for appearance.

The arresting officer was a Sergeant Skepley.

Swearing, he threw down the form. He was well known in the town. Any other member of the force, he told himself, would have given him a simple warning or, at worst, a summons which could be mailed in with a nominal fine. Skepley, he remembered, had a reputation for toughness. Recalling the sergeant's steady, somewhat bulging eyes and compressed lips, Marinson concluded that he was not merely tough but actually sadistic.

After another drink, he decided to fight the case. He'd call Boatner's law firm tomorrow morning. They had a branch in nearby Hartford. He knew young Millward who was in charge of it. Millward would get him off the hook if anybody could.

He felt better after the third drink. He poured a

fourth, sprawling back in his chair with a sigh of relative contentment. As he glanced toward the mantel, he noticed the Haitian doll.

He set down his drink and crossed the room.

Flicking his forefinger against one of the wooden drums attached to the figure, he triggered the feathered doll into motion. Bobbing, nodding and swaying, it performed a macabre little dance.

"Zombique!" he commanded, "make Sergeant Skepley drop dead!"

"Dead, dead, dead!" he repeated as the dance slowed and the puppet came to rest.

Returning to his chair, he decided to finish off the bottle of Scotch.

He woke up with a nagging hangover the next morning. Maria was fretful and feverish and didn't want to eat.

He telephoned Boatner's law office in Hartford before ten o'clock. Millward hadn't arrived yet. He left no message but said he'd call back.

He tried again shortly before eleven. Millward had arrived but was in conference and couldn't be disturbed. Did he want to leave a message? Muttering, he hung up.

After pacing the floor for a few minutes, he went up to see Maria.

She was reading in bed and seemed somewhat better. He told her he had to talk to Millward but hadn't been able to reach him by telephone.

Maria laid down her book. "Tyler, you're so restless, you're making me nervous! Why don't you just drive into Hartford and see Millward?"

When he murmured something about leaving her alone, she scoffed. "The phone's next to my bed and anyway I'm better. You've been wound up tight ever since that directors' meeting. You don't need to fuss over me. Go and talk to Millward. Something's making you positively jumpy!"

Picking up her book, she waved a mock goodbye.

He kissed her and grinned. "If I were a doctor, you'd be my favorite patient! All right. I'll see you later then."

He drove to Hartford, taking his time down Farmington Avenue. When he arrived at Boatner's, Millward had already left for lunch. He went out for a cocktail and a sandwich and came back an hour later.

This time Millward was in. Tyler told his story, getting angry all over again.

Millward sat back, put his fingertips together and pushed up his glasses. Marinson observed that he was beginning to get paunchy.

Millward's smile held a tinge of deprecation. "Things aren't the way they used to be, Tyler. At least not here in Connecticut. To quash something like this is almost impossible. The best we can do is get some delays and stall for the right judge. With luck, you'll hang onto your license. This Skepley must have a reputation and you did have a sick wife at home. We'll see what we can do."

Marinson thanked him and stood up. He felt a keen sense of disappointment. A few years ago, in New York, Millward would have taken the ticket and torn it up in front of him. Then there'd be a slap on the back and a drink from Millward's private flask.

He started homeward in a thoughtful mood, vaguely troubled and apprehensive. His money and presence, he reflected, no longer seemed to matter as much as formerly.

He drove through the small center of Barsted, noticing that it appeared nearly deserted.

As he swung into Postgate Road, which led to his house, an ambulance pulled into view. It wasn't going very fast and the siren wasn't on. He stared into it as it passed. A figure lay in the back, covered with a blanket.

He stopped, hesitated and very nearly backed around to follow the ambulance. He changed his mind and drove on, feeling his stomach constrict. Postgate Road lay in a relatively isolated area. There were only two houses besides his own on the entire length of it.

Ten minutes later he topped the rise which led to his house and the bottom fell out of his world.

There was no house—only a smoking sprawl of blackened timbers, brick chimneys and collapsed pipes, sagging crazily in every direction.

He managed to stop the car.

As he sat transfixed, a man in a corduroy suit came over. It was someone he recognized but he couldn't recall who it was.

"Take it easy, Mr. Marinson. We did all we could. I'm sorry, awful sorry."

Staring around, Marinson saw the Barsted Volunteer Fire Company trucks, police cars and at least a dozen civilian cars. His lawn, he decided, would be a frightful mess.

Abruptly, he started the car. "I'm going after my wife," he said. "She was in that ambulance."

People were hovering around the car. A hand closed on his wrist.

Someone stood there, looking mournful, shaking his head.

"Your wife wasn't in the ambulance, Mr. Marinson."

He got out of the car, suddenly furious. "What *is* this? Of course it was my wife. What are you telling—?"

He stopped and stared toward the smoking ruins of his house. His eyes sought the others' eyes. Not a single pair of them would meet his own.

A sob shook him. He ran toward the twisted, blackened debris. "Maria!"

Someone put an arm around his shoulder. He looked up dully and turned away, then stopped, puzzled. "My wife's body . . . You say—Who was in the ambulance?"

A familiar voice replied. "That was Sergeant Skepley in the ambulance. He's dead. He came by here on patrol, far as we can figure out, saw the place on fire and ran to see if anyone was inside. He never made it. He dropped dead halfway between his car and the house. Heart attack, we think. Massive. Shortly after, I guess, the Confords saw flames shooting over the trees and called the fire volunteers. They got here in record time but too late. Your wife must have been overcome with smoke. She never—got out."

Marinson stumbled toward the ruins. He stopped, staring.

The living-room's brick chimney and its attached marble mantel were still standing.

Although its feathers had been burned off, the Haitian doll remained on the mantel shelf. The fine-grained wood from which it was carved had somehow survived the sudden inferno of flames.

A wind had risen, buffeting against the miniature drums fastened to the tiny figure.

Bobbing, swaying and bowing, it executed a bizarre little dance of death.

THE PATTERN

Bill Pronzini

At 11:23 P.M. on Saturday, the twenty-sixth of April, a
small man wearing rimless glasses and a dark gray
business suit walked into the detective squad room in
San Francisco's Hall of Justice and confessed to the
murders of three Bay Area housewives whose bodies
had been found that afternoon and evening.

Inspector Glenn Rauxton, who first spoke to the
small man, thought he might be a crank. Every major
homicide in any large city draws its share of oddballs
and mental cases, individuals who confess to crimes
in order to attain public recognition in otherwise unsub-
stantial lives, or because of some secret desire for
punishment; or for any number of reasons which can
be found in the casebooks of police psychiatrists. But
it wasn't up to Rauxton to make a decision either way.
He left the small man in the company of his partner,
Dan Tobias, and went in to talk to his immediate
superior, Lieutenant Jack Sheffield.

"We've got a guy outside who says he's the killer
of those three women today, Jack," Rauxton said.
"Maybe a crank, maybe not."

Sheffield turned away from the portable typewriter at
the side of his desk; he had been making out a report
for the chief's office. "He come in of his own volition?"

Rauxton nodded. "Not three minutes ago."

"What's his name?"

"He says it's Andrew Franzen."

"And his story?"

"So far, just that he killed them," Rauxton said. "I didn't press him. He seems pretty calm about the whole thing."

"Well, run his name through the weirdo file, and then put him in one of the interrogation cubicles," Sheffield said. "I'll look through the reports again before we question him."

"You want me to get a stenographer?"

"It would probably be a good idea."

"Right," Rauxton said, and went out.

Sheffield rubbed his face wearily. He was a lean, sinewy man in his late forties, with thick graying hair and a curving, almost falconic nose. He had dark-brown eyes that had seen most everything there was to see, and been appalled by a good deal of it; they were tired, sad eyes. He wore a plain blue suit, and his shirt was open at the throat. The tie he had worn to work when his tour started at four P.M., which had been given to him by his wife and consisted of interlocking, psychedelic-colored concentric circles, was out of sight in the bottom drawer of his desk.

He picked up the folder with the preliminary information on the three slayings and opened it. Most of it was sketchy: telephone communications from the involved police forces in the Bay Area, a precursory report from the local lab, a copy of the police Telex which he had had sent out statewide as a matter of course following the discovery of the first body, and which had later alerted the other authorities in whose areas the two subsequent corpses had been found. There was also an Inspector's Report on that first and only death in San Francisco, filled out and signed by Rauxton. The last piece of information had come in less than a half-hour earlier, and he knew the facts of the case by memory; but Sheffield was a meticulous cop and he liked to have all the details fixed in his mind.

The first body was of a woman named Janet Flanders, who had been discovered by a neighbor at four-fifteen that afternoon in her small duplex on 39th Avenue, near Golden Gate Park. She had been killed by several blows about the head with an as yet unidentified blunt instrument.

The second body, of one Viola Gordon, had also been found by a neighbor—shortly before 5:00 P.M.—in her neat, white frame cottage in South San Francisco. Cause of death: several blows about the head with an unidentified blunt instrument.

The third body, Elaine Dunhill, had been discovered at 6:37 P.M. by a casual acquaintance who had stopped by to return a borrowed book. Mrs. Dunhill lived in a modest cabin-style home clinging to the wooded hillside above Sausalito Harbor, just north of San Francisco. She, too, had died as a result of several blows about the head with an unidentified blunt instrument.

There were no witnesses, or apparent clues, in any of the killings. They would have, on the surface, appeared to be unrelated if it had not been for the conceivably coincidental facts that each of the three women had died on the same day, and in the same manner. But there were other cohesive factors as well—factors which, taken in conjunction with the surface similarities, undeniably linked the murders.

Item: each of them had been between the ages of thirty and thirty-five, on the plump side, and blonde.

Item: each of them had been orphaned non-natives of California, having come to the San Francisco Bay Area from different parts of the Midwest within the past six years.

Item: each of them had been married to traveling salesmen who were home only short periods each month, and who were all—according to the information garnered by investigating officers from neighbors and friends—currently somewhere on the road.

Patterns, Sheffield thought as he studied the folder's contents. Most cases had one, and this case was no exception. All you had to do was fit the scattered pieces of its particular pattern together, and you would have your answer. Yet the pieces here did not seem to join logically, unless you concluded that the killer of the woman was a psychopath who murdered blond, thirtyish, orphaned wives of traveling salesmen for some perverted reason of his own.

That was the way the news media would see it, Sheffield knew, because that kind of slant always sold copies, and attracted viewers and listeners. They would try to make the case into another Zodiac thing, or the Boston Strangler. The radio newscast he had heard at the cafeteria across Bryant Street, when he had gone out for supper around nine, had presaged the discovery of still more bodies of Bay Area housewives and had advised all women whose husbands were away to remain behind locked doors. The announcer had repeatedly referred to the deaths as "the bludgeon slayings."

Sheffield had kept a strictly open mind. It was, for all practical purposes, his case—the first body had been found in San Francisco, during his tour, and that gave him jurisdictional priority in handling the investigation. The cops in the two other involved cities would be in constant touch wth him, as they already had been. He would have been foolish to have made any premature speculations not based solely on fact, and Sheffield was anything but foolish. Anyway, psychopath or not, the case still promised a hell of a lot of not very pleasant work.

Now, however, there was Andrew Franzen.

Crank? Or multiple murderer? Was this going to be one of those blessed events—a simple case? Or was Franzen only the beginning of a long series of very large headaches?

Well, Sheffield throught, *we'll find out soon enough.*

He closed the folder and got to his feet and crossed to the door of his office.

In the squad room, Rauxton was just closing one of the metal file cabinets in the bank near the windows. He came over to Sheffield and said, "Nothing on Franzen in the weirdo file, Jack."

Sheffield inclined his head and looked off toward the row of glass-walled interrogation cubicles at the rear of the squad room. In the second one, he could see Dan Tobias propped on a corner of the bare metal desk inside; the man who had confessed, Andrew Franzen, was sitting with his back to the squad room, stiffly erect in his chair. Also waiting inside, stoically seated in the near corner, was one of the police stenographers.

Sheffield said, "Okay, Glenn, let's hear what he has to say."

He and Rauxton went over to the interrogation cubicle and stepped inside. Tobias stood, and shook his head almost imperceptibly to let Sheffield and Rauxton know that Franzen hadn't said anything to him. Tobias was tall and muscular, with a slow smile and big hands and—like Rauxton—a strong dedication to the life's work he had chosen.

He moved to the right corner of the metal desk, and Rauxton to the left corner, assuming set positions like football halfbacks running a bread-and-butter play. Sheffield, the quarterback, walked behind the desk, cocked one hip against the edge and leaned forward slightly, so that he was looking down at the small man sitting with his hands flat on his thighs.

Franzen had a round, inoffensive pink face with tiny-shelled ears and a Cupid's-bow mouth. His hair was brown and wavy, immaculately cut and shaped, and it saved him from being nondescript; it gave him a certain boyish character, even though Sheffield placed his age at around forty. His eyes were brown and liquid, like those of a spaniel, behind his rimless glasses.

Sheffield got a ball-point pen out of his coat pocket and tapped it lightly against his front teeth; he liked to have something in his hands when he was conducting an interrogation. He broke the silence, finally, by saying, "My name is Sheffield. I'm the lieutenant in charge here. Now before you say anything, it's my duty to advise you of your rights."

He did so, quickly and tersely, concluding with, "You understand all of your entitled rights as I've outlined them, Franzen?"

The small man sighed softly and nodded.

"Are you willing, then, to answer questions without the presence of counsel?"

"Yes, yes."

Sheffield continued to tap the ball-point pen against his front teeth. "All right," he said at length. "Let's have your full name."

"Andrew Leonard Franzen."

"Where do you live?"

"Here in San Francisco."

"At what address?"

"Nine-oh-six Greenwich."

"Is that a private residence?"

"No, it's an apartment building."

"Are you employed?"

"Yes."

"Where?"

"I'm an independent consultant."

"What sort of consultant?"

"I design languages between computers."

Rauxton said, "You want to explain that?"

"It's very simple, really," Franzen said tonelessly. "If two business firms have different types of computers, and would like to set up a communication between them so that the information stored in the memory banks of each computer can be utilized by the other, they call me. I design the linking electronic connections between the two computers, so that each can understand the other; in effect, so that they can converse."

"That sounds like a very specialized job," Sheffield said.

"Yes."

"What kind of salary do you make?"

"Around forty thousand a year."

Two thin, horizontal frown lines appeared in Sheffield's forehead. Franzen had the kind of vocation that bespoke of intelligence and upper-class respectability; why would a man like that want to confess to the brutal murders of three simple-living housewives? Or an even stranger question: if his confession was genuine, what was his reason for the killings?

Sheffield said, "Why did you come here tonight, Franzen?"

"To confess." Franzen looked at Rauxton. "I told this man that when I walked in a few minutes ago."

"To confess to what?"

"The murders."

"What murders, specifically?"

Franzen sighed deeply. "The three women in the Bay Area today."

"Just the three?"

"Yes."

"No others whose bodies maybe have not been discovered as yet?"

"No, no."

"Suppose you tell us why you decided to turn yourself in?"

"Why? Because I'm guilty. Because I killed them."

"And that's the only reason?"

Franzen was silent for a moment. Then slowly, he said, "No, I suppose not. I went walking in Aquatic Park when I came back to San Francisco this afternoon, just walking and thinking. The more I thought, the more I knew that it was hopeless. It was only a matter of time before you would have found out I was the one, a matter of a day or two. I guess I could have run, but I wouldn't know how to begin to do that.

I've always done things on impulse, things I would never do if I stopped to think about them. That's how I killed them, on some insane impulse; if I had thought about it I never would have done it. It was so useless . . ."

Sheffield exchanged glances with the two inspectors, and then he said, "You want to tell us how you did it, Franzen?"

"What?"

"How did you kill them?" Sheffield asked. "What kind of weapon did you use?"

"A tenderizing mallet," Franzen said without hesitation.

Tobias asked, "What was that again? What was that you said?"

"A tenderizing mallet. One of those big wooden things with serrated ends that women keep in the kitchen to tenderize a piece of steak."

It was very silent in the cubicle now. Sheffield looked at Rauxton, and then at Tobias; they were all thinking the same thing: the police had released no details to the news media as to the kind of weapon involved in the slayings, other than the general information that it was a blunt instrument. But the initial lab report on the first victim—and the preliminary observations on the other two—stated that the wounds of each had been made by a roughly square-shaped instrument, which had sharp "teeth" capable of making a series of deep indentations as it bit into the flesh. A mallet such as Franzen had just described fitted those characteristics exactly.

Sheffield asked, "What did you do with this mallet, Franzen?"

"I threw it away."

"Where?"

"In Sausalito, into some bushes along the road."

"Do you remember the location?"

"I think so."

"Then you can lead us there later on?"

"I suppose so, yes."

"Was Elaine Dunhill the last woman you killed?"

"Yes."

"What room did you kill her in?"

"The bedroom."

"Where in the bedroom?"

"Beside her vanity."

"Who was your first victim?" Rauxton asked.

"Janet Flanders."

"You killed her in the bathroom, is that right?"

"No, no, in the kitchen . . ."

"What was she wearing?"

"A flowered housecoat."

"Why did you strip her body?"

"I didn't. Why would I—"

"Mrs. Gordon was the middle victim, right?" Tobias asked.

"Yes."

"Where did you kill *her?*"

"The kitchen."

"She was sewing, wasn't she?"

"No, she was canning," Franzen said. "She was canning plum preserves. She had mason jars and boxes of plums and three big pressure cookers all over the table and the stove . . ."

There was wetness in Franzen's eyes now. He stopped talking and took his rimless glasses off and wiped at the tears with the back of his left hand. He seemed to be swaying slightly on the chair.

Sheffield, watching him, felt a curious mixture of relief and deep sadness. The relief was due to the fact that there was no doubt in his mind—nor in the minds of Rauxton and Tobias; he could read their eyes—that Andrew Franzen was the slayer of the three women. They had thrown detail and "trip-up" questions at him, one right after another, and he had had all the right answers; he knew particulars that had also not been given to the news media, that no crank could possibly have known, that only the murderer could have been aware of. The case had turned out to be one of the simple ones, after all, and it was all but wrapped up now; there would be no more "bludgeon slayings," no public hue and cry, no attacks on police inefficiency in the press, no pressure from the commissioner or the mayor. The deep sadness was the result of twenty-six years of police work, of living with death and crime every day, of looking at a man who seemed to be the essence of normalcy and yet who was a cold-blooded multiple murderer.

Why? Sheffield thought. That was the big question. *Why did he do it?*

He said, "You want to tell us the reason, Franzen? Why you killed them?"

The small man moistened his lips. "I was very happy, you see. My life had some meaning, some challenge. I was fulfilled—but they were going to destroy everything." He stared at his hands. "One of them had found out the truth—I don't know how—and tracked down the other two. I had come to Janet this morning, and she told me that they were going to expose me, and I just lost my head and picked up the mallet and killed her. Then I went to the others and killed them. I couldn't stop myself; it was as if I were moving in a nightmare."

"What are you trying to say, Franzen?" Sheffield asked very softly. "What was your relationship with those three women?"

The tears in Andrew Franzen's eyes shone like tiny diamonds in the light from the overhead fluorescents. "They were my wives," he said.

PIPE DREAM

Alan Dean Foster

It was the aroma of tobacco that first attracted her, an aroma delicate enough to demand notice, distinctive enough to bludgeon aside the mundane odor of cigarette and cigar. It was the first different thing she'd encountered all evening.

She'd hoped to meet someone at least slightly interesting at Norma's little get-together. Thus far, though, Norma's guest list had been unswervingly true in reflecting Norma's tastes. Emma had only been fooling herself in hoping it would be otherwise.

There, there it was again: open wood fires and honeysuckle; really different, not bitter or sharp at all.

The vacuity of her excuse as she slipped away was matched only by the vacuousness of the young man she left, holding his half-drained martini and third or fourth proposition, but the tall football player didn't need sympathy. He shrugged away the brushoff and immediately corralled another of Norma's friends.

The owner of the pipe was surprise number two. He looked as out of place at the party as a Mozart concerto. Instead of a girl on his lap, he cradled a fat book. He'd isolated himself in a near-empty corner of the sunken livingroom.

She put a hand on the back of his high-backed easy chair. "Hi," she said.

He looked up. "Hello," absently spoken, then back to the book.

Her interest grew. He might be playing indifferent deliberately—but she didn't think so. If he were interested, he sure faked otherwise well. Men did not usually dismiss Emma with an unconcerned hello, nor did they pass over her face with a casual glance and totally avoid the interesting territory beneath. She was piqued.

There was an unclaimed footstool nearby. She pulled it up next to the bookcase and sat down facing him. He didn't look up.

The man was well-tanned, no beard or moustache (another anomaly). His dark wavy hair was tinged with gray at the sharp bottom of modest sideburns. He might even be over forty. His jaw was pronounced, but otherwise his features were small, almost childlike. Even so, there was something just a little frightening about him.

She didn't scare easily. "I couldn't help noticing your tobacco."

"Hmmm?" He glanced up again.

"Your tobacco. Noticing it."

"Oh, really?" He looked pleased, took the pipe out of his mouth and admired it. "It's a special blend. Made for me. I'm glad you like it." He peered at her with evident amusement. "I suppose next you'll tell me you love the smell of a man's pipe."

"As a matter of fact, usually I can't stand it. That's what makes yours nice. Sweet."

"Thanks again." Was that a faint accent, professionally concealed?

He almost seemed prepared to return to his book. A moment's hesitation, then he shut it with a snap. Back it slipped into its notch in the bookcase. She eyed the spine to identify the work.

"Dürer. You like Dürer, then?"

"Not as art. But I do like the feel of a new book." He gestured negligently at the bookcase. "These are all new books." A little smile turned up the corners of his mouth.

"It says '1962' on the spine of that one," she observed.

"Well, not new, then. Say, 'unused.' No, I'm not crazy about Dürer as an artist. But his work has some real value from a medical history standpoint."

Emma sat back on the foostool and clasped a knee with both hands. This had the intended effect of raising her skirt provocatively. He took no notice as she asked, "In what do you specialize?"

"How marvelous!" he said. "She does not say, 'Are you a doctor?' but immediately goes on to 'in what do you specialize?' assuming the obvious. It occurs to me, young lady, that behind that starlet façade and comic-book body, there may be a brain."

"Please, good sir," she mock-pleaded, "you flatter me unmercifully. And I am not a 'starlet,' I'm an actress. To forestall your next riposte, I'm currently playing in a small theater to very good reviews and very small audiences. In *A Midsummer Night's Dream,* and it's *not* a rock musical, you know."

He was nodding. "Good, good."

"Do I get a gold star on my test, teacher?" she pouted.

"Two. To answer your question, if you're really curious, I happen to specialize in endocrinology. You," he continued comfortably, "do not appear to be adversely affected where my field is concerned. Please don't go and make an idiot of me by telling me about your thyroid problems since the age of five."

She laughed. "I won't."

"Isn't this a delightful party?"

"Oh yes," she deadpanned. "Delightful."

He really smiled then, a wide, honest grin, white crescent cracking the tan. "If you're interested in art, I have a few pieces you might appreciate. Oils, pen-and-ink, no etchings." Grin. "The people in them don't move, but they're more full of life than this bunch."

"I think I'd like that." She smiled back.

It was a longer drive than she'd expected. In Los Angeles, that means something; a good twenty minutes north of Sunset, up Pacific Coast Highway, then down a short, bumpy road.

The house was built on pilings out from a low cliff, to the edge of the ocean. The sea hammered the wood incessantly, December songs boiling up from the basement.

"Like something to drink?" he asked.

She was examining the den; cozy as mittens, masculine as mahogany; hatch-cover table; old, very unmod, supremely comfortable chairs; a big fat brown elephant of a couch in which you could vanish.

"Can you make a ginger snap?" she asked.

His eyebrows rose. "With or without pinching her?"

"With."

"I think so. A minute."

Behind the couch, the wide picture window opened onto a narrow porch, that overhanging a black sea. The crescent of lights from Santa Monica Bay had the look of a flattened Rio de Janeiro, unblinking in the clear winter night. Northward, the hunchback of Point Dume thrust out of the water.

The opposite wall was one huge bookcase. Most of them were medical tomes, titles stuffed with Latin nouns. There were several shelves of volumes in German, a single one in French, yet another in what seemed like some sort of Scandinavian language.

Crowded into a small corner of the north wall, almost in embarrassment, were a group of plaqued diplomas from several eastern institutions and, to match the books, one in German and another in French.

The art, of which there wasn't much, consisted mostly of small pieces. Picasso she expected, but not the original Dalis, nor the Winslow Homer, the charming Wyeth sketches, some English things she didn't recognize, and the framed anatomical drawings of da Vinci—not originals, of course. Over the fireplace, in a massive oak frame, hung a glowing Sierra Nevada landscape by Bierstadt. A distinctive collection . . . just like its owner, she mused.

"With pinch."

She whirled, missed a breath. "You startled me!"

"Fair play. You've already done the same to me, tonight."

She took the glass, walked over to the couch, sat and sipped. "Very slight pinch," she murmured appreciatively.

He walked over and sat down next to her.

"I wouldn't expect you to be the sort to go to many of Norma's parties," she said.

"What that the name of our charming hostess? No, I don't." There was a long rack holding twenty-odd pipes on the table. A lazy Susan full of different tobaccos rested at one end. He selected a new pipe, began stuffing it. "If you believe it, I was invited by one of my patients."

She giggled. The drink was perfect.

"I'm afraid it's true," he said. "She was concerned for my supposed monastic existence. Poor Mrs. Marden." He put pipe to lips, took out a box of matches.

"Let me," she said, the lighter from her purse already out.

"Uh-uh. Not with that." He gently pushed her hand away. The wrist tingled after he removed his hand.

"Gas flame spoils the flavor. Not every smoker notices it, but I do."

She reached out, took the box of Italian wax matches. She struck one and leaned forward. As he puffed the tobacco alight, one hand slipped into her décolletage.

"I didn't think you were wearing a foundation garment."

"Oh, come on!" She blew out the match. His hand was moving gently now. "You sound like a construction engineer!"

"I apologize. You know, you're very fortunate."

She was beginning to breathe unevenly. "How . . . so?"

"Well," he began in a professional tone, "the under-curve of a woman's breast is more sensitive than the top. Many aren't sufficiently well endowed to experience the difference. Not a problem you have to face."

"What," she said huskily, brushing his cheek, "does the book say about the bottom lip, versus the top?"

"As to that," he put the pipe on the table and leaned much, much closer, "opinion is still somewhat divided . . ."

New Year's Day came and went, as usual utterly the same as an old year's day.

It wasn't an affair, of course, but more like a fair. A continuing, wonderful, slightly mad fair, like the fair at Sorochinsk in Petroushka, but there were no puppets here. Walt never shouted at her, never had a mean word. He was unfailingly gentle, polite, considerate, with just the slightest hint of devilry to keep things spicy.

He had fewer personal idiosyncrasies than any man she'd ever met. The only thing that really seemed to bother him was any hint of nosiness on her part. A small problem, since he'd been quite candid about his background without being asked, and about his work.

She'd been a little surprised to learn about the two previous marriages, but since there were no children, nothing tying him to the past, her concern quickly vanished.

Next Tuesday was his birthday. She was determined to surprise him, but with what? Clothes? He had plenty of clothes and was no fashion plate anyway. She couldn't afford a painting of any quality. Besides, choosing art for someone was an impossible job. Electronic gadgetry, the modern adult male's equivalent of Tinker Toys and Lincoln Logs, didn't excite him.

Then she thought of the tobacco. Of course! She'd have some of his special blend prepared. Whenever he lit a pipe he'd think of her.

Now, she considered, looking around the sun-dappled den, where would I hide if I were a tin of special tobacco? There must be large tins around somewhere. The lazy Susan didn't hold much and it was always full, though she never saw him replenishing it. Of course, she couldn't ask him. That would spoil the surprise.

It wasn't hidden, as it turned out; just inconspicuous, in a place she'd had no reason to go. There was a small storage room, a second bedroom, really, in the front of the beach house. It held still more books and assorted other things, including an expensive and unused set of golf clubs.

The tobacco tins were in an old glass cabinet off in one dark, cool corner. The case was locked, but the key was on top of the cabinet. Standing on tiptoe, she could just reach it.

Hunt as she did, though, giving each tin a thorough inspection, there was nothing one could call a special blend. There were American brands, and Turkish, Arabic, and Brazilian, and even a small, bent tin from some African country that had changed its name three times in the past ten years, but no special blends.

She closed the cabinet and put back the key. In frustration she gave the old highboy a soft kick. There was a click. The bottom foot or so of the cabinet looked like solid maple, but it wasn't, because a front panel swung out an inch or so.

She knelt, opened it all the way.

Inside, there were eight large tins on two shelves. Each was wrapped in what looked like brown rice paper or thin leather, but was neither. In fine, bold script across the front of each someone had written: SPECIAL

BLEND, Prepared Especially For DR. WALTER SCOTT. Under this were the various blend names: Liz Granger, Virginia Violet, and so on.

She pulled out one tin and examined it patiently. That was all—no address, no telephone number, nothing. She went over each tin carefully, with identical results. Just special blend, prepared especially for . . . and the blend name. Nothing to indicate who prepared it, where it was purchased.

The paper on the final tin was slightly torn. She handled it carefully and inspected the tear. Something was stamped into the metal of the tin, almost concealed by the wrapping. Gently she peeled a little aside.

Yes, an oval stamp had been used on the tin. They probably all carried it. It was hard to make out . . . the stamp was shallow.

Peter van Eyck, The Smoke Nook . . . and an address right on Santa Monica Boulevard!

She found a little scrap of paper, wrote down the name and address. Then she smoothed the torn paper (or was it leather?) as best she could, replaced the tin on its shelf and shut the panel. It snapped closed with another click of the old-fashioned latch.

For much of its length, Santa Monica Boulevard is like the back of a movie set—a street where all the store fronts, you're certain, have their faces to the alleys and their backsides to the boulevard.

She was almost convinced she'd misread the address, but on the third cruise past, she spotted it. It was just a door in an old two-story building.

After parking, she found the door unlocked, the stairs inside reasonably clean. At the top of the landing she looked left, went right. She knocked on number five once and walked in. The overpowering pungent odor of tobacco hit her immediately. Bells on the door jangled for a second time as she closed it.

Someone in the back of the room said, "Just a minute!" Twice that later, there appeared the proprietor—

short, fat, a fringe of hair running all around his head from chin to cheeks, into sideburns, over the ear and around back, like a cut-on-the-dotted-line demarcation. He was at least in his sixties, but most of the wrinkles were still fat wrinkles, not age wrinkles. His voice was smooth, faintly accented. He smiled. "Well! If I had more clients like you, young lady, I might not consider retiring."

"Thanks. Anyhow," she said, "you can't retire. At least, not until tonight. I'm here to buy a birthday present for a special friend, who seems to have everything."

The owner put on a pleased expression. "What does he like, you tell me. Imported cigars? Pipe tobacco? Snuff?" He winked knowingly, an obscene elf. "Perhaps something a little more unusual? Mexican, say, or Taiwanese?"

"And the opium den in the attic." She smiled back. "No, I'm afraid not. My friend buys his tobacco from you regularly . . ."

"He has good taste."

". . . a special blend you make for him."

"My dear, I make special blends for many people, and not only here in Los Angeles. It's a fine art, and young people today . . ." He sighed. "Some of my best customers, their names would startle you. Who is your friend?"

"Dr. Walter Scott."

Smile, good-bye. Grin, vanished. Humor, to another universe.

"I see." All of a sudden, he was wary of her. "Does the doctor know that you are doing this?"

"No. I want to surprise him."

"I daresay." He looked at his feet. "I am afraid, dear lady, I cannot help you."

None of this made any sense. "Why not? Can't you just . . . blend it, or whatever else it is you do? I don't need it till next week."

"You must understand, dear lady, that this is a very

special blend. I can prepare most of it. But one ingredient always stays the same, and Dr. Scott always
supplies that himself. It's like saffron in paella, you
know. Without the tiny pinch of saffron, you have nothing, soup. Without the doctor's little additive . . ." He
shrugged.

"Haven't you tried to find out what it is, for yourself?" she pressed.

"Of course. But the doctor, he only smiles. I don't
blame him for protecting the secret of his blend. Such
a marvelous sweetness it gives the smoke, I tell you!"
The tobacconist shook his head, fringe bobbing. "No,
I cannot help you. Excuse me." He headed for the back
of the room.

"Well, I like that!" She walked out the door, paused
halfway down the stairs. Odd. Oh well, she'd buy him
that antique hurricane lamp he'd admired in Ports
O'Call.

It was raining as she drove out to the house.
Wednesdays he worked late and she was sure he could
use some company. She shivered deliciously. So could
she.

Pacific Coast Highway was a major artery. Thanks
to the rain and fog, the number of four-wheeled cor-
puscles was greatly reduced tonight; typical South-
ern California rain—clean, cold, tamer than back East.

She let herself in quietly.

Walt was shoving another log into the fireplace. He
was sucking on the usual pipe, a gargoylish meerschaum
this time. After the wet run from the driveway the fire
was a sensuous, delightful inferno, howling like a
chained orange cat.

She took off the heavy, wet coat, strolled over to the
stand near the warmth. The heat was wonderful. She
kissed him but this time the fire's enthusiasm wasn't
matched.

"Something wrong, Walt?" She grinned. "Mrs. Norris
giving you trouble about her glands again?"

"No, no, not that," he replied quietly. "Here, I made you a ginger snap."

The drink was cool and perfect as always.

"Well, tell me, then, what is it?" She went and curled up on the couch. The fire was a little too hot.

He leaned against the stone mantel, staring down into the flames. The only light in the room came from the fireplace. His face assumed biblical shadows. He sighed.

"Emma, you know what I think of women who stick their noses in where they shouldn't."

"Walt?" *Damn,* he must have noticed the new tear in the tobacco tin wrapping! "I don't know what you mean, darling."

The handsome profile turned to full-face. "You've been in my tobacco, haven't you?"

"Oh, all right. I confess, darling. Yes, I was in your precious hoard."

"Why?" There was more than a hint of mild curiosity in his voice. It seemed to come from another person entirely.

She pressed back into the couch and shivered. It was the sudden change in temperature from outside, of course. "Gee, Walt, I didn't think you'd be so . . . so upset."

"Why?" he repeated. His eyes weren't glowing; just the reflection from the fire, was all.

She smiled hopefully. "I was going to surprise you for your birthday. I wanted to get you some of your special blend and really surprise you. Don't think I'm going to tell you what I got you now, either!"

He didn't smile. "I see. I take it you didn't obtain my blend?"

"No, I didn't. I went to your tobacco place . . ."

"You went to my tobacco place . . ." he echoed.

"Yes, on Santa Monica. The address was under the paper, or whatever that wrapping is." She blinked, shook herself. Was she that tired? She took another sip of the drink. It didn't help. In fact, she seemed to grow drowsier. "That nice Mr. . . . I can't remember his name . . . he . . . excuse me, Walt. Don't know why I'm so . . . sleepy."

"Continue. You went to the shop."

"Yes. The owner said he couldn't make any of your blend for me because (fog) you always brought one of the (*so* tired) ingredients yourself and he didn't know what it was. So I had to get you something else."

"Why?" he said again. Before she could answer, "Why must you all know *everything?* Each the Pandora." He took up a poker, stirred the fire. It blazed high, sparks bouncing drunkenly off the iron rod.

She finished the drink, put the glass down on the table. It seemed to waver. She leaned back against the couch.

"I'm sorry, Walt. Didn't think you'd get so . . . upset."

"It's all right, Emma."

"Funny . . . about those . . . tins. Eight of them. Two were . . . named Anna Mine and Sue deBlakely."

"So?" He fingered the poker.

"Well," she giggled, "weren't those the . . . names of your two ex-wives?"

"I'm very sentimental, Emma."

She giggled again, frowned. Falling asleep would spoil the whole evening. Why couldn't she keep her damn eyes open? "In fact . . . all your blends had female . . . names."

"Yes." He walked over to her, stared down. His eyes seemed to burn . . . reflection from the fire again . . . and his face swam, blurred. "You're falling asleep, Emma." He moved her empty glass carefully to one end of the table. It was good crystal.

"Can't . . . understand it. So . . . tired . . ."

"Maybe you should take a little rest, Emma. A good rest."

"Rest . . . maybe . . ."

His arms cradled her. "Lie here, Emma. Next to the fire. It'll warm you." He put her down on the carpet across from the fronting brick. The flames pranced hellishly, anxiously, searing the red-hot brick interior to an inferno.

"Warm . . . hot, Walt," she mumbled sleepily. Her voice was thick uncertain. "Lower it?"

"No, Emma." He took the poker, jabbed and pushed the logs back against the rear of the fireplace. Funny, she'd never noticed how big it was, for such a modest house.

Her eyes closed. There was silence for several minutes. As he bent and touched her, they fluttered open again, just a tiny bit.

"Walt . . ." Her voice was barely audible and he had to lean close to hear.

"Yes?"

"What . . . special ingredient . . . ?"

There was a sigh before he could reply and her eyes closed again. He tossed two more logs on the fire, adjusted them on the iron. Then he knelt, grabbed her under the arms. Her breathing was shallow, faint.

He put his mouth close to her ear and whispered: "Ashes, my love. Ashes."

SHOTTLE BOP

Theodore Sturgeon

I'd never seen the place before, and I lived just down
the block and around the corner. I'll even give you the
address, if you like. "The Shottle Bop," between
Twentieth and Twenty-first streets, on Tenth Avenue
in New York City. You can find it if you go there looking for it. Might even be worth your while, too.

But you'd better not.

"The Shottle Bop." It got me. It was a small shop
with a weather-beaten sign swung from a wrought crane,
creaking dismally in the late fall wind. I walked past it,
thinking of the engagement ring in my pocket and how
it had just been handed back to me by Audrey, and
my mind was far removed from such things as shottle
bops. I was thinking that Audrey might have used a
gentler term than "useless" in describing me; and her
neatly turned remark about my being a "constitutional
psychopathic incompetent" was as uncalled-for as it
was spectacular. She must have read it somewhere,
balanced as it was by "And I wouldn't marry you if
you were the last man on earth!" which is a notably
worn cliché.

"Shottle Bop!" I muttered, and then paused, wonder-
ing where I had picked up such oddly rhythmic syllables

with which to express myself. I'd seen it on that sign, of
course, and it had caught my eye. "And what," I asked
myself, "might be a Shottle Bop?" Myself replied
promptly, "Dunno. Toddle back and have a look." So
toddle I did, back along the east side of Tenth, wonder-
ing what manner of man might be running such an establishment in pursuance of what kind of business. I
was enlightened on the second point by a sign in the
window, all but obscured by the dust and ashes of apparent centuries, which read:

WE SELL BOTTLES

There was another line of small print there. I rubbed
at the crusted glass with my sleeve and finally was able
to make out

With things in them

Just like that:

WE SELL BOTTLES
With things in them

Well of course I went in. Sometimes very delightful
things come in bottles, and the way I was feeling, I
could stand a little delighting.

"Close it!" shrilled a voice, as I pushed through the
door. The voice came from a shimmering egg adrift in
the air behind the counter, low-down. Peering over, I
saw that it was not an egg at all, but the bald pate of an
old man who was clutching the edge of the counter, his
scrawny body streaming away in the slight draft from
the open door, as if he were made of bubbles. A mite
startled, I kicked the door with my heel. He immediately
fell on his face, and then scrambled smiling to his feet.

"Ah, its good to see you again," he rasped.

I think his vocal cords were dusty, too. Everything
else here was. As the door swung to, I felt as if I were

inside a great dusty brain that had just closed its eyes. Oh yes, there was light enough. But it wasn't the lamp-light and it wasn't daylight. It was like—like light reflected from the cheeks of pale people. Can't say I enjoyed it much.

"What do you mean, 'again'?" I asked irritably. "You never saw me before."

"I saw you when you came in and I fell down and got up and saw you again," he quibbled, and beamed. "What can I do for you?"

"Oh," I said. "Well, I saw your sign. What have you got in a bottle that I might like?"

"What do you want?"

"What've you got?"

He broke into a piping chant—I remember it yet, word for word:

> *"For half a buck, a vial of luck*
> *Or a bottle of nifty breaks*
> *Or a flask of joy, or Myrna Loy*
> *For luncheon with sirloin steaks.*
>
> *"Pour out a mug from this old jug,*
> *And you'll never get wet in rains.*
> *I've bottles of grins and racetrack wins*
> *And lotions to ease your pains.*
>
> *"Here's bottles of imps and wet-pack shrimps*
> *From a sea unknown to man,*
> *And an elixir to banish fear,*
> *And the sap from the pipes of Pan.*
>
> *"With the powered horn of a unicorn*
> *You can win yourself a mate;*
> *With the rich hobnob; or get a job—*
> *It's yours at a lowered rate."*

"Now wait right there!" I snapped. "You mean you actually sell dragon's blood and ink from the pen of Friar Bacon and all such mumbo-jum?"

He nodded rapidly and smiled all over his improbable face.

I went on—"The genuine article?"

He kept on nodding.

I regarded him for a moment. "You mean to stand there with your teeth in your mouth and your bare face hanging out and tell me that in this day and age, in this city and in broad daylight, you sell such trash and then expect me—me, an enlightened intellectual—"

"You are very stupid and twice as bombastic," he said quietly.

I glowered at him and reached for the doorknob—and there I froze. And I mean froze. For the old man whipped out an ancient bulb-type atomizer and squeezed a couple of whiffs at me as I turned away; and so help me, *I couldn't move!* I could cuss, though, and boy, did I.

The proprietor hopped over the counter and ran over to me. He must have been standing on a box back there, for now I could see he was barely three feet tall. He grabbed my coat tails, ran up my back and slid down my arm, which was extended doorward. He sat down on my wrist and swung his feet and laughed up at me. As far as I could feel, he weighed absolutely nothing.

When I had run out of profanity—I pride myself on never repeating a phrase of invective—he said, "Does that prove anything to you, my cocky and unintelligent friend? That was the essential oil from the hair of the Gorgon's head. And until I give you an antidote, you'll stand there from now till a week text Nuesday!"

"Get me out of this," I roared, "or I smack you so hard you lose your brains through the pores in your feet!"

He giggled.

I tried to tear loose again and couldn't. It was as if all my epidermis had turned to high-carbon steel. I began cussing again, but quit in despair.

"You think altogether too much of yourself," said

the proprietor of the Shottle Bop. "Look at you! Why, I wouldn't hire you to wash my windows. You expect to marry a girl who is accustomed to the least of animal comfort, and then you get miffed because she turns you down. Why does she turn you down? Because you won't get a job. You're a nogood. You're a bum. He, he! And you have the nerve to walk around telling people where to get off. Now if I were in your position I would ask politely to be released, and then I would see if anyone in this shop would be good enough to sell you a bottle full of something that might help out."

Now I never apologize to anybody, and I never back down, and I never take any guff from mere tradesmen. But this was different. I'd never been petrified before, nor had my nose rubbed in so many galling truths. I relented. "O.K., O.K.; let me break away then. I'll buy something."

"Your tone is sullen," he said complacently, dropping lightly to the floor and holding his atomizer at the ready. "You'll have to say, Please. Pretty please."

"Pretty please," I said, almost choking with humiliation.

He went back of the counter and returned with a paper of powder which he had me sniff. In a couple of seconds I began to sweat, and my limbs lost their rigidity so quickly that it almost threw me. I'd have been flat on my back if the man hadn't caught me and solicitously led me to a chair. As strength dribbled back into my shocked tissues, it occurred to me that I might like to flatten this hobgoblin for pulling a trick like that. But a strange something stopped me—strange because I'd never had the experience before. It was simply the idea that once I got outside I'd agree with him for having such a low opinion of me.

He wasn't worrying. Rubbing his hands briskly, he turned to his shelves. "Now let's see . . . what would be best for you, I wonder? Hm-m-m. Success is something you couldn't justify. Money? You don't know how to spend it. A good job? You're not fitted for one."

He turned gentle eyes on me and shook his head. "A sad case. *Tsk, tsk.*" I crawled. "A perfect mate? Nup. You're too stupid to recognize perfection, too conceited to appreciate it. I don't think that I can—Wait!"

He whipped four or five bottles and jars off the dozens of shelves behind him and disappeared somewhere in the dark recesses of the store. Immediately there came sounds of violent activity—clinkings and little crashes; stirrings and then the rapid susurrant grating of a mortar and pestle; then the slushy sound of liquid being added to a dry ingredient during stirring; and at length, after quite a silence, the glugging of a bottle being filled through a filtering funnel. The proprietor reappeared triumphantly bearing a four-ounce bottle without a label.

"This will do it!" he beamed.

"That will do what?"

"Why, cure you!"

"Cure—" My pompous attitude, as Audrey called it, had returned while he was mixing. "What do you mean 'cure'? I haven't got anything!"

"My dear little boy," he said offensively, "you most certainly have. Are you happy? Have you ever been happy? No. Well, I'm going to fix all that up. That is, I'll give you the start you need. Like any other cure, it requires your cooperation.

"You're in a bad way, young fellow. You have what is known in the profession as retrogressive metempsychosis of the ego in its most malignant form. You are a constitutional unemployable; a downright sociophagus. I don't like you. Nobody likes you."

Feeling a little bit on the receiving end of a blitz, I stammered, "W-what do you aim to do?"

He extended the bottle. "Go home. Get into a room by yourself—the smaller the better. Drink this down, right out of the bottle. Stand by for developments. That's all."

"But—what will it do to me?"

"It will do nothing *to* you. It will do a great deal *for*

you. It can do as much for you as you want it to. But
mind me, now. As long as you use what it gives you for
your self-improvement, you will thrive. Use it for self-
gratification, as a basis for boasting, or for revenge, and
you will suffer in the extreme. Remember that, now."

"But what is it? How——"

"I am selling you a talent. You have none now.
When you discover what kind of a talent it is, it will be
up to you to use it to your advantage. Now go away. I
still don't like you."

"What do I owe you?" I muttered, completely snowed
under by this time.

"The bottle carries its own price. You won't pay anything unless you fail to follow my directions. Now will
you go, or must I uncork a bottle of jinn—and I don't
mean London Dry?"

"I'll go," I said. I'd seen something swirling in the
depths of a ten-gallon carboy at one end of the counter,
and I didn't like it a bit. "Good-bye."

"Bood-gye," he returned.

I went out and I headed down Tenth Avenue and
I turned east up Twentieth Street and I never looked
back. And for many reasons I wish now that I had, for
there was, without doubt, something very strange about
that Shottle Bop.

I didn't simmer down until I got home; but once I
had a cup of black Italian coffee under my belt I felt
better. I was skeptical about it at last. I was actually inclined to scoff. But somehow I didn't want to scoff too
loudly. I looked at the bottle a little scornfully, and
there was a certain something about the glass of it that
seemed to be staring back at me. I sniffed and threw
it up behind some old hats on top of the closet, and
then sat down to unlax. I used to love to unlax. I'd put
my feet on the doorknob and slide down in the up-
holstery until I was sitting on my shoulder blades, and
as the old saying has it, "Sometimes I sets and thinks,
and sometimes I just sets." The former is easy enough,
and is what even an accomplished loafer has to go

through before he reaches the latter and more blissful state. It takes years of practice to relax sufficiently to be able to "just set." I'd learned it years ago.

But just as I was about to slip into the vegetable status, I was annoyed by something. I tried to ignore it. I manifested a superhuman display of lack of curiosity, but the annoyance persisted. A light pressure on my elbow, where it draped over the arm of the chair. I was put in the unpleasant predicament of having to concentrate on what it was; and realizing that concentration on anything was the least desirable thing there could be, I gave up finally, and with a deep sigh, opened my eyes and had a look.

It was the bottle.

I screwed up my eyes and then looked again, but it was still there. The closet door was open as I had left it, and its shelf almost directly above me. Must have fallen out. Feeling that if the damn thing were on the floor it couldn't fall any farther, I shoved it off the arm of the chair with my elbow.

It bounced. It bounced with such astonishing accuracy that it wound up in exactly the same spot it had started from—on the arm of the easy chair, by my elbow. Startled, I shoved it violently. This time I pushed it hard enough to send it against the wall, from which it rebounded to the shelf under my small table, and thence back to the chair arm—and this time it perched cozily against my shoulder. Jarred by the bouncing, the stopper hopped out of the bottle mouth and rolled into my lap; and there I sat, breathing the bittersweet fumes of its contents, feeling frightened and silly as hell.

I grabbed the bottle and sniffed. I'd smelled that somewhere before—where was it? Uh—oh, yes; that mascara the Chinese honkytonk girls use in Frisco. The liquid was dark—smoky black. I tasted it cautiously. It wasn't bad. If it wasn't alcoholic, then the old man in the shop had found a darn good substitute for alcohol. At the second sip I liked it and at the third I really enjoyed it and there wasn't any fourth because by then the little bottle was a dead marine. That was about the time I remembered the name of the black ingredient with the funny smell. Kohl. It is an herb the Orientals use to make it possible to see supernatural beings. Silly superstition!

And then the liquid I'd just put away, lying warm and comfortable in my stomach, began to fizz. Then I think it began to swell. I tried to get up and couldn't. The room seemed to come apart and throw itself at me piecemeal, and I passed out.

Don't you ever wake up the way I did. For your own sake, be careful about things like that. Don't swim up out of a sodden sleep and look around you and see all those things fluttering and drifting and flying and creeping and crawling around you—puffy things dripping blood, and filmy, legless creatures, and little bits and snatches of pasty human anatomy. It was awful. There was a human hand afloat in the air an inch away from my nose; and at my startled gasp it drifted away from me, fingers fluttering in the disturbed air from my breath. Something veined and bulbous popped out from under my chair and rolled across the floor. I heard a faint clicking, and looked up into a gnashing set of jaws without any face attached. I think I broke down and cried a little. I know I passed out again.

The next time I awoke—must have been hours later, because it was broad daylight and my clock and watch had both stopped—things were a little better. Oh, yes, there were a few of the horrors around. But somehow they didn't bother me much now. I was practically convinced that I was nuts; now that I had the conviction, why worry about it? I dunno; it must have been one of the ingredients in the bottle that had calmed me down so. I was curious and excited, and that's about all. I looked around me and I was almost pleased.

The walls were green! The drab wallpaper had turned to something breathtakingly beautiful. They were covered with what seemed to be moss; but never moss like that grew for human eyes to see before. It was long and thick, and it had a slight perpetual movement—not that of a breeze, but of growth. Fascinated, I moved over and looked closely. Growing indeed, with all the quick magic of spore and cyst and root and growth again to spore; and the swift magic of it was only a part of the magical whole, for never was there such a green. I put my hand to touch and stroke it, but I felt only the wallpaper. But when I closed my fingers on it, I could feel that light touch of it in the palm of my hand, the weight of twenty sunbeams, the soft resilience of jet-darkness in a closed place. The sensation was a delicate ecstasy, and never have I been happier than I was at that moment.

Around the baseboards were little snowy toadstools, and the floor was grassy. Up the hinged side of the closet door climbed a mass of flowering vines, and their petals were hued in tones indescribable. I felt as if I had been blind until now, and deaf, too; for now I could hear the whispering of scarlet, gauzy insects among the leaves and the constant murmur of growth. All around me was a new and lovely world, so delicate that the wind of my movements tore petals from the flowers, so real and natural that it defied its own impossibility. Awestruck, I turned and turned, running from wall to wall, looking under my old furniture, into my old books; and everywhere I looked I found newer and more beautiful things to wonder at. It was while I was flat on my stomach looking up at the bed springs, where a colony of jewel-like lizards had nested, that I first heard the sobbing.

It was young and plaintive, and had no right to be in my room where everything was so happy. I stood up and looked around, and there in the corner crouched the translucent figure of a little girl. She was leaning back against the wall. Her thin legs were crossed in front of her, and she held the leg of a tattered toy elephant dejectedly in one hand and cried into the other. Her hair was long and dark, and it poured and tumbled over her face and shoulders.

I said, "What's the matter, kiddo?" I hate to hear a child cry like that.

She cut herself off in the middle of a sob and shook the hair out of her eyes, looking up and past me, all fright and olive skin and big, filled violet eyes. "Oh!" she squeaked.

I repeated, "What's the matter? Why are you crying?"

She hugged the elephant to her breast defensively, and whimpered, "W-where are you?"

Surprised, I said, "Right here in front of you, child. Can't you see me?"

She shook her head. "I'm scared. Who are you?"

"I'm not going to hurt you. I heard you crying, and I wanted to see if I could help you. Can't you see me at all?"

"No," she whispered. "Are you an angel?"

I guffawed. "By no means!" I stepped closer and put my hand on her shoulder. The hand went right through her and she winced and shrank away, uttering a little wordless cry. "I'm sorry," I said quickly. "I didn't mean . . . you can't see me at all? I can see you."

She shook her head again. "I think you're a ghost," she said.

"Do tell!" I said. "And what are you?"

"I'm Ginny," she said. "I have to stay here, and I have no one to play with." She blinked, and there was a suspicion of further tears.

"Where did you come from?" I asked.

"I came here with my mother," she said. "We lived in lots of other rooming houses. Mother cleaned floors in office buildings. But this is where I got so sick. I was sick a long time. Then one day I got off the bed and came over here but then when I looked back I was still on the bed. It was awful funny. Some men came and put the 'me' that was on the bed onto a stretcher-thing and took it—me—out. After a while Mummy left, too. She cried for a long time before she left, and when I called to her she couldn't hear me. She never came back, and I just got to stay here."

"Why?"

"Oh, I got to. I—don't know why. I just—got to."

"What do you do here?"

"I just stay here and think about things. Once a lady lived here, had a little girl just like me. We used to play together until the lady watched us one day. She carried on somethin' awful. She said her little girl was possessed. The girl kept callin' me, 'Ginny! Ginny! Tell Mamma you're here!'; an' I tried, but the lady couldn't see me. Then the lady got scared an' picked up her little girl an' cried, an' so I was sorry. I ran over here an' hid, an' after a while the other little girl forgot about me, I guess. They moved," she finished with pathetic finality.

I was touched. "What will become of you, Ginny?"

"I dunno," she said, and her voice was troubled. "I guess I'll just stay here and wait for Mummy to come back. I been here a long time. I guess I deserve it, too."

"Why, child?"

She looked guiltily at her shoes. "I couldn' stand feelin' so awful bad when I was sick. I got up out of bed before it was time. I shoulda stayed where I was. That is what I get for quittin'. But Mummy'll be back; just you see."

"Sure she will," I muttered. My throat felt tight. "You take it easy, kid. Any time you want someone to talk to, you just pipe up. I'll talk to you any time I'm around."

She smiled, and it was a pretty thing to see. What a raw deal for a kid! I grabbed my hat and went out.

Outside things were the same as in the room to me. The hallways, the dusty stair carpets wore new garments of brilliant, nearly intangible foliage. They were no longer dark, for each leaf had its own pale and different light. Once in a while I saw things not quite so pretty. There was a giggling thing that scuttled back

and forth on the third floor landing. It was a little in-
distinct, but it looked a great deal like Barrel-head
Brogan, a shanty-Irish bum who'd returned from a
warehouse robbery a year or so ago, only to shoot
himself accidentally with his own gun. I wasn't sorry.

Down on the first floor, on the bottom step, I saw
two youngsters sitting. The girl had her head on the
boy's shoulder, and he had his arms around her, and
I could see the banister through them. I stopped to
listen. Their voices were faint, and seemed to come
from a long way away.

He said, "There's one way out."

She said, "Don't talk that way, Tommy!"

"What else can we do? I've loved you for three years,
and we still can't get married. No money, no hope—no
nothing. Sue, if we did do it, I just *know* we'd always
be together. Always and always—"

After a long time she said, "All right, Tommy. You
get a gun, like you said." She suddenly pulled him
even closer. "Oh, Tommy, are you sure we'll always be
together just like this?"

"Always," he whispered, and kissed her. "Just like
this."

Then there was a long silence, while neither moved.
Suddenly they were as I had first seen them, and he
said:

"There's only one way out."

And she said, "Don't talk that way, Tommy!"

And he said, "What else can we do? I've loved you
for three years—" It went on like that, over and over
and over.

I felt lousy. I went on out into the street.

It began to filter through to me what had happened.
The man in the shop had called it a "talent." I couldn't
be crazy, could I? I didn't *feel* crazy. The draught from
the bottle had opened my eyes on a new world. What
was this world?

It was a thing peopled by ghosts. There they were—
storybook ghosts, and regular haunts, and poor damned

souls—all the fixings of a storied supernatural, all the things we have heard about and loudly disbelieved and secretly wonder about. So what? What had it all to do with me?

As the days slid by, I wondered less about my new, strange surroundings, and gave more and more thought to that question. I had bought—or been given—a talent. I could see ghosts. I could see all parts of a ghostly world, even the vegetation that grew in it. That was perfectly reasonable—the trees and birds and fungi and flowers. A ghost world is a world as we know it, and a world as we know it must have vegetation. Yes, I could see them. But they couldn't see me!

O.K.; what could I get out of it? I couldn't talk about it or write about it because I wouldn't be believed, and besides, I had this thing exclusive, as far as I knew; why cut a lot of other people in on it?

On what, though?

No, unless I could get a steer from somewhere, there was no percentage in it for me that I could see. And then, about six days after I took that eye-opener, I remember the one place where I might get that steer.

The Shottle Bop!

I was on Sixth Avenue at the time, trying to find something in a five-and-dime that Ginny might like. She couldn't touch anything I brought her but she enjoyed things she could look at—picture books and such. By getting her a little book on photographs of trains since the "De Witt Clinton," and asking her which of them was like ones she had seen, I found out approximately how long it was she'd been there. Nearly eighteen years. Anyway, I got my bright idea and headed for Tenth Avenue and the Shottle Bop. I'd ask that old man—he'd tell me. And when I got to Twenty-first Street, I stopped and stared. Facing me was a blank wall. The whole side of the block was void of people. There was no sign of a shop.

I stood there for a full two minutes not even daring to think. Then I walked downtown toward Twentieth, and then uptown to Twenty-first. Then I did it again. No shop. I wound up without my question answered— what was I going to do with this "talent"?

I was talking to Ginny one afternoon about this and that when a human leg, from the knee down, complete and puffy, drifted between us. I recoiled in horror, but Ginny pushed it gently with one hand. It bent under the touch, and started toward the window, which was open a little at the bottom. The leg floated toward the crack and was sucked through like a cloud of cigarette smoke, reforming again on the other side. It bumbled against the pane for a moment and then ballooned away.

"My gosh!" I breathed. "What *was* that?"

Ginny laughed. "Oh, just one of the Things that's all 'e time flying around. Did it scare you? I used to be scared, but I saw so many of them that I don't care any more, so's they don't light on me."

"But what in the name of all that's disgusting are they?"

"Parts." Ginny was all childish *savoir-faire*.

"Parts of what?"

"People, silly. It's some kind of a game, *I* think. You see, if someone gets hurt and loses something—a finger or an ear or something, why, the ear—the *inside* part of it, I mean, like me being the inside of the 'me' they carried out of here—it goes back to where the person who owned it lived last. Then it goes back to the place before that, and so on. It doesn't go very fast. Then when something happens to a whole person, the 'inside' part comes looking for the rest of itself. It picks up bit after bit—Look!" she put out a filmy forefinger and thumb and nipped a flake of gossamer out of the air.

I learned over and looked closely; it was a small section of semitransparent human skin, ridged and whorled.

"Somebody must have cut his finger," said Ginny matter-of-factly, "while he was living in this room. When something happens to um—you see! He'll be back for it!"

"Good heavens!" I said. "Does this happen to every-one?"

"I dunno. Some people have to stay where they are —like me. But I guess if you haven't done nothing to deserve bein' kept in one place, you have to come all around pickin' up what you lost."

I'd thought of more pleasant things in my time.

For several days I'd noticed a gray ghost hovering up and down the block. He was always on the street, never inside. He whimpered constantly. He was—or had been—a little inoffensive man of the bowler hat and starched collar type. He paid no attention to me— none of them did, for I was apparently invisible to them. But I saw him so often that pretty soon I realized that I'd miss him if he went away. I decided I'd chat with him the next time I saw him.

I left the house one morning and stood around for a few minutes in front of the brownstone steps. Sure enough, pressing through the flotsam of my new, weird co-existent world, came the slim figure of the wraith I had noticed, his rabbit face screwed up, his eyes deep and sad, and his swallowtail coat and striped waistcoat immaculate. I stepped up behind him and said, "Hi!"

He started violently and would have run away, I'm sure, if he'd known where my voice was coming from.

"Take it easy, pal," I said. "I won't hurt you."

"Who are you?"

"You wouldn't know if I told you," I said. "Now stop shivering and tell me about yourself."

He mopped his ghostly face with a ghostly handker-chief, and then began fumbling nervously with a gold toothpick. "My word," he said. "No one's talked to me for years. I'm not quite myself, you see."

"I see," I said. "Well, take it easy. I just happen to've noticed you wandering around here lately. I got curious. You looking for somebody?"

"Oh, no," he said. Now that he had a chance to talk about his troubles, he forgot to be afraid of this mysterious voice from nowhere that had accosted him. "I'm looking for my home."

"Hm-m-m," I said. "Been looking for a long time?"

"Oh, yes." His nose twitched. "I left for work one morning a long time ago, and when I got off the ferry at Battery Place I stopped for a moment to watch the work on that newfangled elevated railroad they were building down there. All of a sudden there was a loud noise—my goodness! It was terrible—and the next thing I knew I was standing back from the curb and looking at a man who looked just like me! A girder had fallen, and—my word!" He mopped his face again. "Since then I have been looking and looking. I can't seem to find anyone who knows where I might have lived, and I don't understand all the things I see floating around me, and I never thought I'd see the day when grass would grow on lower Broadway—oh, it's terrible." He began to cry.

I felt sorry for him. I could easily see what had happened. The shock was so great that even his ghost had amnesia! Poor little egg—until he was whole, he could find no rest. The thing interested me. Would a ghost react to the usual cures for amnesia? If so, then what would happen to him?

"You say you got off a ferryboat? Then you must have lived on the Island . . . Staten Island, over there across the bay!"

"You really think so?" He stared through me, puzzled and hopeful.

"Why sure! Say, how'd you like me to take you over there? Maybe we can find your house."

"Oh, that would be splendid! But—oh, my, what will my wife say?"

I grinned. "She might want to know where you've been. Anyway, she'll be glad to see you back, I imagine. Come on; let's get going!"

I gave him a shove in the direction of the subways and strolled along behind him. Once in a while I got a stare from a passer-by for walking with one hand out in front of me and talking into thin air. It didn't bother me very much. My companion, though, was very self-conscious about it, for the inhabitants of his world screeched and giggled when they saw him doing practically the same thing. Of all the humans, only I was invisible to them, and the little ghost in the bowler hat blushed from embarrassment until I thought he'd burst.

We hopped a subway—it was a new experience for him, I gathered—and went down to South Ferry. The subway system in New York is a very unpleasant place to one gifted as I was. Everything that enjoys lurking in the dark hangs out there, and there is quite a crop of dismembered human remains. After this day I took the bus.

We got a ferry without waiting. The little gray ghost got a real kick out of the trip. He asked me about the ships in the harbor and their flags, and marveled at the dearth of sailing vessels. He *tsk, tsked* at the Statue of Liberty; the last time he had seen it, he said, was while it still had its original brassy gold color, before it got its patina. By this I placed him in the late seventies; he must have been looking for his home for over sixty years!

We landed at the Island, and from there I gave him his head. At the top of Fort Hill he suddenly said, "My name is John Quigg. I live at 45 Fourth Avenue!" I've never seen anyone quite so delighted as he was by the discovery. And from then on it was easy. He turned left again, straight down for two blocks and again right. I noticed—he didn't—that the street was marked "Winter Avenue." I remembered vaguely that the streets in this section had been numbered years ago.

He trotted briskly up the hill and then suddenly stopped and turned vaguely. "I say, are you still with me?"

"Still here," I said.

"I'm all right now. I can't tell you how much I appreciate this. Is there anything I could do for you?"

I considered. "Hardly. We're of different times, you know. Things change."

He looked, a little pathetically, at the new apartment house on the corner and nodded. "I think I know what happened to me," he said softly. "But I guess it's all right . . . I made a will, and the kids were grown." He sighed. "But if it hadn't been for you I'd still be wandering around Manhattan. Let's see—ah; come with me!"

He suddenly broke into a run. I followed as quickly as I could. Almost at the top of the hill was a huge old shingled house, with a silly cupola and a complete lack of paint. It was dirty and it was tumble-down, and at the sight of it the little fellow's face twisted sadly. He gulped and turned through a gap in the hedge and down beside the house. Casting about in the long grass, he spotted a boulder sunk deep into the turf.

"This is it," he said. "Just you dig under that. There is no mention of it in my will, except a small fund to keep paying the box rent. Yes, a safety-deposit box, and the key and an authority are under that stone. I hid it"— he giggled—"from my wife one night, and never did get a chance to tell her. You can have whatever's any good to you." He turned to the house, squared his shoulders, and marched in the side door, which banged open for him in a convenient gust of wind. I listened for a moment and then smiled at the tirade that burst forth. Old Quigg was catching real hell from his wife, who'd sat waiting for over sixty years for him! It was a bitter stream of invective, but—well, she must have loved him. She couldn't leave the place until she was complete, if Ginny's theory was correct, and she wasn't really complete until her husband came home! It tickled me. They'd be all right now!

I found an old pinchbar in the drive and attacked the ground around the stone. It took quite a while and made my hands bleed, but after a while I pried the stone up and was able to scrabble around under it. Sure enough, there was an oiled silk pouch under there. I caught it up and carefully unwrapped the strings around it. Inside was a key and a letter addressed to a New York bank, designating only "Bearer" and authorizing the use of the key. I laughed aloud. Little old meek and mild John Quigg, I'd bet, had set aside some "mad money." With a layout like that, a man could take a powder without leaving a single sign. The son-of-a-gun! I would never know just what it was he had up his sleeve, but I'll bet there was a woman in the case. Even fixed up with his will! Ah, well—I should kick!

It didn't take me long to get over to the bank. I had a little trouble getting into the vaults, because it took quite a while to look up the box in the old records. But I finally cleared the red tape, and found myself the proud possessor of just under eight thousand bucks in small bills—and not a yellowback among 'em!

Well, from then on I was pretty well set. What did I do? Well, first I bought clothes, and then, I started out to cut ice for myself. I clubbed around a bit and got to know a lot of people, and the more I knew the more I realized what a lot of superstitious dopes they were. I couldn't blame anyone for skirting a ladder under which crouched a genuine basilisk, of course, but what the heck—not one in a thousand have beasts under them! Anyway, my question was answered. I dropped two grand on an elegant office with drapes and dim indirect lighting, and I got me a phone installed and a little quiet sign on the door—Psychic Consultant. And, boy, I did all right.

My customers were mostly upper crust, because I came high. It was generally no trouble to get contact with people's dead relatives, which was usually what they wanted. Most ghosts are crazy to get in contact with this world anyway. That's one of the reasons that almost anyone can become a medium of sorts if he tries hard enough; Lord knows that it doesn't take much to contact the average ghost. Some, of course, were not available. If a man leads a pretty square life, and kicks off leaving no loose ends, he gets clear. I never did find out where these clear spirits went to. All I knew was that they weren't to be contacted. But the vast majority of people have to go back and tie up those loose ends after they die—righting a little wrong here, helping someone they've hindered, cleaning up a bit of dirty work. That's where luck itself comes from, I do believe. You don't get something for nothing.

If you get a nice break, it's been arranged that way by someone who did you dirt in the past, or someone who did wrong to your father or your grandfather or your great-uncle Julius. Everything evens up in the long run, and until it does, some poor damned soul is wandering around the earth trying to do something about it. Half of humanity is walking around crabbing about its tough breaks. If you and you and you only knew what dozens of powers were begging for the chance to help you if you'll let them! And if you let them, you'll help clear up the mess they've made of their lives here, and free them to go wherever it is they go when they've cleaned up. Next time you're in a jam, go away somewhere by yourself and open your mind to these folks. They'll cut in and guide you all right, if you can drop your smugness and your mistaken confidence in your own judgment.

I had a couple of ghostly stooges to run errands for me. One of them, an ex-murderer by the name of One-eye Rachuba, was the fastest spook ever I saw, when it came to locating a wanted ancestor; and then there was Professor Grafe, a frog-faced teacher of social science who'd embezzled from a charity fund and fallen into the Hudson trying to make a getaway. He could trace the most devious genealogies in mere seconds, and deduce the most likely whereabouts of the ghost of a missing relative. The pair of them were all the office force I could use, and although every time they helped out one of my clients they came closer to freedom for themselves, they were both so entangled with their own sloppy lives that I was sure of their services for years.

But do you think I'd be satisfied to stay where I was making money hand over fist without really working for it? Oh, no. Not me. No, I had to big-time. I had to brood over the events of the last few months, and I had to get dramatic about that screwball Audrey, who really wasn't worth my trouble. It wasn't enough that I'd prove Audrey wrong when she said I'd never amount to anything. And I wasn't happy when I thought about the gang. I had to show them up.

I even remembered what the little man in the Shottle Bop had said to me about using my "talent" for bragging or for revenge. I figured I had the edge on everyone, everything. Cocky, I was. Why, I could send one of my ghostly stooges out any time and find out exactly what anyone had been doing three hours ago come Michaelmas. With the shade of the professor at my shoulder, I could back-track on any far-fetched statement and give immediate and logical reasons for back-tracking. No one had anything on me, and I could out-talk, out-maneuver, and out-smart anyone on earth. I was really quite a fellow. I began to think, "What's the use of my doing as well as this when the gang on the West Side don't know anything about it?" and "Man, would that half-wit Happy Sam burn up if he saw me drifting down Broadway in my new six-thousand-dollar roadster!" and "To think I used to waste my time and tears on a dope like Audrey!" In other words, I was tripping up on an inferiority complex. I acted like a veridam fool, which I was. I went over to the West Side.

It was a chilly, late winter night. I'd taken a lot of trouble to dress myself and my car so we'd be bright and shining and would knock some eyes out. Pity I couldn't brighten my brains up a little.

I drove up in front of Casey's poolroom, being careful to do it too fast, and concentrating on shrieks from the tires and a shuddering twenty-four cylinder roar from the engine before I cut the switch. I didn't hurry to get out of the car, either. Just leaned back and lit a fifty-cent cigar, and then tipped my hat over one ear and touched the horn button, causing it to play "Tuxedo Junction" for forty-eight seconds. Then I looked over toward the pool hall.

Well, for a minute I thought that I shouldn't have come, if that was the effect my return to the fold was going to have. And from then on I forgot about everything except how to get out of here.

There were two figures slouched in the glowing doorway of the pool room. It was up a small side street, so short that the city had depended on the place, an old institution, to supply the street lighting. Looking carefully, I made out one of the silhouetted figures as Happy Sam, and the other was Fred Bellew. They just looked out at me; they didn't move; they didn't say anything, and when I said, "Hiya, small fry—remember me?" I noticed that along the darkened walls flanking the bright doorway were ranked the whole crowd of them—the whole gang. It was a shock; it was a little too casually perfect. I didn't like it.

"Hi," said Fred quietly. I knew he wouldn't like the big-timing. I didn't expect any of them to like it, of course, but Fred's dislike sprang from distaste, and the others from resentment, and for the first time I felt a little cheap. I climbed out over the door of the roadster and let them have a gander at my fine feathers.

Sam snorted and said, "Jellybean!" very clearly. Someone else giggled, and from the darkness beside the building came a high-pitched, "Woo-woo!"

I walked up to Sam and grinned at him. I didn't feel like grinning. "I ain't seen you in so long I almost forgot what a heel you were," I said. "How you making?"

"I'm doing all right," he said, and added offensively, "I'm still *working* for a living."

The murmur that ran through the crowd told me that the really smart thing to do was to get back into that

shiny new automobile and hoot along out of there. I
stayed.

"Wise, huh?" I said weakly.

They'd been drinking, I realized—all of them. I was
suddenly in a spot. Sam put his hands in his pockets and
looked at me down his nose. He was the only short man
that ever could do that to me. After a thick silence he
said:

"Better get back to yer crystal balls, phony. We like
guys that sweat. We even like guys that have rackets, if
they run them because they're smarter or tougher than
the next one. But luck and gab ain't enough. Scram."

I looked around helplessly. I was getting what I'd
begged for. What had I expected, anyway? Had I
thought that these boys would crowd around and
shake my hand off for acting this way?

They hardly moved, but they were all around me
suddenly. If I couldn't think of something quickly, I
was going to be mobbed. And when those mugs started
mobbing a man, they did it up just fine. I drew a
deep breath.

"I'm not asking for anything from you, Sam. Nothing; that means advice; see?"

"You're gettin' it?" he flared. "You and your see-
anses. We heard about you. Hanging up widdow-
women for fifty bucks a throw to talk to their 'dear departed'! P-sykik investigator! What a line! Go on; beat
it!"

I had a leg to stand on now. "A phony, huh? Why
I'll bet I could put a haunt on you that would make
that hair of yours stand up on end, if you have guts
enough to go where I tell you to."

"You'll bet? That's a laugh. Listen at that, gang."
He laughed, then turned to me and talked through one
side of his mouth. "All right, you wanted it. Come on,
rich guy; you're called. Fred'll hold stakes. How about
ten of your lousy bucks for every one of mine? Here,
Fred—hold this sawbuck."

"I'll give you twenty to one," I said half hysterically. "And I'll take you to a place where you'll run up against the homeliest, plumb-meanest old haunt you ever heard of."

The crowd roared. Sam laughed with them, but didn't try to back out. With any of that gang, a bet was a bet. He'd taken me up, and he'd set odds, and he was bound. I just nodded and put two century notes into Fred Bellew's hand. Fred and Sam climbed into the car, and just as we started, Sam leaned out and waved.

"See you in hell, fellas," he said. "I'm goin' to raise me a ghost, and one of us is going to scare the other one to death!"

I honked my horn to drown out the whooping and hollering from the sidewalk and got out of there. I turned up the parkway and headed out of town.

"Where to?" Fred asked after a while.

"Stick around," I said, not knowing.

There must be some place not far from here where I could find an honest-to-God haunt, I thought, one that would make Sam backtrack and set me up with the boys again. I opened the compartment in the dashboard and let Ikey out. Ikey was a little twisted imp who'd got his tail caught in between two sheets of steel when they were assembling the car, and had to stay there until it was junked.

"Hey, Ike," I whispered. He looked up, the gleam of the compartment light shining redly in his bright little eyes. "Whistle for the professor, will you? I don't want to yell for him because those mugs in the back seat will hear me. They can't hear you."

"O.K., boss," he said; and putting his fingers to his lips, he gave vent to a blood-curdling, howling scream.

That was the prof's call-letters, as it were. The old man flew ahead of the car, circled around and slid in beside me through the window, which I'd opened a crack for him.

"My goodness," he panted, "I wish you wouldn't

summon me to a location which is traveling with this high degree of celerity. It was all I could do to catch up with you."

"Don't give me that, Professor," I whispered. "You can catch a stratoliner if you want to. Say, I have a guy in the back who wants to get a real scare from a ghost. Know of any around here?"

The professor put on his ghostly pince-nez. "Why, yes. Remember my telling you about the Wolfmeyer place?"

"Golly—he's bad."

"He'll serve your purpose admirably. But don't ask me to go there with you. None of us ever associates with Wolfmeyer. And for heaven's sake, be careful."

"I guess I can handle him. Where is it?"

He gave me explicit directions, bade me good night and left. I was a little surprised; the professor traveled around with me a great deal, and I'd never seen him refuse a chance to see some new scenery. I shrugged it off and went my way. I guess I just didn't know any better.

I headed out of town and into the country to a certain old farmhouse. Wolfmeyer, a Pennsylvania Dutchman, had hung himself there. He had been, and was, a bad egg. Instead of being a nice guy about it all, he was the rebel type. He knew perfectly well that unless he did plenty of good to make up for the evil, he'd be stuck where he was for the rest of eternity. That didn't seem to bother him at all. He got surly and became a really bad spook. Eight people had died in that house since the old man rotted off his own rope. Three of them were tenants who had rented the place, and three were hobos, and two were psychic investigators. They'd all hung themselves. That's the way Wolfmeyer worked. I think he really enjoyed haunting. He certainly was thorough about it anyway.

I didn't want to do any real harm to Happy Sam. I just wanted to teach him a lesson. And look what happened!

We reached the place just before midnight. No one had said much, except that I told Fred and Sam about Wolfmeyer, and pretty well what was to be expected from him. They did a good deal of laughing about it, so I just shut up and drove. The next item of conversation was Fred's, when he made the terms of the bet. To win, Sam was to stay in the house until dawn. He wasn't to call for help and he wasn't to leave. He had to bring in a coil of rope, tie a noose in one end and string the other up on "Wolfmeyer's Beam"—the great oaken beam on which the old man had hung himself, and eight others after him. This was an added temptation to Wolfmeyer to work on Happy Sam, and was my idea. I was to go in with Sam, to watch him in case the thing became too dangerous. Fred was to stay in the car a hundred yards down the road and wait.

I parked the car at the agreed distance and Sam and I got out. Sam had my tow rope over his shoulder, already noosed. Fred had quieted down considerably, and his face was dead serious.

"I don't think I like this," he said, looking up the road at the house. It hunched back from the highway, and looked like a malign being deep in thought.

I said, "Well, Sam? Want to pay up now and call it quits?"

He followed Fred's gaze. It sure was a dreary-looking place, and his liquor had fizzed away. He thought a minute, then shrugged and grinned. I had to admire the rat. "Hell, I'll go through with it. Can't bluff me with scenery, phony."

Surprisingly, Fred piped up, "I don't think he's a phony, Sam."

The resistance made Sam stubborn, though I could see by his face that he knew better. "Come on, phony," he said and swung up the road.

We climbed into the house by way of a cellar door that slanted up to a window on the first floor. I hauled out a flashlight and lit the way to the beam. It was only one of many that delighted in turning the sound of one's footsteps into laughing whispers that ran round and round the rooms and halls and would not die. Under the famous beam the dusty floor was dark-stained.

I gave Sam a hand in fixing the rope, and then clicked off the light. It must have been tough on him then. I didn't mind, because I knew I could see anything before it got to me, and even then, no ghost could see me. Not only that, for me the walls and floors and ceilings were lit with the phosphorescent many-hued glow of the ever-present ghost plants. For its eerie effect I wished Sam could see the ghost-molds feeding greedily on the stain under the beam.

Sam was already breathing heavily, but I knew it would take more than just darkness and silence to get his goat. He'd have to be alone, and then he'd have to have a visitor or so.

"So long, kid," I said, slapping him on the shoulder, and I turned and walked out of the room.

I let him hear me go out of the house and then I crept silently back. It was without doubt the most deserted place I have ever seen. Even ghosts kept away from it, excepting, of course, Wolfmeyer's. There was just the luxurious vegetation, invisible to all but me, and the deep silence rippled by Sam's breath. After ten minutes or so I knew for certain that Happy Sam had more guts than I'd ever have credited him with. He had to be scared. He couldn't—or wouldn't—scare himself.

I crouched down against the walls of an adjoining room and made myself comfortable. I figured Wolfmeyer would be along pretty soon. I hoped earnestly that I could stop the thing before it got too far. No use in making this any more than a good lesson for a wiseacre. I was feeling pretty smug about it all, and I was totally unprepared for what happened.

I was looking toward the doorway opposite when I realized that for some minutes there had been the palest of pale glows there. It brightened as I watched; brightened and flickered gently. It was green, the green of things moldy and rotting away; and with it came a subtly harrowing stench. It was the smell of flesh so very dead that it had ceased to be really odorous. It was utterly horrible, and I was honestly scared out of my wits. It was some moments before the comforting thought of my invulnerability came back to me, and I shrank lower and closer to the wall and watched.

And Wolfmeyer came in.

His was the ghost of an old, old man. He wore a flowing, filthy robe, and his bare forearms thrust out in front of him were stringy and strong. His head, with its tangled hair and beard, quivered on a broken, ruined neck like the blade of a knife just thrown into soft wood. Each slow step as he crossed the room set his head to quivering again. His eyes were alight; red they were, with deep green flames buried in them. His canine teeth had lengthened into yellow, blunt tusks, and they were like pillars supporting his crooked grin. The putrescent green glow was a horrid halo about him. He was a bright and evil thing.

He passed me completely unconscious of my presence and paused at the door of the room where Sam waited by the rope. He stood just outside it, his claws extended, the quivering of his head slowly dying. He stared in at Sam, and suddenly opened his mouth and howled. It was a quiet, deadly sound, one that might have come from the throat of a distant dog, but, though I couldn't see into the other room, I knew that Sam had jerked his head around and was staring at the ghost. Wolfmeyer raised his arms a trifle, seemed to totter a bit, and then moved into the room.

I snapped myself out of the crawling terror that gripped me and scrambled to my feet. If I didn't move fast—

Tiptoeing swiftly to the door, I stopped just long enough to see Wolfmeyer beating his arms about erratically over his head, a movement that made his robe flutter and his whole figure pulsate in the green light; just long enough to see Sam on his feet, wide-eyed, staggering back and back toward the rope. He clutched his throat and opened his mouth and made no sound, and his head tilted, his neck bent, his twisted face gaped at the ceiling as he clumped backward away from the ghost and into the ready noose. And then I leaned over Wolfmeyer's shoulder, put my lips to his ear, and said:

"*Boo!*"

I almost laughed. Wolfmeyer gave a little squeak, jumped about ten feet, and, without stopping to look around, high-tailed out of the room so fast that he was just a blur. That was one scared old spook!

At the same time Happy Sam straightened, his face relaxed and relieved, and sat down with a bump under the noose. That was as close a thing as ever I want to see. He sat there, his face soaking wet with cold sweat, his hands between his knees, staring limply at his feet.

"That'll show you!" I exulted, and walked over to him. "Pay up, scum, and you may starve for that week's pay!" He didn't move. I guess he was plenty shocked.

"Come on!" I said. "Pull yourself together, man! Haven't you seen enough? That old fellow will be back any second now. On your feet!"

He didn't move.

"Sam!"

He didn't move.

"*Sam!*" I clutched at his shoulder. He pitched over sideways and lay still. He was quite dead.

I didn't do anything and for a while I didn't say anything. Then I said hopelessly, as I knelt there, "Aw, Sam. Sam—cut it out, fella."

After a minute I rose slowly and started for the door. I'd taken three steps when I stopped. Something was happening! I rubbed my hand over my eyes. Yes, it is— it was getting dark! The vague luminescence of the vines and flowers of the ghost world was getting dimmer, fading, fading—

But that had never happened before!

No difference. I told myself desperately, it's happening now, all right. *I got to get out of here!*

See? You see. It was the stuff—the damn stuff from the Shottle Bop. It was wearing off! When Sam died it . . . it stopped working on me! Was this what I had to pay for the bottle? Was this what was to happen if I used it for revenge?

The light was almost gone—and now it was gone. I couldn't see a thing in the room but one of the doors. Why could I see the doorway? What was that pale-green light that set off its dusty frame?

Wolfmeyer! *I got to get out of here!*

I couldn't see ghosts any more. Ghosts could see me now. I ran. I darted across the dark room and smashed into the wall on the other side. I reeled back from it, blood spouting from between the fingers I slapped to my face. I ran again. Another wall clubbed me. Where was that other door? I ran again, and again struck a wall. I screamed and ran again. I tripped over Sam's body. My head went through the noose. It whipped down on my windpipe, and my neck broke with an agonizing crunch. I floundered there for half a minute, and then dangled.

Dead as hell, I was. Wolfmeyer, he laughed and laughed.

Fred found me and Sam in the morning. He took our bodies away in the car. Now I've got to stay here and haunt this damn old house. Me and Wolfmeyer.

THE MAGNUM

Jack Ritchie

Amos Weatherlee clutched a magnum of champagne in one hand and a hammer in the other.

He paused in the wide doorway of the hotel bar.

At this hour of the afternoon, the barroom was nearly empty except for three women in one booth with Pink Ladies and a middle-aged man alone in another.

Weatherlee approached him and extended the hammer. "Pardon me, but I would regard it as an extreme favor if you would smash my bottle."

Harry Sloan studied him warily. "Don't you think that would make quite a mess?"

Weatherlee's silver-gray hair was somewhat disheveled and he spoke with a slight slur. "I never thought of that. You don't suppose that the bartender has a basin or something like that we could use?"

Sloan sipped his whiskey and soda. "If you're really set on smashing that bottle, why don't you do it yourself?"

Weatherlee sighed. "I tried. I really tried. Captain O'Reilly did too. So did Carruthers and Larson and Cooper and I don't know how many more. It was quite a wild night."

"What was?"

"Our club meeting a year ago."

Sloan's attention was distracted by the procession of a dozen elderly men filing through the hotel entrance. At least half of them walked with canes. They moved slowly across the lobby toward the open doors of a private dining room.

Sloan showed some interest. "Who in the world are they?"

"Our club," Weatherlee said. "It's our annual reunion. The members just finished a sight-seeing bus tour of the city and now we're going to have dinner." He watched as the group entered the dining room. "We were all members of the same National Guard Company. We formed the club right after the war."

"World War I?"

"No," Weatherlee said. "The Spanish American War."

Sloan regarded him skeptically.

"That's Captain O'Reilly," Weatherlee said. "Wearing the broad-brimmed campaign hat." He sat down. "How old do you think I am?"

"I haven't the faintest idea."

"Ninety," Weatherlee said proudly. "I was eighteen when I enlisted."

"Sure," Sloan said. "And I suppose you were a member of Teddy Roosevelt's Rough Riders and charged up San Juan hill?"

"No. Actually our outfit never got beyond Tampa before the war ended. Our only casualties were to yellow fever."

"You look pretty spry for ninety."

"I am," Weatherlee said firmly. "I take a brisk half-hour walk every day and I'm still in full possession of all my faculties. In full possession."

"Sure," Sloan said. "Sure."

"Of course we weren't all the same age when we formed the club. Captain *O'Reilly*, for instance, our oldest man, was thirty-six. Twice as old as I at the time.

He joined the club more in the spirit of good-fellowship, rather than really expecting to drink the bottle."

Sloan eyed the magnum of champagne. "Just what kind of a club was this?"

"A Last Man club. Perhaps you've heard of them? We founded ours in 1898. Right after the war ended and we were waiting to get shipped home. We wanted one hundred members, but actually we could get only ninety-eight to sign up."

"And those are the survivors? What's left?"

"Oh, no. Those are only the members who could make it. The others are in hospitals, old age homes, and the like."

Sloan did some mental arithmetic. "You said that Captain O'Reilly was thirty-six when the club formed in 1898?"

"Yes."

"Are you telling me that Captain O'Reilly is now one hundred and eight years old?"

"That's right. Our oldest man."

"And at ninety, you're the youngest?"

"Yes," Weatherlee said. "And, I'm Custodian of the Bottle. According to our by-laws, the youngest surviving member is Custodian of the Bottle."

Sloan finished his drink. "Just how many club members are still alive?"

"Ninety-five."

Sloan stared at him for a few moments. "You mean to tell me that only three of you people have died since 1898?"

Weatherlee nodded. "There was Meyer. He died in a train accident back in 1909. Or was it 1910? And McMurty. He stayed in the Guard and worked himself up to full colonel before he was killed in the Argonne in 1918. And Iverson. He died of acute appendicitis in 1921."

Sloan considered his empty glass and then sighed. "Care for a drink?"

Weatherlee smiled affably. "I guess one more won't hurt. I'll take whatever you're having."

Sloan caught the bartender's eye and held up two fingers.

Weatherlee leaned forward and lowered his voice. "Actually this isn't the original champagne bottle. I broke that in 1924."

Sloan studied it again.

"It happened at our convention that year," Weatherlee said. "I was riding the elevator at the time. In those days they didn't operate as smoothly as they do now. There was this sudden jerk as the operator stopped at my floor. The suitcase I was carrying sprang open and the bottle dropped to the floor. Couldn't have fallen more than a foot, but there it lay, shattered on the floor."

Weatherlee shook his head at the memory. "I was absolutely panic-stricken. I mean here I was the custodian of the club's bottle—a great responsibility—and there it lay, shattered on the elevator floor. Luckily I was the only passenger on the elevator at the time. No one but the operator knew what had happened."

"So you went out and bought another bottle?"

"No. I didn't see how I could duplicate it anywhere. The bottle was quite distinctive. Purchased in Tampa, twenty-six years before."

Sloan indicated the bottle. "Then what is that?"

"It was the elevator operator who saved me," Weatherlee said. "He went out and got an *exact* duplicate."

"How did he manage to do that?"

"I haven't the faintest idea. He seemed a little evasive, now that I remember, but I was too overjoyed to press him. He was really most apologetic about the accident. Most solicitous. Took care of the mess in the elevator and brought the new bottle to my room fifteen minutes later. Wouldn't even let me pay for it. Claimed that the entire incident was really his doing and wouldn't accept a cent."

Sloan took his eyes from the magnum. "You said

something about Captain O'Reilly trying to break the bottle?"

"Yes. Last year at our meeting. I still don't know exactly why he tried it. But I do remember that he kept staring at the bottle all evening. That year I was the Treasurer and I'd just finished reading my report. We had $4,900 in the treasury. Our dues are actually almost nominal, but still after all those years and compounded interest, it reached that sum."

The bartender brought the drinks. Sloan paid him and took a swallow of his whiskey and soda. "So what about O'Reilly?"

Weatherlee watched the bartender leave. "Oh, yes. Well, just as I finished, he rose suddenly to his feet and began slashing at the bottle with his cane and shouting, 'That damn bottle! That damn bottle!' And then it seemed as though nearly everyone else went bad too. They shouted and cursed and smashed at the bottle, some even with chairs. I really don't know how it would all have ended if the waiters and other hotel people hadn't rushed in and restrained them."

"But they didn't break the bottle?"

"No. It was most remarkable. The blows were really resounding, and yet it didn't break. I thought about that all year. All this long year."

Weatherlee took a deep breath. "I arrived here early this morning. I am not a drinking man, but on impulse I bought a pint of whiskey and took it up to my room. I just sat there drinking and staring at that bottle. I even forgot all about the bus tour. And then I don't know what came over me, but I picked up an ashtray— one of those heavy glass things that are practically indestructible—and struck the bottle. Again and again, until finally the *ashtray* broke."

Weatherlee took the handkerchief from his breastcoat pocket. "I was in a perfect frenzy. I rushed out of my room with the bottle and down the hallway I found one of those maintenance closets with its door open. There was a hammer on one of the shelves. I put the magnum of champagne into the stationary tub in the cubicle and struck it again and again with the hammer."

"But the bottle still didn't break?"

Weatherlee dabbed lightly at his forehead with the handkerchief. "But what was most ghastly of all was that all the time I was trying to smash that bottle, I had the feeling that someone, somewhere, was *laughing* at me."

He glared at the magnum. "And then suddenly, the *conviction,* the *certainty,* came to me that neither I, nor *anybody* in the club could destroy that bottle. If it were done, it had to be done by someone on the outside."

Sloan frowned at his drink. "Just *why* do you want to destroy that bottle in the first place?"

Weatherlee sighed. "I don't know. I just know that I *do.*"

They were both silent for almost a minute and then Sloan said. "This elevator operator. What did he look like?"

"The elevator operator? Rather a distinguished sort of a person. I remember thinking at the time that he wasn't at all what one would expect of an elevator operator. Rather tall. Dark hair, dark eyes."

One of the doors of the dining room across the lobby opened and a waiter stepped out. He came into the bar. "Mr. Weatherlee, we're serving now."

Weatherlee nodded. "Yes. I'll be there in a moment."

Sloan waited until the waiter was out of hearing. "When did you say you broke the original bottle?"

"In 1924."

"And nobody's died since then?"

"Nobody's died since 1921. That was when Iverson got his acute appendicitis."

Sloan stared at the bottle again. "I'd like to join your club."

Weatherlee blinked. "But that's impossible."

"Why is it impossible?"

"Well . . . for one thing, you didn't belong to our National Guard company."

"Do your by-laws say anything about members having to belong to that particular company? Or any company at all?"

"Well, no. But it was *assumed*. . . ."

"And you did say that you never did fill your membership quota? Only ninety-eight people signed up? That leaves a vacancy of two, doesn't it?"

"Yes, but you are so much younger than any of the rest of us. It would be unfair for us to have to compete with you for the bottle."

"Look," Sloan said. "I'm not a rich man, but I'll match what's in the treasury, dollar for dollar."

"That's very kind of you," Weatherlee said a bit stiffly, "but if you should outlive all of us, and that seems likely, you'd get it all back anyhow."

Sloan smiled patiently. "I'll sign an affidavit renouncing all claim to what's in the treasury."

Weatherlee rubbed his neck. "I don't know. I'm not the final authority on anything like this. I'm not even an officer this year, unless you want to count being Custodian of the bottle. I really don't know what the procedure would be in a case like this. I suppose we'll have to take a vote or something."

He rose and put the magnum under his arm. "I suppose there's no harm in asking, but frankly I think they'll turn you down."

Sloan put his hand on the hammer. "Better leave this here with me."

Sloan came to Weatherlee's room at nine-thirty the next morning.

He took an envelope from his pocket and handed it to Weatherlee.

Weatherlee nodded acceptance. "To be quite honest, I was a bit surprised that the club decided to accept you. Not without exception, of course. Captain O'Reilly was quite against it."

Sloan moved to the bureau and picked up the magnum of champagne.

Weatherlee blinked. "What are you doing?"

"Taking the bottle with me. You told me yourself that according to the club's by-laws, the youngest member is Custodian of the Bottle."

"Yes, but. . . ."

Sloan opened the door to the corridor. He smiled broadly. "We wouldn't want you to go around asking strange people to break it, now would we?"

When Sloan was gone, Weatherlee locked the door.

He went to the bathroom and began removing the make-up from his face. As he worked, a half century disappeared.

Maybe he could have taken Sloan for more than five thousand, but you never know. Getting too greedy could have blown the whole deal.

He smiled.

Finding the sucker was the hardest part of it.

But once you did, and learned approximately how much he could part with without undue pain, you went about arranging the set-up. That included going to the nearest Old Soldiers' Home and offering to treat a dozen of their oldest veterans to a dinner.

And the old boys did so enjoy an afternoon out.

VOICES
IN THE DUST

Gerald Kersh

I landed on the northeast coast with tinned goods and other trade goods such as steel knives, beads and sweet chocolate, intending to make my way to the ruins of Annan.

A chieftain of the savages of the central belt warned me not to go to The Bad Place. That was his name for the ancient ruins of the forgotten city of Annan, a hundred miles to the southeast. Some of the tribesmen called it The Dead Place or The Dark Place. He called it The Bad Place. He was a grim but honorable old ruffian, squat and hairy and covered with scars. Over a pot of evil-smelling black beer—they brew it twice a year, with solemn ceremony, and everyone gets hideously drunk—he grew communicative, and, as the liquor took hold of him, boastful. He showed me his tattooing; every mark meant something, so that his history was pricked out on his skin. When a chieftain of the central belt dies he is flayed and his hide is hung up in the hut that is reserved for holy objects; so he lives in human memory.

Showing his broken teeth in a snarling smile, he pointed to a skillfully executed fish on his left arm; it proved that he had won a great victory over the fish eaters of the north. A wild pig on his chest celebrated the massacre of the pig men of the northwest. He told

Gerald Kersh

me a bloody story, caressing a black-and-red dog that lay at his feet, and watched me with murderous yellow eyes. Oh, the distances he had traveled, the men he had killed, the women he had ravished, the riches he had plundered! He knew everything. He liked me—had I not given him a fine steel knife? So he would give me some good advice.

"I could keep you here if I liked," he said, "but you are my friend, and if you want to go, you may go. I will even send ten armed men with you. You may need them. If you are traveling southward you must pass through the country of the red men. They eat men when they can catch them, and move fast; they come and go. Have no fear, however, of the bird men. For a handful of beads and a little wire—especially wire—they will do anything. My men will not go with you to The Bad Place. Nobody ever goes to The Bad Place. Even I would not go to The Bad Place, and I am the bravest man in the world. Why must you go? Stay. Live under my protection. I will give you a wife. Look. You can have her." He jerked a spatulate thumb in the direction of a big, swarthy girl with greased hair who squatted, almost naked, a couple of yards away. "She is one of mine. But you can have her. No man has touched her yet. Marry her. Stay."

I said, "Tell me, why have you—even you, chief— stayed away from that place?"

He grew grave. "I fear no man and no beast," he said.

"But——"

"But"—he gulped some more black beer—"there are Things."

"What things?"

"Things. Little people." He meant fairies. "I'll fight anything I can see. But what of that which man cannot see? Who fights that? Stay away from The Bad Place. Marry her. Stay here. Feel her—fat! Don't go. Nobody goes. . . . *hup!* I like you. You are my friend. You must stay here."

I gave him a can of peaches. He crowed like a baby. "You are my friend," he said, "and if you want to go, then go. But if you get away, come back."

"*If?*" I said. "I am not much afraid of what I cannot see. First I see. Then I believe. I cannot fear that which I do not believe."

His eyebrows knotted, his fists knotted, and he bared his teeth. "Are you saying that what I say is not true?" he shouted.

"King . . . great chief," I said, "I believe, I believe. What you say is true."

"If I had not given my word, I should have had you killed for that," he grunted. "But I have gi-given my word. . . . *hup!* My—my word is a word. I . . . you . . . go, go!"

Next morning he was ill. I gave him magnesia in a pot of water, for which he expressed gratitude. That day I set out with ten squat, sullen warriors—killers, men without fear.

But when we came in sight of the place that was called The Bad Place, The Dark Place or The Dead Place, they stopped. For no consideration would they walk another step forward. I offered each man a steel knife. Their terror was stronger than their desire. "Not even for that," said their leader.

I went on alone.

It was a Dead Place because there was no life in it, and therefore it was also a Dark Place. No grass grew there. It had come to nothingness. Not even the coarse, hardy weeds that find a roothold in the uncooled ashes of burned-out buildings pushed their leaves out of its desolation. Under the seasonal rain it must have been a quagmire. Now, baked by the August sun, it was a sort of ash heap, studded with gray excrescences that resembled enormous cinders. A dreary, dark-gray, powdery valley went down; a melancholy dust heap of a hill crept up and away. As I looked I saw something writhe and come up out of the hillside; it came down

toward me with a sickening, wriggling run, and it was
pale gray, like a ghost. I drew my pistol. Then the
gray thing pirouetted and danced. It was nothing but
dust, picked up by a current of warm air. The cold hand
that had got hold of my heart relaxed, and my heart
fell back into my stomach, where it had already sunk.

I went down. This place was so dead that I was grateful for the company of the flies that had followed me.
The sun struck like a floodlight out of a clean blue sky;
every crumb of grit threw a clear-cut black shadow
in the dust. A bird passed, down and up, quick as the
flick of a whip, on the trail of a desperate dragonfly. Yet
here, in a white-hot summer afternoon, I felt that I was
going down, step by step, into the black night of the
soul. This was a Bad Place.

The dust clung to me. I moved slowly between half-
buried slabs of shattered granite. Evening was coming.
A breeze that felt like a hot breath on my neck stirred
the ruins of the ancient city; dust devils twisted and
flirted and fell; the sun grew red. At last I found something that had been a wall, and pitched my tent close
to it. Somehow it was good to have a wall behind me.
There was nothing to be afraid of—there was absolutely
nothing. Yet I was afraid. What is it that makes a comfortable man go out with a pickax to poke among the
ruins of ancient cities? I was sick with nameless terror.
But fear breeds pride. I could not go back. And I was
tired, desperately tired. If I did not sleep, I should break.

I ate and lay down. Sleep was picking me away,
leaf by leaf. Bad Place . . . Dead Place . . . Dark Place
. . . little people. . . .

Before I fell asleep I thought I heard somebody singing a queer, wailing song: *"Oh-oo, oh-oo, oh-oo!"* It
rose and descended—it conveyed terror. It might have
been an owl or some other night bird, or it might
have been the wind in the ruins or a half dream. It
sounded almost human, though. I started awake,
clutching my pistol. I could have sworn that the wail

was forming words. What words? They sounded like
some debased sort of Arabic:

> *"Ookil'karabin*
> *Ookil'karabin,*
> *Isapara, mibanara,*
> *Ikil'karabin,*
> *Ookil'karabin."*

As I sat up, the noise stopped. *Yes,* I thought, *I was
dreaming.* I lay back and went to sleep. Centuries of
silence lay in the dust.

All the same, in that abominable loneliness I felt
that I was not alone. I woke five times before dawn to
listen. There was nothing. Even the flies had gone away.
Yet when day broke I observed that something strange
had happened.

My socks had disappeared. In the dust—that powdery dust in which the petal of a flower would have left
its imprint—there were no tracks. Yet the flap of my
tent was unfastened and my socks were gone.

For the next three days I sifted the detritus of that
dead city, fumbling and feeling after crumbs of evidence,
and listening to the silence. My pickax pecked out nothing but chips of stone and strange echoes. On the second
day I unearthed some fragments of crumbling glass
and shards of white, glazed pottery, together with a
handful of narrow pieces of iron which fell to nothing
as I touched them. I also found a small dish of patterned
porcelain, on which were five letters—ESDEN—part of
some inscription. It was sad and strange that this poor
thing should have survived the smashing of the huge
edifices and noble monuments of that great city. But
all the time I felt that someone or something was watching me an inch beyond my field of vision.

On the third day I found a red drinking vessel, intact, and a cooking pot of some light white metal, with

marks of burning on the bottom of it and some charred powder inside. The housewife to whom this pot belonged was cooking some sort of stew, no doubt, when the wrath of God struck the city.

When the blow fell that city must have ceased to be in less time than it takes to clap your hands; it fell like the cities of the plain when the fire came down from heaven. Here, as in the ruins of Pompeii, one might discover curiously pathetic ashes and highly individual dust. I found the calcined skeleton of a woman, clutching, in the charred vestiges of loving arms, the skeletal outline of a newly born child. As I touched these remains they broke like burnt paper. Not far away, half-buried in a sort of volcanic cinders, four twisted lumps of animal charcoal lay in the form of a cross, the center of which was a shapeless mass of glass; this had been a sociable drinking party. This lump of glass had melted and run into a blob the outlines of which suggested the map of Africa. But in the equatorial part of it, so to speak, one could distinguish the base of a bottle.

I also found a tiny square of thin woven stuff. It must have been a handkerchief, a woman's handkerchief. Some whimsey of chance let it stay intact. In one corner of it there was embroidered a roman letter A. Who was A? I seemed to see some fussy, fastidious gentlewoman, discreetly perfumed—a benevolent tyrant at home, but every inch a lady. Deploring the decadence of the age, she dabbed this delicate twenty-five square inches of gauzy nothingness at one sensitive nostril. Then—psst!—she and the house in which she lived were swept away in one lick of frightful heat. And the handkerchief fluttered down on her ashes.

Near by, untouched by time and disaster, stood a low wall of clay bricks. On this wall was an inscription in chalk. A child must have scrawled it. It said: LYDIA IS A DIRTY PIG. Below it lay the unidentifiable remains of three human beings. As I looked, the air currents stirred the dust. Swaying and undulating like a ballet dancer, a fine gray powdery corkscrew spun up and threw itself at my feet.

That night, again, I thought I heard singing. But what was there to sing? Birds? There were no birds. Nevertheless, I lay awake. I was uneasy. There was no moon. I saw that my watch said 12:45. After that I must have slipped into the shallow end of sleep, because I opened my eyes—instinct warned me to keep still—and saw that more than two hours had passed. I felt, rather than heard, a little furtive sound. I lay quiet and listened. Fear and watchfulness had sharpened my ears. In spite of the beating of my heart I heard a "tink-tink" of metal against metal. My flashlight was under my left hand; my pistol was in my right. I breathed deeply. The metal clinked again. Now I knew where to look. I aimed the flashlight at the noise, switched on a broad beam of bright light, and leaped up with a roar of that mad rage which comes out of fear. Something was caught in the light. The light paralyzed it. The thing was glued in the shining, white puddle; it had enormous eyes. I fired at it—I mean, I aimed at it and pressed my trigger, but had forgotten to lift my safety catch. Holding the thing in the flashlight beam, I struck at it with the barrel of the pistol. I was cruel because I was afraid. It squealed, and something cracked. Then I had it by the neck. If it was not a rat, it smelled like a rat. *"Oh-oo, oh-oo, oh-oo!"* it wailed, and I heard something scuffle outside. Another voice wailed, *"Oh-oo, oh-oo, oh-oo!"* A third voice picked it up. In five seconds the hot, dark night was full of a most woe-begone crying. Five seconds later there was silence, except for the gasping of the cold little creature under my hand.

I was calm now, and I saw that it was not a rat. It was something like a man—a little, distorted man. The light hurt it, yet it could not look away; the big eyes contracted, twitching and flickering, out of a narrow and repulsive face fringed with pale hair.

"Oh, oh, oh," it said—the wet, chisel-toothed mouth was quivering on the edge of a word.

I noticed then that it was standing on something gray; I looked again, and saw my woolen jacket. It had been trying to take this jacket away. But in the right-hand pocket there was a coin and a small key; they had struck together and awakened me.

I was no longer afraid, so I became kind. "Calm," I said, as one talks to a dog. "Calm, calm, calm! Quiet now, quiet!"

The little white one held up a wrist from which dropped a skinny, naked hand like a mole's paw, and whispered, *"Oh-oo."*

"Sit!" I said.

It was terrified and in pain. I had broken its wrist. I should say his wrist; he was a sort of man; a male creature, wretched, filthy and dank, dwarfish, debased; greenish-white, like milkdew, smelling like mildew, cold and wetly yielding like mildew; rat-toothed, rat-eared and chinless, yet not unlike a man. If he had stood up-right, he would have been about three feet tall.

This, then, was the nameless thing that had struck such terror into the bloody old chieftain of the savages of the middle belt—this bloodless, chinless thing with-out a forehead, whose limbs were like the tendrils of a creeping plant that sprouts in the dark, and who cringed, twittering and whimpering, at my feet. Its eyes were large, like a lemur's. The ears were long, pointed and almost transparent; they shone sickly pink in the light, and I could see that they were reticulated with thin, dark veins. There had been some attempt at cloth-ing—a kind of primitive jacket and leggings of some thin gray fur, tattered and indescribably filthy. My stomach turned at the feel of it and its deathly, musty smell.

This, then was one of the fairies, one of the little people of The Dead Place, and I had it by the neck.

I may say, at this point, that I have always be-lieved in fairies. By "fairies," I do not mean little del-icate, magical, pretty creatures with butterfly wings, living among the flowers and drinking nectar out of bluebell blossoms. I do not believe in such fairies. But I do believe in the little people—the gnomes, elves, pucks, brownies, pixies and leprechauns of legend. Belief in these little people is as old as the world, universal and persistent. In the stories, you remember, the outward appearance of the little people is fairly constant. They are dwarfish. They have big eyes and long, pointed features. They come out at night, and have the power to make themselves invisible. Sometimes they are mischievous.

It is best to keep on the good side of the little people, because they can play all kinds of malevolent tricks— spoil the butter, frighten the cows, destroy small objects. You will have observed that they have no power seriously to injure mankind, yet they carry with them the terror of the night. In some parts of the world peasants placate the little people by leaving out a bowl of hot porridge or milk for them to drink, for they are always hungry and always cold. Note that.

Every child has read the story of the Cold Lad of the Hill. A poor cobbler, having spent his last few coins on a piece of leather, fell asleep, too tired to work. When he awoke in the morning, he found that the leather had been worked with consummate skill into a beautiful pair of slippers. He sold these slippers and bought a larger piece of leather, which he left on the bench, together with a bowl of hot soup. Then he pretended to fall asleep and saw, out of the corner of his eye, a tiny, pale, shivering, naked man who crept in and set to work with dazzling speed. Next morning there were two pairs of slippers. This went on for several days. Prosperity returned to the house of the cobbler. His wife, to reward the little man, knitted him a little cloak with a hood. They put the garment on the bench. That night the little man came again. He saw the cloak and hood, put them on with a squeal of joy, capered up and down the cobbler's bench admiring himself, and at last sprang out of the window, saying, "I have taken your cloak, I have taken your hood, and the Cold Lad of the Hill will do no more good." He never appeared again. He had got what he wanted—a woolen cloak with a hood.

The little people hate the cold, it appears. Now, if they are sensitive to cold and hunger, as all the stories indicate, they must be people of flesh and blood. Why not? There are all kinds of people. There is no reason why, in the remote past, certain people should not have gone to live underground, out of the reach of fierce and powerful enemies. For example, there used to be a race of little men in North Britain called the Picts. History records them as fierce and cunning little border raiders —men of the heather, who harried the Roman garrisons in ancient times and stole whatever they could lay their hands on. These Picts—like the African Bushmen, who, by the way, were also little people—could move so quickly and surely that they seemed to have a miraculous gift of invisibility. In broad daylight a Pict could disappear, and not a single heather blossom quivered over his hiding place. The Picts disappeared off the face of the earth at last. Yet, for centuries, in certain parts of Scotland, the farmers and shepherds continued to fear them. They were supposed to have gone underground, into the caves, whence they sometimes emerged to carry off a sheep, a woman, a cooking pot or a child.

It seems to me not unreasonable to assume that, during the long-drawn-out period of strife on the western borders of Britain, certain little weak people went underground and made a new life for themselves secure in the darkness of the caves. Living in the dark, of course, they would grow pale. After many generations they would have developed a cat's faculty for seeing in the dark.

The little people are supposed to know the whereabouts of great buried treasures. This also is possible. Their remote ancestors may have taken their riches with them to bury, meaning to unearth them in safer times which never came. Again, these strange underground men, who knew every stone, every tree and every tuft of grass in their country, may easily have come across treasures buried by other men. In how many fairy tales has one read of the well-disposed little one who left behind him a bright gold coin?

I am convinced that ever since frightened men began to run away and hide there have been little people—in other words, fairies. And such was the nightmarish little thing that trembled in my grip that night in the tent.

I remembered, then, how frightened I had been. As I thought of all the awe that such creatures had inspired through the ages, I began to laugh. The little man—I had better call him a man—listened to me. He stopped whimpering. His ears quivered, then he gave out a queer, breathless, hiccuping sound, faint as the ticking of a clock. "Are you human?" I asked.

He trembled, and laboriously made two noises, *"Oonern."*

He was trying to repeat what I had said. I led him to an angle of the tent, so that he could not escape, and tied up his wrist with an elastic plaster. He looked at it, gibbering. Then I gave him a piece of highly sweetened chocolate. He was afraid of that too.

I bit off a corner and chewed it, saying, "Good. Eat."

I was absurdly confident that, somehow, he would understand me. He tried to say what I had said——*"Oh-ee"*—and crammed the chocolate into his mouth. For half a second he slobbered, twitching with delight, then the chocolate was gone. I patted his head. The touch of it made me shudder, yet I forced my hand to a caress. I was the first man on earth who had ever captured a fairy; I would have taken him to my bosom. I smiled at him. He blinked at me. I could see by the movement of his famished little chest that he was a little less afraid of me. I found another piece of chocolate and offered it to him. But in doing so, I lowered my flashlight. The chocolate was flicked out of my hand. I was aware of something that bobbed away and ran between my legs. Before I could turn, the little man was gone. The flap of the tent was moving. If it had not been for that and a stale dirty smell, I might have thought I had been dreaming. I turned the beam of my flashlight to the ground. This time the little man had left tracks.

As I was to discover, the little people of The Dead Place used to cover their tracks by running backward on all fours and blowing dust over the marks their hands and feet had made. But my little man had not had time to do this tonight.

Dawn was beginning to break. I filled my pockets with food and set out. Nothing was too light to leave a mark in that place, but the same quality that made the fine dust receptive made every mark impermanent. I began to run. The little man's tracks resembled those of a gigantic mole. The red-dust sun was up and the heat of the day was coming down, when I came to the end of his trail. He had scuttled under a great, gray heap of shattered stone. This had been a vast—possibly a noble—building. Now it was a rubbish heap, packed tight by the inexorable pull of the earth through the centuries. Here was fairyland, somewhere in the depths of the earth.

Enormous edifices had been crushed and scattered like burned biscuits thrown to the wild birds. The crumbs were identifiable. The shape of the whole was utterly lost. The loneliness was awful. Inch by inch I felt myself slipping into that spiritual twilight which sucks down to the black night of the soul. The tracks of the little man had disappeared—the dust was always drifting and the contours of the lost city were perpetually changing. Yesterday was a memory. Tomorrow was a dream. Then tomorrow became yesterday—a memory, and memory blurred and twirled away with the dust devils. I was sick. There was bad air in the ruins of Annan. I might have died or run away, if there had not been the thunderstorm.

It threatened for forty-eight hours. I thought that I

was delirious. Everything was still—dreadfully still. The
air was thick and hard to breathe. It seemed to me that
from some indefinable part of the near distance I heard
again that thin, agonized singing which I had heard
once before. Male and female voices wailed a sort of
hymn:

> *"Ah-h-h, Balasamo,*
> *Balasamo! Oh!*
> *Sarnacorpano! Oh-oh!*
> *Binno Mosha,*
> *Sada Rosha,*
> *Chu mila Balasamo! Oh!"*

Then the storm broke, and I thanked God for it. It
cleared the air and it cleared my head. The sky seemed
to shake and reverberate like a sheet of iron. Lightning
feinted and struck, and the rain fell. Between the thun-
der I could still hear the singing. As dawn came, the
storm rumbled away and the aspect of the ruins was
changed. Annan wore a ragged veil of mist. Thin mud
was running away between the broken stones. The sun
was coming up and in a little while the dust would return, but for the moment the rain had washed the face
of the ruin.

So I found the lid of the underworld. It was a disk
of eroded metal that fitted a hole in the ground. I struck
it with my hammer; it fell to pieces. The pieces dropped
away, and out of the hole in the ground there rose a
musty, sickening, yet familiar smell. The hole was the
mouth of an ancient sewer. I could see the rusty remains
of a metal ladder. The top rung was solid—I tried it
with my foot. The next rung supported my weight. I
went down.

The fifth rung broke, and I fell. I remember that I
saw a great white light; then a great dark. Later—I do
not know how much later—I opened my eyes. I knew
that I was alive, because I felt pain. But I was not lying where I had fallen. I could see no circle of daylight

such as I had seen, in falling, at the mouth of the man-
hole. There was nothing to be seen; I was in the dark.
And I could hear odd little glottal voices.

"Water!" I said.

"*Ah-awa,*" said a thin, whining voice. Something that
felt like a cracked earthenware saucer was pressed
against my lips. It contained a spoonful or two of cold
water—half a mouthful. The cracked earthenware
saucer was taken away empty and brought back full. I
took hold of it to steady it. It was a little cupped hand,
a live hand.

I knew then that I had fallen down into the underground world of the little people that haunt the desolate
ruin called Annan, or The Bad Place. I was in fairyland. But my right leg was broken. My flashlight was
broken and I was in the dark. There was nothing to be
done. I could only lie still.

The little people squatted around me in a circle. One
high, ecstatic, piping voice began to sing:

> *"Ookil'karabin,*
> *Ookil'karabin!"*

Thirty or forty voices screeched:

> *"Isapara, mibanara,*
> *Ikil'karabin!"*

Then, abruptly, the singing stopped. Something was
coming. These little people knew the art of making fire
and understood the use of light. One of them was holding a tiny vessel in which flickered a dim, spluttering
flame no larger than a baby's fingernail. It was not what
we would call illumination. It was better than darkness; it permitted one to see, at least, a shadow. You
will never know the comfort that I found in that tiny
flame. I wept for joy. My sobbing jolted my broken
leg, and I must have fainted. I was a wounded man,
remember. Shivering in a wet cold that came from me

and not from the place in which I lay, I felt myself rising on waves of nausea out of a horrible emptiness.

The little people had gone, all but one. The one that stayed had my elastic plaster on his left wrist. His right hand was cupped, and it held water, which I drank. Then he made a vague gesture in the direction of my pockets—he wanted chocolate. I saw this in the light of the little lamp, which still flickered. His shadow danced; he looked like a rat waltzing with a ghost. I had some chocolate in my pocket, and gave him a little. The light was dying. I pointed at it with a forefinger, and gesticulated up, up, up with my hands. He ran away and came back with another lamp.

I can tell you now that the oil that feeds those little lamps is animal fat—the fat of rats. The wicks of the lamps are made of twisted rat hair. The little men of Annan have cultivated rats since they went underground. There are hereditary rat herds, just as there used to be hereditary shepherds and swineherds. I have learned something—not much—of the habits of the little men of the dust in Annan. They dress in rat-skin clothes and have scraped out runs, or burrows, which extend for miles to the thirty-two points of the compass. They have no government and no leaders. They are sickly people. They are perishing.

Yet they are men of a sort. They have fire, although they cannot tolerate the glare of honest daylight. They have—like all of their kind—a buried treasure of useless coins. They have the vestiges of a language, but they are always cold. The poor creature whose wrist I broke had wanted my woolen jacket; now I gave it to him, and he wept for joy. They cultivate fungi—which I have eaten, not without relish—to augment their diet of the rank meat which they get by butchering the gray creatures that provide them with food, fat and fur. But they are always hungry. The rats are getting slower and less reliable in their breeding; the herds are thinning out.

My little man kept me supplied with meat and water. In the end I began to understand the meaning of his whisperings and snuffling underworld language. This fairy, this man of the dust of Annan, was kind to me in his way. He adored me as a fallen god. Sometimes, when I raved and wept in delirium, he ran away. But he always came back. My leg was throbbing. I knew that infection was taking hold of the wound, and began to lose hope down in the dark. I tried to detach my mind from the miserable condition of my body. I listened to the strange songs of the rat people. It was through the chant *Balasamo* that I learned their language. It came to me in a flash of revelation as I lay listening. *Balasamo, Balasamo,* the tune wove in and out. It gave me no peace. I had heard something like it at home. Doctor Opel had been lecturing on ancient music.

Suddenly I understood. I remembered.

> *Balasamo,*
> *Balasamo,*
> *Sarnacorpano!*

This was a song five hundred years old. It used to be a marching song during World Wars One, Two and Three. The words, which time had corrupted and misery debased, should have been:

> *Bless 'em all,*
> *Bless 'em all,*
> *Sergeants and corporals and all!*
> *There'll be no promotion*
> *This side of the ocean,*
> *So cheer up, my lads, bless 'em all!*

Similarly, *Ookil'karabin* meant Who Killed Cock Robin. And, of course, "Annan" came down, whine by whine, through "Unnon" and "Lunnon" from "London"! The little people spoke archaic English. I could see, then, something of their melancholy history. I could see the proud city dwellers going down to become shelter dwellers at the outbreak of the Atom War, the Ten-Minute War of 19— 19—— I forget the exact date. My head is swimming. My little rat man watches me with terrified eyes. Somewhere his people are singing. But the light is dying, and so am I.

THE ODOR
OF MELTING

Edward D. Hoch

The thing he remembered most vividly from the last instant before the plane hit the cresting Atlantic waves was
the odor of melting, the pungent wisp of a smell which
told him the electric circuits had gone. Then there was
no time for anything else—no time to reach the
passenger compartment, no time for anything but a
clawing endeavor to survive.

He couldn't have lived long in the freezing waters,
but it seemed that he bobbed like Ishmael for days,
the only survivor of this black disaster, clinging to one
of the plane's seats until at last some unseen hands were
lifting him. Perhaps he was bound for heaven, or for
hell. He no longer cared. He merely slipped into a quiet
slumber where the dreams were thick and deep, like
the waters of the Atlantic . . .

When he opened his eyes, some time later, a man in
white slacks and a white turtleneck sweater was bending
over him. He was aware of the man's face, and of the
coolness of the sheets against his naked body, and
nothing more.

"How do you feel?" the man asked.

"I—I don't know. I expected to be dead. Where am
I?"

The man smiled and felt the pilot's forehead. "We

saw the crash and pulled you out of the water. You're very lucky. It's an awfully big ocean."

Now he was aware of the gentle swaying of the room, and he knew he was on a boat of some sort. "What ship is this?" he asked.

"The yacht Indos." The man smiled at the pilot's blank expression. "Owned by J. P. Galvan. Perhaps you've heard of him."

He tried to connect the name with something in his memory, and then suddenly everything else flooded back. "The President!" he gasped. "The President was on the plane! I must—"

He was struggling to get out of bed, but the man restrained him. "You were the only survivor. There is nothing you can do now."

"How long have I been here?"

"You've been sleeping. It's almost seven hours since we pulled you from the water."

"But . . . my God, I've got to get word to Washington!"

"That's been taken care of. They know you're here."

"But the President! I've got to tell them what happened. I was the pilot—it was my responsibility!"

"Rest for a while. Mr. Galvan will want to speak with you soon." The man turned and went out, perhaps to summon the owner of the yacht.

Alone between the cool white sheets, he ran over the whole thing again in his mind. He'd been the chief pilot of the presidential plane for only six months when the President of the United States decided on a flying trip to France and West Germany. The visit, and the high-level talks that accompanied it, had been most successful. The President and his advisors had been pleased when they finally boarded the plane in Paris for the return flight.

They were more than an hour out to sea when it happened, suddenly and without warning. An autumn storm blowing up from the tropics—perhaps an offshoot of some distant hurricane—had hurled a single lightning bolt at the plane, knocking out the radio and electrical systems. It was a freak accident that shouldn't have happened; but it did.

He remembered then the odor of melting as the plastic insulation began to go, remembered even seeing the yacht, a single speck on the vast expanse of storm-tossed waves. Suddenly the plane would no longer function. It was a dead thing, dead beneath his prodding hands.

He had screamed something at his copilot, frantically pressing every emergency button within reach. They'd got the auxiliary radio transmitter to function for a few seconds, but he'd only managed a brief gasping of words—"Going down, rush help!"—before that too fizzled into a spectrum of sparks.

He remembered the water, and then nothing else until now. "How long was I in there?" he asked the man in slacks when he returned. "It seemed like hours."

"We had you out in about twenty minutes."

"No one else?"

The man shook his head. "No one else." He offered him a cigarette and added, "Mr. Galvan is coming down to talk to you."

"Fine." The cigarette tasted good. "Are you Mr. Galvan's son?"

"Nothing so important. I'm only his secretary. You may call me—" he hesitated, then finished, "Martin."

The cabin door opened and a small, middle-aged man entered. He wore a dark-blue nautical jacket with brass buttons, and a captain's cap that seemed oddly out of place above his thin, pale features. "You would be John Harris, the pilot of the plane," he said without preliminaries. "I am J. P. Galvan."

He partly lifted himself from the bunk to shake the man's hand. Memory stirred again, and this time it was a magazine article he'd read some time back. J. P. Galvan, international banker, a man who gloried in the power to manipulate fortunes in world currency. "Thank you for saving me," he said.

"It was nothing. A stroke of luck on your part, that the plane came down so close to my yacht. But I was sorry for the others. Your President—a fine man."

"Do you have a radio I could listen to? I'd like to know what they're saying."

Galvan nodded and sat down beside the bunk. "All in due course. First, tell me what happened."

The yacht had begun a gentle rocking and Harris was aware for the first time that the engines had been cut. He wondered why. He wondered if they were perhaps preparing to shift him to a larger ship, possibly an American warship that had reached the search area.

"The electrical system failed," he told Galvan, going through the story as he remembered it, reliving once more the unexpected fury of the brief storm. "There was no change to save the President, or even get off a radio message."

Galvan smiled slightly. "Oh, but you did get off a message, Mr. Harris."

"What?"

"Your new President—who has already been sworn into office—is under the impression that the plane was shot down by the Russians."

"What!" He sat up in the bunk again, this time with a sudden cold sweat forming over his body. "How could he think that?"

"They picked up a few garbled words. *Russians* was the only one they understood."

He thought back to that hasty final message. *Rush help* could have sounded like *Russians* in the static of the storm-swept airwaves. "But that's terrible! That could start a war!"

"Exactly," Galvan agreed.

"I've got to use your radio at once! I have to get the truth to Washington!"

But the small man restrained him. "There is plenty of

time for that. Your new President took the oath of office almost immediately, even though the search for survivors still continues. I am most anxious to see how he handles the situation."

"How he handles it! We could be at war any minute now, and the President might be powerless to prevent a nuclear holocaust."

Galvan sighed. "Mr. Harris, my business is power. I have made a career out of the skillful manipulation of monkeys. Don't you see? I have in my hands now the greatest single power a man has ever had! I have the power to stop World War III, or to let it proceed."

Harris rolled over on the bunk, sweating freely now. "That's crazy talk! It couldn't have gone that far yet."

"No?" Galvan motioned to his secretary. "Turn on the speaker for the short-wave radio."

The secretary vanished for a moment and then reappeared as a hidden wall speaker suddenly came to life. ". . . no further word. Meanwhile, the great Atlantic search continues. A hundred aircraft and two dozen ships have now converged on the general area in which the President's plane went down. Some bits of wreckage *have* been sighted, but there is no trace of survivors at this hour. Meanwhile, in Washington, both houses of Congress have gone into an extraordinary all-night session to hear an urgent address by the new President. It is expected that the President will attempt to calm those who are calling for an immediate declaration of war with Russia. But on the basis of the presidential pilot's last words before the crash, it is becoming obvious that the pressure of an aroused public could plunge the United States and Russia into war within another twenty-four hours. Moscow has denied all knowledge of the missing plane, but it is known that Russian fishing boats were in the vicinity. Now for a direct report from . . ."

"We're got to stop them," Harris interrupted from the bunk. "We've got to—"

Galvan signaled the secretary to turn off the speaker. "You see, Mr. Harris, that is my problem. *Should* I stop them?"

For the first time he felt the fear—not only for the others, but for himself. "What do you mean? I can stop them if you won't. You told them you'd rescued me." Overhead somewhere, one of the search planes dipped low and then climbed again. It was the first one he'd heard. *"You did tell them, didn't you?"*

Galvan blinked and stepped closer to the bunk. "We have told them nothing, Mr. Harris. The crew does not understand English. Only the three of us know you are here. There has been no radio communication with the searchers."

The pilot slumped back on his pillow, knowing now, yet not quite knowing all of it. "What do you plan to do?"

"I have been in touch with bankers in London, Rome, Rio, and Paris. There is much to be said for letting the war—this long-postponed confrontation— take place at last. Your Presidents have been men of peace, and even the Russians have shown no eagerness for world conflict. An event like this, today, is needed to plunge the world into chaos."

"You want that?"

"I do not know, Mr. Harris. It might be more profitable for me to buy and sell against the market, realizing that I could produce your evidence at the last possible moment—"

"But this *is* the last possible moment," he told Galvan. "Once the first missile is launched, by either side, it will be too late."

There was an insistent buzzing of a signal from somewhere, and the man in slacks went off to answer it, moving smoothly and silently out of view. When he returned, he spoke to Galvan in a language Harris couldn't understand.

The small man grunted and turned back to the bunk. "An American ship has hailed us—a bit sooner than I expected. I must tell them about you now, or not at all."

Looking up at Galvan, Harris already knew the decision. The owner of the yacht could not now allow him to live, to give even a hint to the waiting world of this fantastic conversation. "You're mad," he said, very quietly.

"Do you think those who are calling for war—do you think they are sane?"

"There's no money in it for you if the whole world goes up in smoke."

Galvan blinked and turned away. "Perhaps I am only tired of the indecision of it all."

"Or mad with the power of this moment." He waited no longer, but threw back the sheet and hurled himself across the cabin at the little man. He grabbed him by the neck and was tightening his grip on the wrinkled throat when the secretary drew a pistol and fired a single shot at close range.

Harris stumbled backward, seeing the two of them—the only two in the world who knew—suddenly tall above him, and he felt very tired as his life drained away. Again there came to him the unmistakable odor of melting, and he wondered if perhaps he was back in the dead plane, if all that went between had been but a drowning man's dream . . .

Or was this the way the earth smelled, as it died?

THE SOUND
OF MURDER

William P. McGivern

The Orient Express stops for an hour or more at the Yugoslav-Trieste border. Customs are a formality as a rule, but the changing of foreign currencies into dinars takes quite a bit of time.

Knowing this, Adam James yawned slightly as the train pulled into Sesana. He wasn't really bored; he merely wished he were in Belgrade, at work, instead of here at the frontier. He rubbed the window of his compartment with the palm of his hand. There was little to see outside—uniformed customs officials waiting to board the train, an oiler walking down the opposite track, and beyond the wooden station, white foothills under a dark sky. It was a cheerless prospect; the hills were huddled together, as if the earth had hunched its shoulders against the bitter weather.

The customs officer knocked and entered, bringing in a touch of coldness on his clothes and breath. He was cordial and efficient, and bowed himself out with a smile a few minutes later. The money-control officer was equally cordial, but his work took more time. Finally he too went away, and Adam sat down with his book, a dull but important one on Yugoslavian politics, and lit his pipe.

However, his moment of peace was brief. The argu-

ment between the couple in the adjoining compartment
flared up again, and he closed his book with a sigh.
They had been at it, off and on, since the Express had
left Trieste an hour or so ago, and the partition between
the compartments was so thin that Adam could hardly
ignore the noise. They spoke Croatian or Serbian,
neither of which he understood, but the anger in their
voices was unmistakable—no matter what the language.

He had noticed them in Trieste where they had
boarded the train. The woman was very attractive, with
light blond hair, clear fresh skin, and the slender, grace-
fully muscled legs of a dancer. She was in her early
thirties, Adam had guessed, and wore a plum-colored
tweed suit under a good fur coat. The man was stout
and florid, with small alert eyes, and a manner of
petulant importance. He was fastidiously turned out in
a black overcoat with a fur-trimmed collar, a black
Homburg, and, rather inevitably Adam had thought, carried a cane. His gray flannel trousers were sharply
creased, and his spats gleamed white against his glossy
black shoes.

There was something about them, some constraint in
their manner, that had caught Adam's attention. They
said little to each other as they waited to board the
train, but there was a quality in the set of their shoulders which indicated they had plenty to say, and were
only waiting for the chance to say it.

Unfortunately for himself, Adam thought, they got
their chance when they were finally alone in their compartment. At first he'd been mildly interested in their
bickering; but as they became angrier and louder, he
had become bored and irritated.

There was a knock on the door, and the conductor
entered. He was a small, neatly built man with quick
intelligent eyes, and had a tiny black mustache above a
generous but cautious mouth.

"Your passport, sir," he said, handing Adam the
slim green gold-lettered booklet. "Everything is in or-

der. You will not be disturbed again until we arrive in Belgrade."

"Thanks, but I haven't been disturbed," Adam said.

The conductor raised his eyebrows. "That's an unusual reaction for an American. Most of you are—well, impulsive. You have no patience."

"Oh, there are all types of Americans," Adam said with a smile. "Also, there are all types of French, British, and even Yugoslavians, I imagine."

"No, you are wrong. Here in Yugoslavia we grow up with the land, and become like it, slow and patient. You Americans are different. Excitable, I mean. You leap at things. That is desirable in some matters, but it can also cause trouble."

"Well, that may be," Adam said. He had spent fifteen years of his life as a foreign correspondent, and his job, reduced to an oversimplification, was to find out what people thought, and why they thought it. He was interested in the conductor's opinions, and he wanted to put the man at ease. He raised a hand as the argument in the next compartment broke out again. "Are they Americans?" he asked innocently.

"No, of course not."

"Well, *they* seem pretty excitable."

The conductor looked blank. Then he smiled good-humoredly. "I asked for that, as you say. No, they are Yugoslavians. The Duvecs—she is a dancer, and he is an actor." The conductor listened to the argument with a little smile. "The artistic temperament," he said. "Well, I must go on with my work. I have not offended you with my directness, eh?"

"Certainly not. Stop by when you get a minute and we'll finish our talk."

"Thank you, I shall try."

The conductor went away and Adam returned to his book. He was grateful, a chapter later, when the train began to move. Sesana was behind them now. They would pass Zagreb sometime after dinner, and be in Belgrade the following morning. He would have been almost cheerful if it weren't for the argument in the next compartment.

The couple had reached a new and higher pitch after a few moments of blessed silence. The woman's voice was shrill now, where before it had been somewhat controlled. The man shouted at her whenever she ceased speaking. This continued for a few moments, and then Adam heard the door of the compartment jerked open energetically. The man shouted a last sentence or two, then the door was banged shut with angry finality. Adam heard the man's heavy footsteps pass his door, and fade away in the direction of the dining-car.

"Well, well," he thought, "peace at last!" There was nothing quite like a door-slamming exit to put an end to an argument. Perversely, however, now that everything was quiet, he lost interest in his book. He decided to have dinner, and finish his reading later— though probably by then the argument would be on again, he thought wryly, and he'd berate himself for missing the present opportunity.

He washed his face, combed his hair, and walked through the lurching train to the dining-car. There were two third-class coaches connected to the *Wagon-Lit,* filled with stolid, impassive soldiers who endured the unheated compartments with the stoic acceptance of domestic animals.

There was no menu on the Express, just the one *préfixe* dinner: Soup, roast veal and vegetables served with a theoretically white, but in fact, orange-colored Dalmatian wine. This was followed by stewed prunes, and thick sweet Turkish coffee.

The man in the fur-trimmed overcoat, Duvec, was seated at the far end of the diner, hungrily and belligerently attacking a bowl of soup. He wore an angrily righteous look, Adam thought, and was probably reviewing the argument with his wife in the most favorable possible light. Duvec wore his overcoat buttoned up to the throat, and occasionally put down his spoon and rubbed his plump hands together to warm them, though the diner wasn't cold; Adam was comfortable enough in his suit-coat.

The sleeping-car conductor entered the diner a few moments later, looking pale and agitated. He glanced about quickly, then striding to Duvec's table, he bent and whispered a few words. Their effect was electric. Duvec sprang to his feet, almost overturning his table, and his mouth opened and closed soundlessly.

"Please come with me," the conductor said in a firm voice.

The two men hurried from the car, the other diners staring after them curiously. Adam frowned at the table-cloth for a moment or so, oddly disturbed. Finally, obeying a compulsion he didn't quite understand, he rose and started back through the train for the sleeping-car. But at the vestibule he was stopped by a blue-uniformed mail-car guard. The man put a hand against Adam's chest.

"You must not enter," he said, in slow, laborious English.

"But this is my car," Adam said.

"You must not come in."

"Has something happened?"

The guard merely shook his round head stubbornly.

At this point the sleeping-car conductor appeared in the opposite vestibule. He opened the door, spoke a few words to the mail-car guard, and the man took his hand from Adam's chest.

"You may come in," the conductor said.

"What has happened?" Adam asked.

"A great tragedy, a great tragedy," the conductor said, rubbing his mustache nervously. Adam became aware that the train was slowing down.

"We're stopping?" he asked.

"Yes, yes. Please come inside."

Adam followed him into the sleeping-car and turned the corner into the aisle. Duvec stood before the open door of his compartment, sobbing terribly. Beyond him, held by two mail-car guards, was a stocky Yugoslavian soldier in a patched and dirty uniform. Duvec turned away from his compartment and sagged weakly against the wall. He beat a fist slowly against his forehead, and his lips opened and closed as if he were praying.

Adam stepped forward and glanced into Duvec's compartment. He knew what he would see. Somehow he had anticipated this; but it was still a jarring, shocking sight. Mrs. Duvec lay on the floor in the careless, undignified sprawl of death. One slender leg was doubled under her body, and a lock of blond hair lay across her pale throat. The bronze handle of a letter-opener—or a knife—protruded from between her breasts.

The train had come to a full stop. There was no sound as Adam stepped back from the compartment except Duvec's hoarse, strangled sobs.

The conductor touched Adam's arm. "You will be good enough to remain in your compartment, please. I have sent a messenger back to the police at Sesana. We will wait until they arrive."

"Naturally," Adam rejoined. "But what happened?"

"It was the soldier. He thought all the passengers were in the dining-car. He came in to pilfer what he could, I imagine. He was surprised when he found the woman here, he lost his head—" The conductor shrugged eloquently. "It is a great tragedy."

The soldier seemed to understand what was being said. His eyes were wild and frightened. He suddenly shouted, *"Nil! Nil!"* and chattered out a stream of words which Adam didn't understand.

"He protests his innocence," the conductor said matter-of-factly. "That is to be expected."

"He lies, he lies!" Duvec said in ragged voice. "He killed my wife, and he must die for it."

"There is no doubt he is guilty," the conductor agreed. "We can establish that easily. Your wife was alive when you left her?"

"Yes, yes! My God, yes!" Duvec cried. He began to

sob again, hopelessly, piteously. "We had a quarrel, a silly, stupid quarrel, and I left in anger. But she was alive, alive as we are now." He glanced at Adam, as if noticing him for the first time. "But *you* must have heard our quarrel."

"Yes, I heard it," Adam said.

"Then you heard our voices until the moment I left."

Adam nodded. "Yes, I heard you."

The conductor shrugged. "Then there is proof that she was alive when her husband left. The soldier admits going into her compartment—but at that point he loses his love for the truth."

"What's his story?" Adam asked.

"He says that Mrs. Duvec was already dead. This is why he attempted to flee, he tells us."

"Who caught him?"

"I had appointed a guard for this car while I worked out space plans with the attendant in the next car," the conductor said. "We get a crowd at Zagreb, and it is necessary to prepare for them in advance, you see. I appointed a guard because the sleeping-car is empty during the dinner hour, and the soldiers—well, you understand how it is with soldiers. The guard, a man from the mail-car, was at the opposite vestibule—that is, he was at the other end of the car from where we now stand. Something caused him to turn and glance down the aisle. He saw the soldier backing out of the Duvecs' compartment. He shouted, and the soldier attempted to run back to his own car. But the guard caught him, fortunately."

"What caused the guard to look down the aisle?"

The conductor raised his eyebrows. "Who can tell? The good Lord, perhaps; it was an impulse—and it apprehended a murderer. The guard will be officially congratulated."

"Yes, yes, of course," Adam muttered. "Catching murderers is always a cause for congratulations. Whose knife did the soldier use, by the way?"

The conductor looked blank. He turned to Duvec, who said, "It was my wife's letter-opener. Perhaps she was using it when the soldier burst in on her."

"That is logical," the conductor said, nodding. "We will get the truth from him, all of it, you will see."

Suddenly the soldier shouted wildly and broke away from his two guards. He ran down the narrow aisle, jerked open the door at the end of the car, and disappeared. The guards lumbered after him, and Duvec screamed, "Get him, get him, the murderer!"

The conductor remained calm. "He cannot leave the train," he said. "The vestibule doors are secured from the outside. That was my first order. He will be caught, never fear."

Adam glanced at Duvec and the conductor, frowning. Finally he said, "excuse me, please," and entered his own compartment. He sat down and lit his pipe.

Something was wrong about all this, wrong as the very devil, and he could feel it in his bones. But how could he prove it? He stretched his long legs out in front of him and rested his head against the back of the seat. Proof . . . Where was it? He puffed on his pipe, trying to recall everything that had happened since the Express left Trieste. He sorted out all the details he could remember, and juggled them into different relationships, turned them upside down and inside out, trying desperately to justify his conviction.

The conductor appeared in his doorway ten minutes later, wearing a small pleased smile. "It is finished," he said. "We have caught him. He sought to hide in the coal-car, but was found."

Adam stood up and began knocking the dottle from his pipe. "That's fine," he said. "The only thing is, you've got the wrong man."

"The wrong man? Impossible! His guilt is proven by his attempt to escape."

"Nonsense. He's simply scared out of his wits. Bring everyone here, and I'll show you the murderer," Adam said, marveling slightly at the ring of confidence in his voice.

The conductor squared his shoulders stubbornly. "This is a police matter, I must remind you."

"Yes, but it won't redound to your credit to present them with an innocent suspect when they arrive."

The conductor rubbed his thin black mustache. "Very well," he said at last. "I am not afraid to test your opinion against mine. I have reached my conclusions logically. I am not in error."

"We'll see," Adam said.

The soldier was brought back down the aisle, securely held by two mail-car guards. He was not more than eighteen, Adam saw, a strongly-built youth with a dull face and black hopeless eyes; obviously he had resigned himself to his fate. Duvec, who still wore his fur-trimmed overcoat, stood at the end of the aisle, occasionally rubbing a hand despairingly over his broad forehead.

Adam was in the doorway of his compartment. The soldier and his guards were at his left, Duvec and the conductor, on his right. They all watched him expectantly.

"This soldier did not kill Mrs. Duvec," Adam said quietly.

"What do you know about it?" Duvec shouted.

"If you will listen, you will find out."

"I will not listen. You have no authority here."

"Silence!" the conductor said, in a sharp voice. "I am in charge until the police arrive. I have given the American permission to speak."

"Thank you," said Adam. "I'll continue. As I have said, the soldier did not kill Mrs. Duvec. I think I can prove that to everyone's satisfaction. First of all, has it not struck you as odd that the guard in this car did not hear Mrs. Duvec scream?"

For an instant there was silence. Then the conductor said, "She was struck down before she could cry out."

However, Adam's question brought a tiny frown to his face.

"I think that's an unlikely explanation," Adam said. "Let's reconstruct what must have happened if the soldier is the murderer. First, he opened the door of the compartment. Mrs. Duvec looked up at him, startled and probably frightened. What would one expect her to do? Scream, of course."

"My wife was no silly maiden," Duvec snapped. "She would not scream at the sight of a man; she would have ordered him from the compartment. That is unquestionably what happened. She asked him to leave, ordered him to leave. He took advantage of that moment to seize the letter-opener from her and plunge it into her heart. Yes, he silenced her before she could scream."

The conductor nodded, looking somewhat relieved. "Yes, certainly that is it," he said.

"No, that isn't it," Adam said. "Why would a strong agile young man use a knife on a woman? If he wanted to silence her, he would use his hands. In the time it would take him to grasp the knife away from her, and strike her down with it, she might have screamed half a dozen times. And yet, I repeat, the guard in this car heard no sound at all from Mrs. Duvec."

The conductor shook his head impatiently. "You are making up theories. We are dealing with facts. According to your own testimony, Mrs. Duvec was alive when her husband left the compartment. She was dead when the soldier left the compartment. Those are the facts. No one but the soldier could have killed her."

"You're wrong, but it's purely my fault," Adam said. "I've misled you. However, I'll clear things up now. There's the murderer," he said—and he pointed at Duvec.

"Monstrous!" Duvec shouted. "I will not stand for these slanders."

"Let me ask you this," Adam said. "Why are you wearing a heavy overcoat in a comfortably heated train?

What is under it, Duvec? Or, more to the point, what *isn't* under it?"

"I don't know what you're talking about," Duvec snapped.

"I'll tell you, then," Adam said. "What *isn't* under that overcoat is your suit-coat—the suit-coat which was bloodied when you murdered your wife. When I saw you in the diner I knew something was odd. You wouldn't have worn an overcoat all the way from Trieste, so you must have put it on before leaving your compartment. However, the emotional fireworks accompanying your departure made it seem unlikely that you would have stopped to put on an overcoat. That routine bit of business would have shattered the effect of your exit. But why wear the coat at all? The train isn't cold. Therefore, I decided, it was worn not for comfort but for camouflage. And what was it you were so eager to camouflage?"

"You are talking like a madman," Duvec said. "My wife was alive when I left her. You know that is true. You said you heard us."

"I said I heard *you*," Adam corrected him. "Duvec, you killed your wife in a moment of rage. This puts you in a tough predicament. There was a witness of sorts to the crime—an auditory witness, in the next compartment—myself, of course. But I could be used to your advantage. You could create the illusion that your wife was alive when you left her by taking both parts of the dialogue for a moment or so before banging out of the compartment. This was no trick for an actor. Meanwhile, as you imitated your wife's voice, you removed your bloodstained suit-coat and got into your overcoat. Then you left the compartment with a final artistic bellow at your wife. The suit-coat, I'll bet, you either hid in your compartment, or threw off the train on the way to the diner. In either event, a search will produce it."

"Talk, talk, talk!" Duvec cried.

"Take off your overcoat," said Adam.

"This is childish nonsense," Duvec said angrily. He unbuttoned his overcoat and flung it open. He wore a gray tweed jacket above gray flannel trousers. There was a little silence, in which Adam felt his stomach contract unpleasantly. "Are you satisfied now?" Duvec said contemptuously.

The conductor had unconsciously placed a hand on Duvec's arm as Adam had talked. Now he removed it hastily. "Forgive me," he said.

"Wait a minute," Adam said, frowning. He had noticed that Duvec wore ruby cuff-links. What was wrong with that?

"No—enough," the conductor said angrily. "There will be no more of these wild accusations."

"No, I'm right," Adam snapped. "He wouldn't wear cuff links with a tweed jacket, any more than he'd wear black shoes with a brown suit. Of course! He changed into the tweed jacket, and hid the blood-stained suit-coat underneath the overcoat. He threw the suit-coat out one of the vestibule doors. He was fairly safe then; at least he had an alibi. But luck joined forces with him and provided the crime with a reasonable suspect. The soldier blundered onto the scene and put Duvec completely into the clear. But it won't work. I'll bet one hundred dollars to a dinar that the police will find a bloodstained flannel jacket within ten miles of this spot."

Duvec began to weep. "I can stand no more!" he cried. "My wife is dead, and I hear myself called her murderer!" He turned aside, still sobbing, and put a hand to the vestibule door for support. The gesture was so natural that no one noticed him reach for the door-knob. He jerked open the door and was into the vestibule before anyone could move. The conductor shouted at the mail-car guards who still held the soldier. They plunged out of the car after Duvec, with the conductor on their heels.

They caught him in the next coach and dragged him back to the sleeping-car. Duvec offered no resistance.

He stared straight ahead with shoulders slumped, and there was an expression of terrible anguish on his face. Adam realized that for the first time since the murder of his wife Duvec had ceased to act.

In a low, trembling voice, he said, "She was going to leave me, you see. I—couldn't stand that. I—couldn't."

Half an hour later the conductor came to Adam's compartment. "You must excuse me," he said, rather sheepishly. "I think of what I said about the excitable Americans, and my face becomes hot with shame. I must apologize."

"Please don't worry about that," Adam said.

"But I do not understand completely. Your proof was not overwhelming, I do not think. And yet you seemed so *sure*."

"I was sure," Adam said. "You see, in the classic tradition, Duvec made one mistake which I didn't bother to mention. When he acted out the scene with his dead wife, he engineered the dialogue badly. He shouted a few last words at her, you will remember, and then banged the door."

The conductor looked blank. Finally he rubbed his mustache and smiled slowly.

"You understand, of course," Adam said. "In Yugoslavia or America, anywhere for that matter, arguments between husbands and wives very seldom end that way. When I realized that, I knew Duvec was guilty. You see Mrs. Duvec wouldn't have let him get away with the last word—if she were alive, that is."

"But of course," the conductor agreed, nodding gravely.

THE INCOME TAX MYSTERY

Michael Gilbert

I qualified as a solicitor before the war and in 1937 I bought a share in a small partnership in the City. Then the War came along and I joined the Infantry. I was already thirty-five and it didn't look as if I was going to see much active service, so I cashed in on my knowledge of German and joined the Intelligence Corps.

When the War was finished, I got back to London and found our old office bombed and the other partner dead. As far as a legal practice can do so, it had vanished. I got a job without any difficulty in a firm in Bedford Row, but I didn't enjoy it. The work was easy enough but there was no real future in it. So I quit and joined the Legal Branch of Inland Revenue.

This may seem even duller than private practice, but in fact it wasn't. As soon as I had finished the subsidiary training in accountancy that all Revenue Officials have to take, I was invited to join a very select outfit known as I.B.A. or Investigation Branch, Active.

If you ask a Revenue official about I.B.A., he'll tell you it doesn't exist. This may simply mean that he hasn't heard of it. Most ordinary Revenue investigation is done by accountants who examine balance sheets, profit and loss accounts, vouchers and receipts, then ask

questions and go on asking questions until the truth
emerges.

Some cases can't be treated like that. They need active investigation. Someone has got to go out and find
the facts. That's where I.B.A. comes in.

It isn't all big cases involving millions of pounds. The
Revenue reckons to achieve the best results by making a few shrewd examples in the right places. One of
our most spectacular coups was achieved when a member of the department once opened a green-grocers
shop and—but that's another story.

When the name of Mr. Portway cropped up in I.B.A.
records, it was natural that the dossier should get
pushed across to me. For Mr. Portway was a solicitor.
I can't remember exactly how he first came to our
notice—you'd be surprised what casual items can set
I.B.A. in motion: a conversation in a railway carriage,
a hint from an insurance assessor, a bit of loud-voiced
boasting in a pub. We don't go in for phone-tapping:
it's inefficient and, from our point of view, quite unnecessary.

The thing about Mr. Portway was simply this: he
seemed to make a very substantial amount of money
without working for it.

The first real confirmation came from a disgruntled
girl who had been hired to look after his books and fired
for inefficiency. Mr. Portway ran a good car, she said;
he dressed well, spent hundreds of pounds at the wine
merchant (she'd seen one of his bills), and conducted
an old-fashioned one-man practice which, by every law
of economics, should have left him broke at the end of
each year.

Some days he had no clients at all, she said, and spent
the morning in his room reading a book (detective
stories, chiefly); then he would take two hours off for
lunch, snooze a little on his return, have a cup of tea,
and go home. On other days a client or two would
trickle in. The business was almost entirely the buying
and selling of houses and the preparation of leases,

mortgages, and sale agreements. Mr. Portway did it all himself. He had one girl to do the typing and look after the outer office, and another (our informant) to keep the books.

I don't suppose you know anything about solicitors' accounting, and I'm not proposing to give you a dissertation on it; but the fact is that solicitors are bound by very strict rules—rules imposed by Act of Parliament and jealously enforced by the Law Society. And quite right, too. Solicitors handle a lot of other people's money.

When we'd made a quiet check to see if Mr. Portway had any private means of his own and learned that he didn't, we decided that this was just the sort of case we ought to have a look at. It wasn't difficult. Mr. Portway knew nothing about figures. However small his staff, he had to have someone with the rudiments of accountancy, or he couldn't have got through his annual audit. We simply watched the periodicals until we saw his advertisement, and I applied for the job.

I don't know if there were any other applicants, but I'm sure I was the only one who professed to know both law and bookkeeping and who was prepared to accept the mouse-like salary he was offering.

Mr. Portway proved to be a small, round, pink-cheeked, white-haired man. One would have said Pickwickian, except that he didn't wear glasses, nor was there anything in the least owl-like about his face. So far as any comparison suggested itself, he looked more like a tortoise. He had a sardonic, leathery, indestructible face, with the long upper lip of a philosopher.

He greeted me warmly and showed me to my room. The office occupied the ground floor and basement of the house. On the right as you came in, and overlooking the paved courtyard and fountain which is all that remains of the old "Inn," was Mr. Portway's sanctum, a very nice room, on the small side, and made smaller by the rows of bookcases full of bound reports. My own room was on the left of the entrance, and even smaller and more austere. Downstairs were storerooms of old files and records and a strongroom which ran back under the pavement.

I have given you some idea of the small scale of things so that you can gather how easy I thought my job was going to be. My guess was that a week would be more than enough to detect any funny business that was going on.

I was quite wrong.

A week was enough to confirm that something *was* wrong. But by the end of a month I hadn't got a step nearer to discovering what it was.

I reported my meagre findings to my superiors.

"Mr. Portway," I said, "has a business which appears to produce, in fees, just about enough to pay the salaries of his two employees, the rent, lighting, and other outgoings, and to leave him no personal income at all. Indeed, in some instances, he has had to make up, from his own pocket, small deficiencies in the office account. Nor does his money come from private means. It is part of my duty as accountant to prepare Mr. Portway's personal tax returns"—(this, it is fair to him to say, was at his own suggestion)—"and apart from a very small holding in War Stock and occasional small earnings for articles on wine, on which he is an acknowledged expert, he has—or at least declares—no outside resources at all. Nevertheless, enjoying as he does a minus income, he lives very well, appears to deny himself little in the way of comfort. He is not extravagant, but I would not hesitate to estimate his personal expenditures at no less than three thousand pounds per annum."

My masters found this report so unsatisfactory that I was summoned to an interview. The head of the department was a tubby and mercurial Welshman, like Lloyd George without the mustache. He was on Christian-name terms with all his staff; but he wasn't a good man to cross.

"Are you asking me to believe in miracles, Michael?" he said. "How can a man have an inexhaustible wallet of notes if he doesn't earn them from somewhere?"

"Perhaps he makes them," I suggested.

Dai elected to take this seriously. "A forger you mean. I wouldn't have thought it likely."

"No," I said. "I didn't quite mean that." (I knew as well as anyone that the skill and organization, to say nothing of the supplies of special paper, necessary for banknote forgery were far beyond the resources of an ordinary citizen.) "I thought he might have a hoard. Some people do, you know. There's nothing intrinsically illegal in it. Suppose he made his money before the war and stowed it away somewhere. In his strongroom downstairs, perhaps. He keeps the keys himself and that's one room no one's allowed inside. Each week he gets out a couple of dozen pound notes and spends them."

Dai grunted. "Why should he trouble to keep up an office? That way he'd save himself money and work. I don't like it, Michael. We're onto something here, boy. Don't let it go."

So I returned to Lombards Inn and kept my eyes and ears open. And as the weeks passed the mystery grew more irritating and seemingly more insoluble.

During the month which ensued I made a very careful calculation. In the course of that single month Mr. Portway acted in the purchase of one house for £5000, and the sale of another at about the same price. He drafted the lease of an office in the City and fixed up a mortgage for an old lady with a Building Society. The income he received for these transactions totaled exactly £171.5.0. And that was just about five pounds *less* than he paid out—to keep his office going for the same period . . .

One day, about three o'clock in the afternoon. I had occasion to take some papers in to him. I found him sitting in the chair beside the fireplace, the *Times* (which he read every day from first to last page) in one hand, and in the other a glass.

He said, "You find me indulging in my secret vice. I'm one of the old school who thinks that claret should be drunk after lunch and burgundy after dinner."

I am fond of French wines myself and he must have seen the quick glance I gave the bottle.

"It's a Pontet Canet," he said, "of 1943. Certainly the best of the war years, and almost the best Château of that year. You'll find a glass in the filing cabinet, Mr. Gilbert."

You can't drink wine standing up. Before I knew what I was doing, we were seated in front of the fireplace with the bottle between us. After a second glass Mr. Portway fell into a mood of reminiscence. I kept my ears open, of course, for any useful information, but only half of me, at that moment, was playing the detective. The other half was enjoying an excellent claret, and the company of a philosopher.

It appeared that Mr. Portway had come to the law late. He had studied art under Bertolozzi, the great Florentine engraver, and had then spent a couple of years in the workshops of Herr Groener, who specialized in intaglios and metal relief work. He took down from the mantelshelf a beautiful little reproduction in copper of the Papal Colophon which he had made himself. Then the first World War, most of which he had spent in Egypt, had disoriented him.

"I felt the need," he said, "of something a little more tangible in my life than the art of metal relievo." He had tried, and failed, to become an architect, and had then chosen the law, mostly to oblige an uncle who had no son.

"There have been Portways," he said, "in Lombards Inn for two centuries. I fear I shall be the last."

The telephone broke up our talk and I went back to my room.

As I thought about things that night, I came to the conclusion that Mr. Portway had presented me with the answer to one problem, in the act of setting me another.

"There have been Portways in Lombards Inn for two centuries." The tie of sentiment? Was that perhaps why he was willing to finance, from his own pocket, a practice which no longer paid him? But where did the money come from? The more you looked at it, the more impossible the whole problem became.

As cashier, remember, I received and paid out every penny the firm earned and spent. And I knew—positively and actually knew—that no money went into Mr. Portway's pocket. On the contrary, almost every month he had to draw a check on his own bank account to keep the office going. Nor did he draw, according to his bank statements, any money from that or any other account.

So from what source did the substantial wad of notes in his wallet come? As you see, I was being driven, step by step, to the only logical conclusion: that he had found some method, some perfectly safe and private method, of manufacturing money.

But not forgery, as the word is usually understood. Despite his bland admissions of an engraver's training, the difficulties were too great. Where would he get the special paper? And such notes as I had seen did not look in the least like forgeries.

I had come to one other conclusion. The heart of the secret lay in the strongroom. This was the one room that no one but Mr. Portway ever visited, the room of which he alone had the key. Try as I would, I had never even glanced inside the door. If he wanted a deed out of it, Mr. Portway would wait until I was at lunch before he went in to fetch it. And he was always the last one to leave the office.

The door of the strongroom was a heavy, old-fashioned affair, and if you have time to study it, and are patient enough, in the end you can get the measure of any lock. I had twice glimpsed the actual key, too, and that is a great help. It wasn't long before I had

equipped myself with keys which I was pretty sure
would open the door. The next thing was to find an
opportunity to use them.

Eventually I hit on quite a simple plan.

At about three o'clock one afternoon I announced
that I had an appointment with the local Inspector
of Taxes. I though it would take an hour or ninety minutes. Would it be all right if I went straight home? Mr.
Portway agreed. He was in the middle of drafting a
complicated conveyance, and looked safely anchored
in his chair.

I went back to my room, picked up my hat, raincoat, and brief case, and tiptoed down to the basement. Quietly I opened the door of one of the storage
rooms; I had used my last few lunch breaks, when I
was alone in the office, to moving a rampart of deed
boxes a couple of feet out from the wall and building
up the top with bundles of old papers. Now I shut the
door behind me and squeezed carefully into my lair.
Apart from the fact that the fresh dust I had disturbed
made me want to sneeze, it wasn't too bad. Soon the
dust particles resettled themselves, and I fell into a
state of somnolence.

It was five o'clock before I heard Mr. Portway moving. His footsteps came down the passage outside, and
stopped. I heard him open the door of the strongroom,
opposite. A pause. The door shut again. The next moment my door opened and the lights sprung on.

I held my breath. The lights went out and the door
closed. I heard the click of the key in the lock. Then
the footsteps moved away.

He was certainly thorough. I even heard him look into
the lavatory. (My first plan had been to lock myself in
it. I was glad now that I had not.) At last the steps
moved away upstairs; more pottering about, the big
outer door slammed shut, and silence came down like a
blanket.

I waited for nearly two hours. The trouble was the

cleaning woman, an erratic old lady called Gertie. She had a key of her own and sometimes she came in the evening, and sometimes early in the morning. I had studied her movements for several weeks. The latest she had ever left the premises was a quarter to eight at night.

By half-past eight I felt it was safe for me to start investigating.

The storage room door presented no difficulties. The lock was on my side and I simply unscrewed it. The strongroom door was a different matter. I had got what is known in the trade as a set of "approximates"— blank keys of the type and, roughly, the shape to open most old locks. My job was to find the one that worked best, and then file it down and fiddle it until it would open the lock. (You can't do this with a modern lock, which is tooled to a hundredth of an inch, but old locks, which rely on complicated convolutions and strong springs, though they look formidable, are actually much easier.)

By half-past ten I heard the sweet click which meant success, and I swung the steel door open, turned on the light switch, and stepped in.

It was a small vault with walls of whitewashed brick, with a run of wooden shelves round two of the sides, carrying a line of black deed boxes. I didn't waste much time on them; I guessed the sort of things they would contain.

On the left, behind the door, was a table and on the table stood a heavy, brass-bound teak box—the sort of thing that might have been built to contain a microscope, only larger. It was locked—with a small, Bramah-type lock which none of my implements was designed to cope with.

I worked for some time at it, but without much hope. The only solution seemed to be to lug the box away with me—it was very heavy, but just portable— and get someone outside to work on it. I reflected that

I should look pretty silly if it did turn out to contain a valuable microscope that one of old Portway's clients had left with him for safekeeping.

Then I had an idea. On the shelf inside the door was a small black tin box with *E. Portway, Personal* painted on the front. It was the sort of thing in which a careful man might keep his War Savings Certificates and Passport. It too was locked, but with an ordinary deed-box lock, which one of the keys on my ring fitted. I opened it, and sure enough, lying on top of the stacked papers inside, the first thing that caught my eye was a worn leather keyholder containing a single, brass Bramah key.

I suddenly felt a little breathless. Perhaps the ventilation was not all it should have been. Moving with deliberation, I fitted the brass key into the tiny keyhole, pressed home, and twisted. Then I lifted the top of the box—and came face to face with Mr. Portway's secret.

At first sight it was disappointing. It looked like nothing more than a small handpress—the sort of thing you use for impressing a company seal, only a little larger. I lifted it out, picked up a piece of clean white paper off the shelf, slid the paper in, and pressed down the handle. Then I released it and extracted the paper.

Imprinted on the paper was a neat orange Revenue Stamp for £20. I went back to the box. Inside was a tray, and arranged in it were dies of various denominations—10s., £1, £2, £5, and upward. The largest was for £100.

I picked one of the dies out and held it up to the light. It was beautifully made. Mr. Portway had not wasted his time at Bertolozzi's Florentine atelier. There was even an arrangement of cogs behind the die by which three figures of the date could be set—tiny, delicate wheels, each a masterpiece of the watchmaker's art.

I heard the footsteps crossing the courtyard, and Mr. Portway was through the door before I even had time to put the die down.

"What are you doing here?" I said stupidly.

"When anyone turns on the strongroom light," he said, "it also turns on the light in my office. I've got a private arrangement with the caretaker of the big block at the end who keeps an eye open for me. If he sees my light on, he telephones me at once."

"I see," I said. Once I had got over the actual shock of seeing him there, I wasn't alarmed. I was half his age and twice his size. "I've just been admiring your private work. Every man his own revenue stamp office. A lovely piece of work, Mr. Portway."

"Is it not?" agreed my employer, blinking up at me under the strong light. I could read in his chelonian face neither fear nor anger, rather a sardonic amusement at the turn of affairs. "Are you a private detective, by any chance?"

"I.B.A.—Investigation Branch of the Inland Revenue."

"And you have been admiring my little machine?"

"My only real surprise is that no one has thought of it before."

"Yes," he said. "It's very useful. To a practising solicitor, of course. I used to find it a permanent source of irritation that my clients should pay more to the Government—who, after all, hadn't raised a finger to earn it—than they did to me. Do you realize that if I act for the purchaser of a London house for £5,000, I get about £43, whilst the Government's share is £100?"

"Scandalous," I agreed. "And so you devised this little machine to adjust the balance. Such a simple and foolproof form of forgery, when you come to think of it." The more I thought of it the more I liked it. "Just think of the effort you would have to spend—to say nothing of obtaining special stocks of paper—if you set out to forge one-hundred-pound notes. Whereas with this machine—a small die, a little pressure—"

"Oh, there's more to it than that," said Mr. Portway airily. "A man would be a fool to forge treasury notes.

They have to be passed into circulation, and each one is a potential danger to its maker. Here, when I have stamped a document, it goes directly into a deed box—and it may not be looked at again for twenty years. Possibly, never."

"As a professional accountant," I said, "that is the angle which appeals to me most. Now, let me see. Take that purchase you were talking about. Your client would give you two checks, one for your fee, which goes through the books in the ordinary way, and a separate one for the stamp duty."

"Made out to cash."

"Made out to cash, of course. Which you would yourself cash at the bank, then come back here—"

"I always took the trouble to walk through the Stamp Office in case anyone should be watching me."

"Very sound precaution," I agreed. "Then you came back here, stamped the document yourself, and put the money in your pocket. It never appeared in your books at all."

"That's precisely right," said Mr. Portway. He seemed gratified at the speed with which I had perceived the finer points of his arrangements.

"There's only one thing I can't quite see," I went on. "You're a bachelor, a man with simple tastes. Could you not—I don't want to sound pompous—but by working a little could you not have made sufficient money legitimately for your reasonable needs?"

Mr. Portway looked at me for a moment, his smile broadening.

"I see," he said, "that you have not had time to examine the rest of this strongroom. My tastes are far from simple, Mr. Gilbert, and owing to the scandalous and confiscatory nature of modern taxation—oh, I beg your pardon, I was forgetting for the moment—"

"Don't apologize," I said. "I have often thought the same thing myself. You were speaking of your expensive tastes—"

Mr. Portway stepped over to a large, drop-fronted

deed box, labeled *Lord Lampeter's Settled Estate,* and
unlocked it with a key from his chain. Inside was a rack
and in the rack I counted the dusty ends of a dozen bottles.

"Château Margaux. The 1934 vintage. I shouldn't
say that even now it has reached its peak. Now here—"
he unlocked *The Dean of Melchester, Family Affairs*—
"I have a real treasure. A Mouton Rothschild of
1924."

"1924!"

"In Magnums. I know that you appreciate a good
wine and since this may perhaps be our last opportunity—"

"Well—"

Mr. Portway took a corkscrew, a decanter, and two
glasses from a small cupboard labeled *Estate Duty
Forms, Miscellaneous,* drew the cork of the Mouton
Rothschild with care and skill, and decanted it with a
steady hand. Then he poured two glasses. We both held
it up to the single unshaded light to note the dark, rich,
almost black color, and took our first ecstatic mouthful. It went down like oiled silk.

"What did you say you had in the other boxes?" I
inquired reverently.

"My preference has been for the great clarets," said
Mr. Portway. "Of course, as I only really started buying
in 1945, I have nothing that you could call a museum
piece. But I picked up a small lot of 1927 Chateau
Talbot which has to be tasted to be believed. And if a
good burgundy was offered, I didn't say no to it." He
gestured toward the *Marchioness of Gravesend* box in
one corner. "There's a 1937 Romanée Conti—but your
glass is empty—"

As we finished the Mouton Rothschild in companion-
able silence I looked at my watch. It was two o'clock
in the morning.

"You will scarcely find any transport to get you
home now," said Mr. Portway. "Might I suggest that the
only thing to follow a fine claret is a noble burgundy?"

"Well—" I said.

I was fully aware that I was compromising my official position. Actually, I think my mind had long since been made up. As dawn was breaking, and the Romanée Conti was sinking in the bottle, we agreed on provisional articles of partnership.

The name of the firm is Portway & Gilbert, of 7 Lombards Inn.

If you are thinking, by any chance, of buying a house—

WATCH FOR IT

Joseph N. Gores

Eric's first one. The very first.

And it went up early.

If I'd been in my apartment on Durant, with the window open, I probably would have heard it. And probably, at 4:30 in the morning, would have thought like any straight that it had been a truck backfire. But I'd spent the night balling Elizabeth over in San Francisco while Eric was placing the bomb in Berkeley. With her every minute, I'd made sure, because whatever else you can say about the federal pigs, they're thorough. I'd known that if anything went wrong, they'd be around looking.

Liz and I heard it together on the noon news, when we were having breakfast before her afternoon classes. She teaches freshman English at SF State.

Eric Whitlach, outspoken student radical on the Berkeley campus, was injured early this morning when a bomb he allegedly was placing under a table in the Student Union detonated prematurely. Police said the explosive device was fastened to a clock mechanism set for 9:30, when the area would have been packed with students. The extent of the young activist's injuries is not known, but

* * *

"God, that's terrible," Liz said with a shudder. She'd been in a number of upper-level courses with both Eric and me. "What could have happened to him, Ross, to make him do . . . something like that?"

"I guess . . . Well, I haven't seen much of him since graduation last June . . ." I gestured above the remains of our eggs and bacon. " 'Student revolutionary'—it's hard to think of Eric that way." Then I came up with a nice touch. "Maybe he shouldn't have gone beyond his M.A. Maybe he should have stopped when we did—before he lost touch."

When I'd recruited Eric without appearing to, it had seemed a very heavy idea. I mean, nobody actually expects this vocal, kinky, Rubin-type radical to go out and set bombs; because they don't. We usually avoid Eric's sort ourselves: they have no sense of history, no discipline. They're as bad as the Communists on the other side of the street, with their excessive regimentation, their endless orders from somewhere else.

I stood up. "Well, baby, I'd better get back across the Bay . . ."

"Ross, aren't you . . . I mean, can't you . . ."

She stopped there, coloring; still a lot of that corrupting Middle America in her. She was ready to try anything at all in bed, but to say right out in daylight that she wanted me to ball her again after class—that still sort of blew her mind.

"I can't, Liz," I said all aw-shucksy, laughing down inside at how *straight* she was. "I *was* his roommate until four months ago, and the police or somebody might want to ask me questions about him."

I actually thought that they might, and nothing brings out pig paranoia quicker than somebody not available for harassment when they want him. But nobody showed up. I guess they knew that as long as they had Eric they could get whatever they wanted out of him just by shooting electricity into his balls or something, like the French pigs in Algeria. I know how the fascists operate.

Beyond possible questions by the pigs, however, I knew there'd be a strategy session that night in Berkeley. After dark at Zeta Books, on Telegraph south of the campus, is the usual time and place for a meet. Armand Marsh let me in and locked the door behind me; he runs the store for the Student Socialist Alliance as a cover. He's a long skinny redheaded cat with ascetic features and quick nervous mannerisms, and is cell-leader for our three-man focal.

I saw that Danzer was in the mailing room when I got there, as was Benny. I didn't like Danzer being there. Sure, he acted as liaison with other Bay Area focals, but he never went out on operations and so he was an outsider. No outsider can be trusted.

"Benny," said Armand, "how badly is Whitlach really hurt?"

Benny Leland is night administrator for Alta Monte Hospital. With his close-trimmed hair and conservative clothes he looks like the ultimate straight.

"He took a big splinter off the table right through his shoulder. Damned lucky that he had already set it and was on his way out when it blew. Otherwise they'd have just found a few teeth and toes."

"So he'd be able to move around?"

"Oh, sure. The injury caused severe shock, but he's out of that now; and the wound itself is not critical." He paused to look pointedly at me. "What I don't understand is how the damned thing went off prematurely."

Meaning I was somehow to blame, since I had supplied Eric with the matériel for the bomb. Armand looked over at me too.

"Ross? What sort of device was it?"

"Standard," I said. "Two sticks of dynamite liberated from that P.G. and E. site four months ago. An electric blasting cap with a small battery to detonate it. Alarm clock timer. He was going to carry the whole thing in a gift-wrapped shoe box to make it less conspicuous. There are several ways that detonation could—"

"None of that is pertinent now," interrupted Danzer. His voice was cold and heavy, like his face. He even looked like a younger Raymond Burr. "Our first concern is this: Will the focal be compromised if they break him down and he starts talking?"

"Eric was my best friend before I joined the focal," I said, "and he was my roommate for four years. But once we had determined it was better to use someone still a student than to set this one ourselves, I observed the standard security procedures in recruiting him. He believes the bombing was totally his own idea."

"He isn't even aware of the *existence* of the focal, let alone who's in it," Armand explained. "There's no way that he could hurt us."

Danzer's face was still cold when he looked over at me, but I had realized he *always* looked cold. "Then it seems that Ross is the one to go in after him."

"If there's any need to go at all," said Benny quickly. I knew what he was thinking. Any operation would entail the hospital, which meant he would be involved. He didn't like that. "After all, if he can't hurt us, why not just . . ." He shrugged.

"Just leave him there? Mmmph." Danzer publishes a couple of underground radical newspapers even though he's only twenty-seven, and also uses his presses to run off porn novels for some outfit in L.A. I think he nets some heavy bread. "I believe I can convince you of the desirability of going in after him. If Ross is willing . . ."

"Absolutely." I kept the excitement from my voice. Cold. Controlled. That's the image I like to project. A desperate man, reckless, careless of self. "If anyone else came through that door, Eric would be convinced

he was an undercover pig. As soon as he sees me, he'll
know that I've come to get him away."

"Why couldn't Ross just walk in off the street as a
normal visitor?" asked Danzer.

"There's a twenty-four-hour police guard on Whitlach's door." Benny was still fighting the idea of a rescue
operation. "Only the doctors and one authorized nurse
per shift get in."

"All right. And Ross *must not* be compromised. If he
is, the whole attempt would be negated, worse than
useless." Which at the moment I didn't understand.
"Now let's get down to it."

As Danzer talked, I began to comprehend why he
had been chosen to coordinate the activities of the
focals. His mind was cold and logical and precise, as
was his plan. What bothered me was my role in that
plan. But I soon saw the error in my objections. I was
Eric's friend, the only one he knew he could trust—
and I had brought him into it in the first place. There
was danger, of course, but that only made me feel better the more I thought of it. You have to take risks
if you are to destroy a corrupt society, because like a
snake with a broken back it still has venom on its
fangs.

It took three hours to work out the operational
scheme.

Alta Monte Hospital is set in the center of a quiet
residential area off Ashby Avenue. It used to be easy
to approach after dark; just walk to the side entrance
across the broad blacktop parking lot. But so many
doctors going out to their cars have been mugged by
heads looking for narcotics that the lot is patrolled
now.

I parked on Benvenue, got the hypo kit and the
cherry bombs from the glove box, and slid them into
my pocket. The thin strong nylon rope was wound
around my waist under my dark blue wind-breaker.
My breath went up in gray wisps on the chilly wet night

air. After I'd locked the car, I held out my hand to
look at it by the pale illumination of the nearest street
lamp. No tremors. The nerves were cool, man. *I* was
cool.

3:23 A.M. by my watch.

In seven minutes, Benny Leland would unlock the
small access door on the kitchen loading dock. He
would relock it three minutes later, while going back
to the staff coffee room from the men's lavatory. I
had to get inside during those three minutes or not at
all.

3:27.

I hunkered down in the thick hedge rimming the lot.
My palms were getting sweaty. Everything hinged on a
nurse who came off work in midshift because her old
man worked screwy hours and she had to be home to
baby-sit her kid. If she was late . . .

The guard's voice carried clearly on black misty air.
"All finished, Mrs. Adamson?"

"Thank God, Danny. It's been a rough night. We lost
one in post-op that I was sure would make it."

"Too bad. See you tomorrow, Mrs. Adamson."

I had a cherry bomb in my rubber-gloved hand now.
I couldn't hear her soft-soled nurse's shoes on the
blacktop, but I could see her long thin shadow come
bouncing up the side of her car ten yards away. I
came erect, threw, stepped back into shadow.

It was beautiful, man; like a sawed-off shotgun in the
silent lot. She gave a wonderful scream, full-throated,
and the guard yelled. I could hear his heavy feet thud-
ding to her aid as he ran past my section of hedge.

I was sprinting across the blacktop behind his back
on silent garage attendant's shoes, hunched as low as
possible between the parked cars in case anyone had
been brought to a window by the commotion. Without
checking my pace, I ran down the kitchen delivery
ramp to crouch in the deep shadow under the edge of
the loading platform.

Nothing. No pursuit. My breath ragged in my chest,

more from excitement than my dash. The watch said 3:31. Beautiful.

I threw a leg up, rolled onto my belly on the platform. Across to the access port in the big overhead accordion steel loading door. It opened easily under my careful fingertips. Benny was being cool, too, producing on schedule for a change. I don't entirely trust Benny.

Hallway deserted, as per the plan. That unmistakable hospital smell. Across the hall, one of those wheeled carts holding empty food trays ready for the morning's breakfasts. Right where it was supposed to be. I put the two cherry bombs on the front left corner of the second tray down, turned, went nine quick paces to the firedoor.

My shoes made slight, scuffing noises on the metal runners. By law, hospital firedoors cannot be locked. I checked my watch: in nineteen seconds, Benny Leland would emerge from the men's room and, as he walked back to the staff coffee room, would relock the access door and casually hook the cherry bombs from the tray. I then would have three minutes to be in position.

It had been 150 seconds when I pulled the third-floor firedoor a quarter-inch ajar. No need to risk looking out: I could visualize everything from Benny's briefing earlier.

"Whitlach's room is the last one on the corridor, right next to the fire stairs," he'd said. "I arranged that as part of my administrative duties—actually, of course, in case we *would* want to get to him. The floor desk with the night duty nurse is around an ell and at the far end of the corridor. She's well out of the way. The policeman will be sitting beside Whitlach's door on a metal folding chair. He'll be alone in the hall at that time of night."

Ten seconds. I held out my hand. No discernible tremor.

Benny Leland, riding alone in the elevator from the

basement to the fourth floor administrative offices, would just be stopping here at the third floor. As the doors opened, he would punch *four* again; as they started to close, he would hurl his two cherry bombs down the main stairwell, and within seconds would be off the elevator and into his office on the floor above. The pig could only think it had been someone on the stairs.

Whoomp! Whump!

Fantastic, man! Muffled, so the duty nurse far down the corridor and around a corner wouldn't even hear them; but loud enough so the pig, mildly alert for a possible attempt to free Whitlach, would have to check . . .

I counted ten, pulled open the firedoor, went the six paces to Eric's now unguarded door. Thirty feet away, the pig's beefy blue-clad back was just going through the access doors to the elevator shaft and the main stairwell.

A moment of absolute panic when Eric's door stuck. Then it pulled free and I was inside. Sweat on my hands under the thin rubber gloves. Cool it now, baby.

I could see the pale blur of Eric's face as he started up from his medicated doze. His light night light cast harsh, antiseptic shadows across his lean face. Narrow stubborn jaw, very bright blue eyes, short nose, wiry, tight-curled brown hair. I felt a tug of compassion: he was very pale and drawn.

But then a broad grin lit up his features. *"Ross!"* he whispered. "How in the hell—"

"No time, baby." My own voice was low, too. I already had the syringe out, was stabbing it into the rubber top of the little phial. "The pig will be back from checking out my diversion in just a minute. We have to be ready for him. Can you move?"

"Sure. What do you want me to—"

"Gimme your arm, baby." I jammed the needle into his flesh, depressed the plunger as I talked. "Painkiller. In case we bump that shoulder getting you out of here, you won't feel anything."

Eric squeezed my arm with his left hand; there were tears in his eyes. How scared that poor cat must have been when he woke up in the hands of the fascist pigs!

"Christ, Ross, I can't believe . . ." He shook his head. "Oh, Jesus, right out from under their snouts! You're beautiful, man!"

I got an arm around his shoulders, as the little clock in my mind ticked off the seconds, weighing, measuring the pig's native stupidity against his duty at the door. They have that sense of duty, all right, the pigs: but no smarts. We had them by the shorts now.

"Gotta get you to the window, cat," I breathed. Eric obediently swung his legs over the edge of the bed.

"Why . . . window . . ." His head was lolling.

I unzipped my jacket to show him the rope wound around my waist. "I'm lowering you down to the ground. Help will be waiting there."

I slid up the aluminum sash, let in the night through the screen. Groovy. Like velvet. No noise.

"Perch there, baby," I whispered. "I want the pig to come in and see you silhouetted, so I can take him from behind, dig?"

He nodded slowly. The injection was starting to take effect. It was my turn to squeeze his arm.

"Hang in there, baby."

I'd just gotten the night light switched off, had gotten behind the door, when I heard the pig's belatedly hurrying steps coming up the hall. Too late, you stupid fascist bastard, much too late.

A narrow blade of light stabbed at the room, widened to a rectangle. He didn't even come in fast, gun in hand, moving down and to the side as he should have. Just trotted in, a fat old porker to the slaughter. I heard his sharp intake of breath as he saw Eric.

"Hey! You! Get away from—"

I was on him from behind. Right arm around the

throat, forearm grip, pull back hard while the left pushes on the back of the head . . .

They go out easily with that grip, any of them. Good for disarming a sentry without using a knife, I had been taught. I hadn't wasted my Cuban sojourn chopping sugar cane like those student straights on the junkets from Canada. I feel nothing but contempt for *these* cats: they have not yet realized that destroying the fabric of society is the only thing left for us.

I dragged the unconscious pig quickly out the door, lowered his fat butt into his chair and stretched his legs out convincingly. Steady pulse. He'd come around in a few minutes; meanwhile, it actually would have been possible to just walk Eric down the fire stairs and out of the building.

For a moment I was tempted; but doing it that way wasn't in the plan. The plan called for the maximum effect possible, and merely walking Eric out would minimize it. Danzer's plan was everything.

Eric was slumped sideways against the window frame, mumbling sleepily. I pulled him forward, letting his head loll on my shoulder while I unhooked the screen and sent it sailing down into the darkness of the bushes flanking the concrete walk below. I could feel the coils of thin nylon around my waist, strong enough in their synthetic strength to lower him safely to the ground.

Jesus, he was one sweet guy. I paused momentarily to run my hand through his coarse, curly hair. There was sweat on his forehead. Last year he took my French exam for me so I could get my graduate degree. We'd met in old Prof Cecil's Western Civ course our junior year, and had been roomies until the end of grad school.

"I'm sorry, baby," I told his semiconscious, sweat-dampened face.

Then I let go and nudged, so his limp form flopped backward through the open window and he was gone,

gone instantly, just like that. Three stories, head-first, to the concrete sidewalk. He hit with a sound like an egg dropped on the kitchen floor. A bad sound, man. One I won't soon forget.

The hall was dark and deserted as I stepped over the pig's out-stretched legs. He'd be raising the alarm soon, but nobody except the other pigs would believe him. Not after the autopsy.

The first sound of sirens came just after I had stuffed the thin surgical gloves down a sewer and was back in my car, pulling decorously away from the curb. The nylon rope, taken along only to convince Eric that I meant to lower him from the window, had been slashed into useless lengths and deposited in a curb-side trash barrel awaiting early morning collection.

On University Avenue, I turned toward an all-night hamburger joint that had a pay phone in the parking lot. I was, can you believe it, ravenous; but more than that, I was horny. I thought about that for a second, knowing I should feel sort of sick and ashamed at having a sexual reaction to the execution. But instead I felt . . . *transfigured*. Eric had been a political prisoner anyway; the pigs would have made sure he wouldn't have lived to come to trial. By his necessary death, *I* would be changing the entire history of human existence. *Me*. Alone.

And there was Liz over in the city, always eager, a receptacle in which I could spend my sexual excitement before she went off to teach. But first, Armand. So he could tell Danzer it was all right to print what we had discussed the night before.

Just thinking of that made me feel elated, because the autopsy would reveal the presence of that massive dose of truth serum I had needled into Eric before his death. And the Establishment news media would do the rest, hinting and probing and suggesting before our underground weeklies even hit the street with our charge against the fascists.

Waiting for Armand to pick up his phone, I composed our headline in my mind:

**PIGS PUMP REVOLUTIONARY HERO FULL
OF SCOPOLAMINE; HE DIVES FROM WINDOW
RATHER THAN FINK ON THE MOVEMENT**

Oh yes, man. Beautiful. Just beautiful. Watch for it.

THE AFFAIR OF THE TWISTED SCARF

Rex Stout

My problems hit a new high that day. What I really felt like doing was to go out for a walk but I wasn't quite desperate enough for that. So I merely beat it down to the office, shutting the door from the hall behind me, and went and sat at my desk with my feet up, leaned back and closed my eyes, and took a couple of deep breaths.

I had made two mistakes. When Bill McNab, garden editor of the *Gazette,* had suggested to Nero Wolfe that the members of the Manhattan Flower Club be invited to drop in some afternoon to look at the orchids, I should have fought it.

And when the date had been set and the invitations sent, and Wolfe had arranged that Fritz and Saul should do the receiving at the front door and I should stay up in the plant-rooms with him and Theodore, mingling with the guests, if I had had an ounce of brains I would have put my foot down. But I hadn't, and as a result I had been up there a good hour and a half, grinning around and acting pleased and happy. . . . "No, sir, that's not a brasso, it's a laelia." . . . "Quite all right, madam—your sleeve happened to hook it. It'll bloom again next year."

It wouldn't have been so bad if there had been something for the eyes. It was understood that the Manhattan Flower Club was choosy about whom it took in, but obviously its standards were totally different from mine. The men were just men; okay as men go. But the women! It was a darned good thing they had picked on flowers to love, because flowers don't have to love back.

There had, in fact, been one—just one. I had got a glimpse of her at the other end of the crowded aisle as I went through the door into the cool-room. From ten paces off she looked absolutely promising, and when I had maneuvered close enough to make her an offer to answer questions if she had any, there was simply no doubt about it—no doubt at all.

The first quick, slanting glance she gave me said plainly that she could tell the difference between a flower and a man, but she just smiled and shook her head, and moved on with her companions, an older female and two males. Later, I had made another try and got another brush-off, and still later, too long later, feeling that the grin might freeze on me for good if I didn't take a recess, I went AWOL by worming my way to the far end of the warm-room and sidling on out.

All the way down the three flights of stairs new guests were coming up, though it was then four o'clock. Nero Wolfe's old brownstone house on West 35th Street had seen no such throng as that within my memory, which is long and good. One flight down, I stopped off at my bedroom for a pack of cigarettes; and another flight down, I detoured to make sure the door of Wolfe's bedroom was locked.

In the main hall downstairs I halted a moment to watch Fritz Brenner, busy at the door with both departures and arrivals, and to see Saul Panzer emerge from the front room, which was being used as a cloakroom, with someone's hat and topcoat. Then, as aforesaid, I entered the office, shutting the door from the hall behind me, went and sat at my desk with my feet up, leaned back and closed my eyes, and took some deep breaths.

I had been there maybe eight or ten minutes, and was getting relaxed and a little less bitter, when the door opened and she came in. Her companions were not along. By the time she had closed the door and turned to me I had got to my feet, with a friendly leer, and had begun, "I was just sitting here thinking—"

The look on her face stopped me. There was nothing wrong with it basically, but something had got it out of kilter. She headed for me, got halfway, jerked to a stop, sank into one of the yellow chairs, and squeaked, "Could I have a drink?"

"Sure thing," I said. I went to the cupboard and got a hooker of old whiskey. Her hand was shaking as she took the glass, but she didn't spill any, and she got it down in two swallows.

"Did I need that!"

"More?"

She shook her head. Her bright brown eyes were moist, from the whiskey, as she gave me a full, straight look with her head tilted up.

"You're Archie Goodwin," she stated.

I nodded. "And you're the Queen of Egypt?"

"I'm a baboon," she declared. "I don't know how they ever taught me to talk." She looked around for something to put the glass on, and I moved a step and reached for it. "Look at my hand shake," she complained.

She kept her hand out, looking at it, so I took it in mine and gave it some friendly but gentle pressure. "You do seem a little upset," I conceded.

She jerked the hand away. "I want to see Nero Wolfe. I want to see him right away, before I change my mind." She was gazing up at me, with the moist brown eyes. "I'm in a fix now, all right! I've made up my mind. I'm going to get Nero Wolfe to get me out of this somehow."

I told her it couldn't be done until the party was over.

She looked around. "Are people coming in here?"

I told her no.

"May I have another drink, please?"

I told her she should give the first one time to settle, and instead of arguing she arose and helped herself. I sat down and frowned at her. Her line sounded fairly screwy for a member of the Manhattan Flower Club, or even for a daughter of one. She came back to her chair, sat, and met my eyes. Looking at her straight like that could have been a nice way to pass the time if there had been any chance for a meeting of minds.

"I could tell you," she said.

"Many people have," I said modestly.

"I'm going to."

"Good. Shoot."

"Okay. I'm a crook."

"It doesn't show," I objected. "What do you do—cheat at Canasta?"

"I didn't say I'm a cheat." She cleared her throat for the hoarseness. "I said I'm a crook. Remind me some day to tell you the story of my life—how my husband got killed in the war and I broke through the gate. Don't I sound interesting?"

"You sure do. What's your line—orchid-stealing?"

"No. I wouldn't be small and I wouldn't be dirty—That's what I used to think, but once you start it's not so easy. You meet people and you get involved. Two years ago four of us took over a hundred grand from a certain rich woman with a rich husband. I can tell you about that one, even names, because she couldn't move, anyhow."

I nodded. "Blackmailers' customers seldom can. What—?"

"I'm not a blackmailer!"

"Excuse me. Mr. Wolfe often says I jump to conclusions."

"You did that time." She was still indignant. "A blackmailer's not a crook; he's a snake! Not that it really matters. What's wrong with being a crook is the other crooks—they make it dirty whether you like it or not. It makes a coward of you, too—that's the worst. I had a friend once—as close as a crook ever comes to having a friend—and a man killed her, strangled her. If I had told what I knew about it they could have caught him, but I was afraid to go to the cops, so he's still loose. And she was my friend! That's getting down toward the bottom. Isn't it?"

"Fairly low," I agreed, eying her. "Of course, I don't know you any too well. I don't know how you react to two stiff drinks. Maybe your hobby is stringing private detectives."

She simply ignored it. "I realized long ago," she went on, as if it were a one-way conversation, "that I had made a mistake. About a year ago I decided to break loose. A good way to do it would have been to talk to someone the way I'm talking to you now, but I didn't have sense enough to see that."

I nodded. "Yeah, I know."

"So I kept putting it off. We got a good one in December and I went to Florida for a vacation, but down there I met a man with a lead, and we followed it up here just a week ago. That's what I'm working on now. That's what brought me here today. This man—" She stopped abruptly.

"Well?" I invited her.

She looked dead serious, not more serious, but a different kind. "I'm not putting anything on him," she declared. "I don't owe him anything, and I don't like him. But this is strictly about me and no one else— only, I had to explain why I'm here. I wish to heaven I'd never come!"

There was no question about that coming from her heart, unless she had done a lot of rehearsing in front of a mirror.

"It got you this talk with me," I reminded her.

She was looking straight through me and beyond. "If only I hadn't come! If only I hadn't seen him!"

She leaned toward me for emphasis. "I'm either too smart or not smart enough; that's my trouble. I should have looked away from him, turned away quick, when I realized I knew who he was, before he turned and saw it in my eyes. But I was so shocked I couldn't help it! I stood there staring at him, thinking I wouldn't have recognized him if he hadn't had a hat on, and then he looked at me and saw what was happening. But it was too late.

"I know how to manage my face with nearly anybody, anywhere, but that was too much for me. It showed so plain that Mrs. Orwin asked me what was the matter with me, and I had to try to pull myself together. Then, seeing Nero Wolfe gave me the idea of telling him; only of course I couldn't right there with the crowd. Then I saw you going out, and as soon as I could break away I came down to find you."

She tried smiling at me, but it didn't work so good. "Now I feel somewhat better," she said hopefully.

I nodded. "That's good whiskey. Is it a secret who you recognized?"

"No. I'm going to tell Nero Wolfe."

"You decided to tell me." I flipped a hand. "Suit yourself. Whoever you tell, what's the good?"

"Why—then he can't do anything to me."

"Why not?"

"Because he wouldn't dare. Nero Wolfe will tell him that I've told about him, so that if anything happened to me he would know it was him, and he'd know who he is—I mean, Nero Wolfe would know—and so would you."

"We would if we had his name and address." I was studying her. "He must be quite a specimen, to scare you that bad. And speaking of names, what's yours?"

She made a little noise that could have been meant for a laugh. "Do you like Marjorie?"

"Not bad. What are you using now?"

She hesitated, frowning.

"For Pete's sake," I protested, "you're not in a vacuum, and I'm a detective. They took the names down at the door."

"Cynthia Brown," she said.

"That's Mrs. Orwin you came with?"

"Yes."

"She's the current customer? The lead you picked up in Florida?"

"Yes. But that's—" She gestured. "That's finished. I'm through."

"I know. There's just one thing you haven't told me, though. Who was it you recognized?"

She turned her head for a glance at the door and then turned it still farther to look behind her.

"Can anyone hear us?" she asked.

"Nope. That other door goes to the front room—today, the cloakroom. Anyhow, this room's sound-proofed."

She glanced at the hall door again, returned to me, and lowered her voice: "This has to be done the way I say."

"Sure; why not?"

"I wasn't being honest with you."

"I wouldn't expect it from a crook. Start over."

"I mean . . ." She used the teeth on the lip again. "I mean I'm not just scared about myself. I'm scared, all right, but I don't just want Nero Wolfe for what I said. I want him to get him for murder, but he has to keep me out of it. I don't want to have anything to do with any cops—not now I don't, especially. If he won't do it that way—Do you think he will?"

I was feeling a faint tingle at the base of my spine. I only get that on special occasions, but this was unquestionably something special. I gave her a hard look and didn't let the tingle get into my voice: "He might, for you, if you pay him. What kind of evidence have you got? Any?"

"I saw him."

"You mean today?"

"I mean I saw him then." She had her hands clasped tight. "I told you—I had a friend. I stopped in at her apartment that afternoon. I was just leaving—Doris was inside, in the bathroom—and as I got near the entrance door I heard a key turning in the lock, from the outside. I stopped, and the door came open and a man came in. When he saw me he just stood and stared. I had never met Doris's bank account, and I knew she didn't want me to. And since he had a key I supposed of course it was him, making an unexpected call; so I mumbled something about Doris being in the bathroom and went past him, through the door and on out."

She paused. Her clasped hands loosened and then tightened again.

"I'm burning my bridges," she said, "but I can deny all this if I have to. I went and kept a cocktail date, and then phoned Doris's number to ask if our dinner date was still on, considering the visit of the bank account. There was no answer, so I went back to her apartment and rang the bell, and there was no answer to that, either. It was a self-service-elevator place, no doorman or hallman, so there was no one to ask anything.

"Her maid found her body the next morning. The papers said she had been killed the day before. That man killed her. There wasn't a word about him—no one had seen him enter or leave. And I didn't open my mouth! I was a rotten coward!"

"And today, all of a sudden, there he is, looking at orchids?"

"Yes."

"Are you sure he knows you recognized him?"

"Yes. He looked straight at me, and his eyes—"

She was stopped by the house phone buzzing. Stepping to my desk, I picked it up and asked it, "Well?"

Nero Wolfe's voice, peevish, came: "Archie!"

"Yes, sir."

"What the devil are you doing? Come back up here!"

"Pretty soon. I'm talking with a prospective client—"

"This is no time for clients! Come at once!"

The connection went. He had slammed it down. I hung up and went back to the prospective client: "Mr. Wolfe wants me upstairs. Do you want to wait here?"

"Yes."

"If Mrs. Orwin asks about you?"

"I didn't feel well and went home."

"Okay. It shouldn't be long—the invitations said two thirty to five. If you want a drink, help yourself. . . . What name does this murderer use when he goes to look at orchids?"

She looked blank.

I got impatient: "What's his name? This bird you recognized."

"I don't know."

"Describe him."

She thought it over a little, gazing at me, and then shook her head. "Not now. I want to see what Nero Wolfe says first."

She must have seen something in my eyes, or thought she did, for suddenly she came up out of her chair and moved to me and put a hand on my arm. "That's all I mean," she said earnestly. "It's not you—I know you're all right. I might as well tell you—you'd never want any part of me anyhow—this is the first time in years, I don't know how long, that I've talked to a man straight —you know, just human. I—" She stopped for a word, and a little color showed in her cheeks. "I've enjoyed it very much."

"Good. Me, too. Call me Archie. I've got to go, but describe him."

But she hadn't enjoyed it that much. "Not until Nero Wolfe says he'll do it," she said firmly.

I had to leave it at that, knowing as I did that in three

more minutes Wolfe might have a fit. Out in the hall
I had the notion of passing the word to Saul and Fritz
to give departing guests a good look, but rejected it
because (a) they weren't there, both of them pre-
sumably being busy in the cloakroom, (b) he might
have departed already, and (c) I had by no means
swallowed a single word of Cynthia's story, let alone
the whole works.

Up in the plant-rooms there were plenty left. When
I came into Wolfe's range he darted me a glance of
cold fury, and I turned on the grin. Anyway, it was a
quarter to five, and if they took the hint on the invitation it wouldn't last much longer.

They didn't take the hint on the dot, but it didn't
bother me because my mind was occupied. I was now
really interested in them—or at least one of them, if he
had actually been there and hadn't gone home.

First, there was a chore to get done. I found the
three Cynthia had been with, a female and two males.

"Mrs. Orwin?" I asked politely.

She nodded at me and said, "Yes?" Not quite tall
enough, but plenty plump enough, with a round, full
face and narrow little eyes that might have been better
if they had been wide open. She struck me as a lead
worth following.

"I'm Archie Goodwin," I said. "I work here."

I would have gone on if I had known how, but I
needed a lead myself.

Luckily one of the males horned in. "My sister?" he
inquired anxiously.

So it was a brother-and-sister act. As far as looks
went he wasn't a bad brother at all. Older than me
maybe, but not much. He was tall and straight, with a
strong mouth and jaw and keen gray eyes. "My sister?"
he repeated.

"I guess so. You are—?"

"Colonel Brown. Percy Brown."

"Yeah." I switched back to Mrs. Orwin: "Miss

Brown asked me to tell you that she went home. I gave her a little drink and it seemed to help, but she decided to leave. She asked me to apologize for her."

"She's perfectly healthy," the colonel asserted. He sounded a little hurt.

"Is she all right?" Mrs. Orwin asked.

"For her," the other male put in, "you should have made it three drinks. Or just hand her the bottle."

His tone was mean and his face was mean, and anyhow that was no way to talk in front of the help in a strange house, meaning me. He was a bit younger than Brown, but he already looked enough like Mrs. Orwin, especially the eyes, to make it more than a guess that they were mother and son.

That point was settled when she commanded him, "Be quiet, Gene!" She turned to the colonel: "Perhaps you should go and see about her?"

He shook his head, with a fond but manly smile at her. "It's not necessary, Mimi. Really."

"She's all right," I assured them, and pushed off, thinking there were a lot of names in this world that could stand a reshuffle. Calling that overweight, narrow-eyed, pearl-and-mink proprietor Mimi was a paradox.

I moved around among the guests, being gracious. Fully aware that I was not equipped with a Geiger counter that would flash a signal if and when I established contact with a strangler, the fact remained that I had been known to have hunches. It would be something for my scrapbook if I picked the killer of Doris Hatten.

Cynthia Brown hadn't given me the Hatten, only the Doris, but with the context that was enough. At the time it had happened, some five months ago, early in October, the papers had given it a big play, of course. She had been strangled with her own scarf, of white silk with the Declaration of Independence printed on it, in her cozy fifth-floor apartment in the West Seventies, and the scarf had been left around her neck, knotted at the back.

The cops had never got within a mile of charging anyone, and Sergeant Purley Stebbins of Homicide had told me that they had never even found out who was paying the rent.

I kept on the go through the plant-rooms, leaving all switches open for a hunch. Some of them were plainly preposterous, but with everyone else I made an opportunity to exchange some words, full face and close up. That took time, and it was no help to my current and chronic campaign for a raise in wages, since it was the women, not the men, that Wolfe wanted off his neck. I stuck at it, anyhow. It was true that if Cynthia was on the level, we would soon have specifications, but I had had that tingle at the bottom of my spine and I was stubborn.

As I say, it took time, and meanwhile five o'clock came and went and the crowd thinned out. Going on five-thirty, the remaining groups seemed to get the idea all at once that time was up and made for the entrance to the stairs.

I was in the moderate-room when it happened, and the first thing I knew I was alone there, except for a guy at the north bench studying a row of dowianas. He didn't interest me, as I had already canvassed him and crossed him off as the wrong type for a strangler; but as I glanced his way he suddenly bent forward to pick up a pot with a flowering plant, and as he did so I felt my back stiffening. The stiffening was a reflex, but I knew what had caused it; the way his fingers closed around the pot, especially the thumbs. No matter how careful you are of other people's property, you don't pick up a five-inch pot as if you were going to squeeze the life out of it.

I made my way around to him. When I got there he was holding the pot so that the flowers were only a few inches from his eyes.

"Nice flower," I said brightly.

He nodded.

He leaned to put the pot back, still choking it. I swiveled my head. The only people in sight, beyond the glass partition between us and the cool-room, were Nero Wolfe and a small group of guests, among whom were the Orwin trio and Bill McNab, the garden editor of the *Gazette*. As I turned my head back to my man he straightened up, pivoted on his heel, and marched off without a word.

I followed him out to the landing and down the three flights of stairs. Along the main hall I was courteous enough not to step on his heel, but a lengthened stride would have reached it. The hall was next to empty. A woman, ready for the street in a caracul coat, was standing there, and Saul Panzer was posted near the front door with nothing to do.

I followed my man on into the front room, now the cloakroom, where Fritz Brenner was helping a guest on with his coat. Of course, the racks were practically bare, and with one glance my man saw his property and went to get it. I stepped forward to help, but he ignored me without even bothering to shake his head. I was beginning to feel hurt.

When he emerged into the hall I was beside him, and as he moved to the front door I spoke: "Excuse me, but we're checking guests out as well as in. Your name, please?"

"Ridiculous," he said curtly, and reached for the knob, pulled the door open, and crossed the sill.

Saul, knowing I must have had a reason for wanting to check him out, was at my elbow, and we stood watching his back as he descended the seven steps of the stoop.

"Tail?" Saul muttered to me.

I shook my head and was parting my lips to mutter something back, when a sound came from behind us that made us both whirl around—a screech from a woman, not loud but full of feeling. As we whirled, Fritz and the guest he had been serving came out of the front room, and all four of us saw the woman in the caracul coat come running out of the office into the hall. She kept coming, gasping something, and the guest, making a noise like an alarmed male, moved to meet her. I moved faster, needing about eight jumps to the office door and two inside. There I stopped.

Of course, I knew the thing on the floor was Cynthia, but only because I had left her in there in those clothes. With the face blue and contorted, the tongue halfway out and the eyes popping, it could have been almost anybody. I knelt down and slipped my hand inside her dress front, kept it there ten seconds, and felt nothing.

Saul's voice came from behind: "I'm here."

I got up and went to the phone on my desk and started dialing, telling Saul "No one leaves. We'll keep what we've got. Have the door open for Doc Vollmer." After only two whirs the nurse answered and put Vollmer on, and I snapped it at him: "Doc, Archie Goodwin. Come on the run. Strangled woman. . . . Yeah, strangled."

I pushed the phone back, reached for the house phone, and buzzed the plant-rooms, and after a wait had Wolfe's irritated bark in my ear: "Yes?"

"I'm in the office. You'd better come down. That prospective client I mentioned is here on the floor strangled. I think she's done, but I've sent for Vollmer."

"Is this flummery?" he roared.

"No, sir. Come down and look at her and then ask me."

The connection went. He had slammed it down. I got a sheet of thin tissue paper from a drawer, tore off a corner, and placed it carefully over Cynthia's mouth and nostrils.

Voices had been sounding from the hall. Now one of them entered the office. Its owner was the guest who had been in the cloakroom with Fritz when the screech came. He was a chunky, broad-shouldered guy with sharp, domineering dark eyes and arms like a gorilla's.

His voice was going strong as he started toward me from the door, but it stopped when he had come far enough to get a good look at the object on the floor.

"Oh, no!" he said huskily.

"Yes, sir," I agreed.

"How did it happen?"

"Don't know."

"Who is it?"

"Don't know."

He made his eyes come away from it and up until they met mine, and I gave him an A for control. It really was a sight.

"The man at the door won't let us leave," he stated.

"No, sir. You can see why."

"I certainly can." His eyes stayed with me, however. "But we know nothing about it. My name is Carlisle, Homer N. Carlisle. I am the executive vice-president of the North American Foods Company. My wife was merely acting under impulse; she wanted to see the office of Nero Wolfe, and she opened the door and entered. She's sorry she did, and so am I. We have an appointment, and there's no reason why we should be detained."

"I'm sorry, too," I told him, "but for one thing if for nothing else; your wife discovered the body. We're stuck worse than you are, with a corpse here in our office. So I guess—Hello, Doc."

Vollmer, entering and nodding at me on the fly, was panting a little as he set his black case on the floor and knelt beside it. His house was down the street and he had had only two hundred yards to trot, but he was taking on weight. As he opened the case and got out the stethoscope, Homer Carlisle stood and watched with his lips pressed tight, and I did likewise until I heard the sound of Wolfe's elevator.

Crossing to the door and into the hall, I surveyed the terrain. Toward the front, Saul and Fritz were calming down the woman in the caracul coat, now Mrs. Carlisle to me. Nero Wolfe and Mrs. Mimi Orwin were emerging from the elevator. Four guests were coming down the stairs: Gene Orwin, Colonel Percy Brown, Bill McNab, and a middle-aged male with a mop of black hair. I stayed by the office door to block the quartet on the stairs.

As Wolfe headed for me, Mrs. Carlisle darted to him and grabbed his arm: "I only wanted to see your office! I want to go! I'm not—"

As she pulled at him and sputtered, I noted a detail: the caracul coat was unfastened, and the ends of a silk scarf, figured and gaily colored, were flying loose. Since at least half of the female guests had sported scarfs, I mention it only to be honest and admit that I had got touchy on that subject.

Wolfe, who had already been too close to too many women that day to suit him, tried to jerk away, but she hung on. She was the big-boned, flat-chested, athletic type, and it could have been quite a tussle, with him weighing twice as much as her and four times as big around, if Saul hadn't rescued him by coming in between and prying her loose. That didn't stop her tongue, but Wolfe ignored it and came on toward me: "Has Dr. Vollmer come?"

"Yes, sir."

The executive vice-president emerged from the office, talking: "Mr. Wolfe, my name is Homer N. Carlisle and I insist—"

"Shut up," Wolfe growled. On the sill of the door to the office, he faced the audience. "Flower lovers," he said with bitter scorn. "You told me, Mr. McNab, a distinguished group of sincere and devoted gardeners. Pfui! . . . Saul!"

"Yes, sir."

"Put them all in the dining-room and keep them there. Let no one touch anything around this door, especially the knob . . . Archie, come with me."

He wheeled and entered the office. Following, I used

my foot to swing the door neatly shut, leaving no crack but not latching it. When I turned, Vollmer was standing, facing Wolfe's scowl.

"Well?" Wolfe demanded.

"Dead," Vollmer told him. "With asphyxiation from strangling."

"How long ago?"

"I don't know, but not more than an hour or two. Two hours at the outside, probably less."

Wolfe looked at the thing on the floor with no change in his scowl, and back at Doc. "Finger marks?"

"No. A constricting band of something with pressure below the hyoid bone. Not a stiff or narrow band; something soft, like a strip of cloth—say, a scarf."

Wolfe switched to me: "You didn't notify the police?"

"No, sir." I glanced at Vollmer and back. "I need a word."

"I suppose so." He spoke to Doc: "If you will leave us for a moment? The front room?"

Vollmer hesitated, uncomfortable. "As a doctor called to a violent death I'd catch the devil. Of course, I could say—"

"Then go to a corner and cover your ears."

He did so. He went to the farthest corner, the angle made by the partition of the bathroom, pressed his palms to his ears, and stood facing us. I addressed Wolfe with a lowered voice:

"I was here and she came in. She was either scared good or putting on a very fine act. Apparently, it wasn't an act, and I now think I should have alerted Saul and Fritz, but it doesn't matter what I now think. Last October a woman named Doris Hatten was killed, strangled, in her apartment. No one got elected. Remember?"

"Yes."

"She said she was a friend of Doris Hatten's and was at her apartment that day, and saw the man that did the strangling, and that he was here this afternoon. She

said he was aware that she had recognized him—that's
why she was scared—and she wanted to get you to
help by telling him that we were wise and he'd better
lay off. No wonder I didn't gulp it down. I realize that
you dislike complications and therefore might want me
to scratch this out, but at the end she touched a soft
spot by saying that she had enjoyed my company, so I
prefer to open up to the cops."

"Then do so. Confound it!"

I went to the phone and started dialing WAtkins
9-8241. Doc Vollmer came out of his corner. Wolfe
was pathetic. He moved around behind his desk and
lowered himself into his own oversized custom-made
number; but there smack in front of him was the object
on the floor, so after a moment he made a face, got
back onto his feet, grunted like an outraged boar, went
across to the other side of the room, to the shelves, and
inspected the backbones of books.

But even that pitiful diversion got interrupted. As I
finished with my phone call and hung up, sudden sounds
of commotion came from the hall. Dashing across, getting fingernails on the edge of the door and pulling it
open, I saw trouble. A group was gathered in the open
doorway of the dining-room, which was across the
hall. Saul Panzer went bounding past me toward the
front.

At the front door, Col. Percy Brown was stiff-arm-
ing Fritz Brenner with one hand and reaching for the
doorknob with the other. Fritz, who is chef and house-
keeper, is not supposed to double in acrobatics, but he
did fine. Dropping to the floor, he grabbed the colonel's
ankles and jerked his feet out from under him.

Then I was there, and Saul, with his gun out; and
there, with us, was the guest with the mop of black hair.

"You fool," I told the colonel as he sat up. "If you'd
got outdoors Saul would have winged you."

"Guilt," said the black-haired guest emphatically.
"The compression got unbearable and he exploded.
I'm a psychiatrist."

"Good for you." I took his elbow and turned him.
"Go back in and watch all of 'em. With that wall mirror
you can include yourself."

"This is illegal," stated Colonel Brown, who had
scrambled to his feet.

Saul herded them to the rear.

Fritz got hold of my sleeve: "Archie, I've got to ask
Mr. Wolfe about dinner."

"Nuts," I said savagely. "By dinner-time this place
will be more crowded than it was this afternoon."

"But he has to eat; you know that."

"Nuts," I said. I patted him on the shoulder. "Excuse
my manners, Fritz; I'm upset. I've just strangled a young
woman."

"Phooey," he said scornfully.

"I might as well have," I declared.

The doorbell rang. It was the first consignment of
cops.

In my opinion, Inspector Cramer made a mistake. It
is true that in a room where a murder has occurred the
city scientists may shoot the works. And they do. But,
except in rare circumstances, the job shouldn't take all
week, and in the case of our office a couple of hours
should have been ample. In fact, it was. By eight o'clock
the scientists were through. But Cramer, like a sap,
gave the order to seal it up until further notice, in
Wolfe's hearing. He knew that Wolfe spent at least
three hundred evenings a year in there, and that was
why he did it.

It was a mistake. If he hadn't made it, Wolfe might
have called his attention to a certain fact as soon as
Wolfe saw it himself, and Cramer would have been
saved a lot of trouble.

The two of them got the fact at the same time, from
me. We were in the dining-room—this was shortly
after the scientists had got busy in the office, and the
guests, under guard, had been shunted to the front room
—and I was relating my conversation with Cynthia
Brown. Whatever else my years as Wolfe's assistant

may have done for me or to me, they have practically turned me into a tape recorder. I gave them the real thing, word for word. When I finished, Cramer had a slew of questions, but Wolfe not a one. Maybe he had already focused on the fact above referred to, but neither Cramer nor I had.

Cramer called a recess on the questions to take steps. He called men in and gave orders. Colonel Brown was to be photographed and fingerprinted, and headquarters records were to be checked for him and Cynthia. The file on the murder of Doris Hatten was to be brought to him at once. The lab reports were to be rushed. Saul Panzer and Fritz Brenner were to be brought in.

They came. Fritz stood like a soldier at attention, grim and grave. Saul, only five feet seven, with the sharpest eyes and one of the biggest noses I have ever seen, in his unpressed brown suit and his necktie crooked—he stood like Saul, not slouching and not stiff. Of course, Cramer knew both of them.

"You and Fritz were in the hall all afternoon?"

Saul nodded. "The hall and the front room, yes."

"Who did you see enter or leave the office?"

"I saw Archie go in about four o'clock—I was just coming out of the front room with someone's hat and coat. I saw Mrs. Carlisle come out just after she screamed. In between those two I saw no one either enter or leave. We were busy most of the time, either in the hall or the front room."

Cramer grunted. "How about you, Fritz?"

"I saw no one." Fritz spoke louder than usual. "I would like to say something."

"Go ahead."

"I think a great deal of all this disturbance is unnecessary. My duties here are of the household and not professional, but I cannot help hearing what reaches my ears. Many times Mr. Wolfe has found the answer to problems that were too much for you. This happened

here in his own house, and I think it should be left
entirely to him."

I yooped, "Fritz, I didn't know you had it in you!"

Cramer was goggling at him. "Wolfe told you to
say that, huh?"

"Bah." Wolfe was contemptuous. "It can't be helped,
Fritz. Have we plenty of ham and sturgeon?"

"Yes, sir."

"Later, probably. For the guests in the front room,
but not the police. . . . Are you through with them, Mr.
Cramer?"

"No." Cramer went back to Saul: "How'd you check
the guests in?"

"I had a list of the members of the Manhattan Flower
Club. They had to show their membership cards. I
checked on the list those who came. If they brought a
wife or husband, or any other guest, I took the names."

"Then you have a record of everybody?"

"Yes."

"About how many names?"

"Two hundred and nineteen."

"This place wouldn't hold that many."

Saul nodded. "They came and went. There wasn't
more than a hundred or so at any one time."

"That's a help." Cramer was getting more and more
disgusted, and I didn't blame him. "Goodwin says he
was there at the door with you when that woman
screamed and came running out of the office, but that
you hadn't seen her enter the office. Why not?"

"We had our backs turned. We were watching a man
who had just left. Archie had asked him for his name
and he had said that was ridiculous. If you want it, his
name is Malcolm Vedder."

"How do you know?"

"I had checked him in with the rest."

Cramer stared. "Are you telling me that you could
fit that many names to that many faces after seeing
them once?"

Saul's shoulders went slightly up and down. "There's more to people than faces. I might go wrong on a few, but not many."

Cramer spoke to a dick standing by the door: "You heard that name, Levy—Malcolm Vedder. Tell Stebbins to check it on that list and send a man to bring him in."

Cramer returned to Saul: "Put it this way: Say I sit you here with that list, and a man or woman is brought in—"

"I could tell you positively whether the person had been here or not, especially if he was wearing the same clothes and hadn't been disguised. On fitting him to his name I might go wrong in a few cases, but I doubt it."

"I don't believe you."

"Mr. Wolfe does," Saul said complacently. "Archie does. I have developed my faculties."

"You sure have. All right; that's all for now. Stick around."

Saul and Fritz went. Wolfe, in his own chair at the end of the dining table, where ordinarily, at this hour, he sat for a quite different purpose, heaved a deep sigh and closed his eyes. I, seated beside Cramer at the side of the table which put us facing the door to the the hall, was beginning to appreciate the problem we were up against.

"Goodwin's story," Cramer growled. "I mean her story. What do you think?"

Wolfe's eyes came open a little. "What followed seems to support it. I doubt if she would have arranged for that"—he flipped a hand in the direction of the office across the hall—"just to corroborate a tale. I accept it."

"Yeah. I don't need to remind you that I know you well and I know Goodwin well. So I wonder how much chance there is that in a day or so you'll suddenly remember that she had been here before, or one or more of the others had, and you've got a client, and there was something leading up to this."

"Bosh," Wolfe said dryly. "Even if it were like that—and it isn't—you would be wasting time, since you know us."

A dick came to relay a phone call from a deputy commissioner. Another dick came in to say that Homer Carlisle was raising the roof in the front room. Meanwhile, Wolfe sat with his eyes shut, but I got an idea of his state of mind from the fact that intermittently his forefinger was making little circles on the polished top of the table.

Cramer looked at him. "What do you know," he asked abruptly, "about the killing of that Doris Hatten?"

"Newspaper accounts," Wolfe muttered. "And what Mr. Stebbins has told Mr. Goodwin, casually."

"Casual is right." Cramer got out a cigar, conveyed it to his mouth, and sank his teeth in it. He never lit one. "Those houses with self-service elevators are worse than walk-ups for a checking job. No one ever sees anyone coming or going. Even so, the man who paid the rent for that apartment was lucky. He may have been clever and careful, but also he was lucky never to have anybody see him enough to give a description of him."

"Possibly Miss Hatten paid the rent herself."

"Sure," Cramer conceded, "she paid it all right, but where did she get it from? No, it was that kind of a set-up. She had only been living there two months, and when we found out how well the man who paid for it had kept himself covered, we decided that maybe he had installed her there just for that purpose. That was why we gave it all we had. Another reason was that the papers started hinting that we knew who he was and that he was such a big shot we were sitting on the lid."

Cramer shifted his cigar one tooth over to the left. "That kind of thing used to get me sore, but what the heck; for newspapers that's just routine. Big shot or not, he didn't need us to do any covering for him—he did too good a job himself. Now, if we're to take it the way this Cynthia Brown gave it to Goodwin, it was the

man who paid the rent. I would hate to tell you what I
think of the fact that Goodwin sat there in your office
and was told he was right here on these premises, and
all he did was—"

"You're irritated," I said charitably. "Not that he
was on the premises, that he *had* been. Also, I was taking it with salt. Also, she was saving specifications for
Mr. Wolfe. Also—"

"Also, I know you. How many of these two hundred
and nineteen people were men?"

"I would say a little over half."

"Then how do *you* like it?"

"I hate it."

Wolfe grunted. "Judging from your attitude, Mr.
Cramer, something that has occurred to me has not
occurred to you."

"Naturally. You're a genius. What is it?"

"Something that Mr. Goodwin told us. I want to
consider it a little."

"We could consider it together."

"Later. Those people in the front room are my guests.
Can't you dispose of them?"

"One of your guests," Cramer rasped, "was a beaut,
all right." He spoke to the dick by the door: "Bring
in that woman—what's her name? Carlisle."

Mrs. Homer N. Carlisle came in with all her
belongings: her caracul coat, her gaily colored scarf,
and her husband. Perhaps I should say that her husband brought her. As soon as he was through the door
he strode across to the dining table and delivered a
harangue.

At the first opening Cramer, controlling himself, said
he was sorry and asked them to sit down.

Mrs. Carlisle did. Mr. Carlisle didn't.

"We're nearly two hours late now," he stated. "I
know you have your duty to perform, but citizens have
a few rights left, thank God. Our presence here is purely adventitious. I warn you that if my name is pub-

lished in connection with this miserable affair, I'll make trouble. Why should we be detained? What if we had left five or ten minutes earlier, as others did?"

"That's not quite logical," Cramer objected. "No matter when you left, it would have been the same if your wife had acted the same. She discovered the body."

"By accident!"

"May I say something, Homer?" the wife put in.

"It depends on what you say."

"Oh," Cramer said significantly.

"What do you mean, oh?" Carlisle demanded.

"I mean that I sent for your wife, not you, but you came with her, and that tells me why. You wanted to see to it that she wasn't indiscreet."

"What's she got to be indiscreet about?"

"I don't know. Apparently you do. If she hasn't, why don't you sit down and relax?"

"I would, sir," Wolfe advised him. "You came in here angry, and you blundered. An angry man is a jackass."

It was a struggle for the executive vice-president, but he made it.

Cramer went to the wife: "You wanted to say something, Mrs. Carlisle?"

"Only that I'm sorry." Her bony hands, the fingers twined, were on the table before her. "For the trouble I've caused."

"I wouldn't say you caused it exactly—except for yourself and your husband." Cramer was mild. "The woman was dead, whether you went in there or not. But if only as a matter of form, it was essential for me to see you, since you discovered the body. That's all there is to it as far as I know."

"How could there be anything else?" Carlisle blurted.

Cramer ignored him. "Goodwin, here, saw you standing in the hall not more than two minutes, probably less, prior to the moment you screamed and ran out of the office. How long had you then been downstairs?"

"We had just come down. I was waiting for my husband to get his things."

"Had you been downstairs before that?"

"No—only when we came in."

"What time did you arrive?"

"A little after three, I think."

"Were you and your husband together all the time?"

"Of course. Well—you know how it is . . . He would want to look longer at something, and I would—"

"Certainly we were," Carlisle said irritably. "You can see why I made that remark about it depending on what she said. She has a habit of being vague."

"I'm not actually vague," she protested. "It's just that everything is relative. Who would have thought my wish to see Nero Wolfe's office would link me with a crime?"

Carlisle exploded. "Hear that? *Link!*"

"Why did you want to see Wolfe's office?" Cramer inquired.

"Why, to see the globe."

I gawked at her. I had supposed that naturally she would say it was curiosity about the office of a great and famous detective. Apparently, Cramer reacted the same as me.

"The globe?" he demanded.

"Yes, I had read about it, and I wanted to see how it looked. I thought a globe that size, three feet in diameter, would be fantastic in an ordinary room— Oh!"

"Oh, what?"

"I didn't see it!"

Cramer nodded. "You saw something else, instead. By the way, I forgot to ask—Did you know her?"

"You mean—her?"

"We had never known her or seen her or heard of her," the husband declared.

"Had you, Mrs. Carlisle?"

"No."

"Of course. She wasn't a member of this flower club. Are you a member?"

"My husband is."

"We both are," Carlisle stated. "Vague again. It's a joint membership. Isn't this about enough?"

"Plenty," Cramer conceded. "Thank you, both of you. We won't bother you again unless we have to. . . . Levy, pass them out."

When the door had closed behind them Cramer glared at me and then at Wolfe. "This is sure a sweet one," he said grimly. "Say it's within the range of possibility that Carlisle is it, and the way it stands right now, why not? So we look into him. We check back on him for six months, and try doing it without getting roars out of him—a man like that in his position. However, it can be done—by three or four men in two or three weeks. Multiply that by what? How many men were here?"

"Around a hundred and twenty," I told him. "But you'll find that at least half of them are disqualified one way or another. As I told you, I took a survey. Say sixty."

"All right, multiply it by sixty. Do you care for it?"

"No," I said.

"Neither do I." Cramer took the cigar from his mouth. "Of course," he said sarcastically, "when she sat in there telling you about him the situation was different. You wanted her to enjoy being with you. You couldn't reach for the phone and tell us you had a self-confessed crook who could put a quick finger on a murderer and let us come and take over. No! You had to save it for a fee for Wolfe!"

"Don't be vulgar," I said severely.

"You had to go upstairs and make a survey! You had to—Well?"

Lieutenant Rowcliff had opened the door and entered. There were some city employees I liked, some I admired, some I had no feeling about, some I could have done without easy—and one whose ears I was going to twist some day. That was Rowcliff. He was tall, strong, handsome, and a pain in the neck.

"We're all through in there, sir," he said importantly. "We've covered everything. Nothing is being taken away, and it is all in order. We were especially careful with the contents of the drawers of Wolfe's desk, and also we—"

"My desk!" Wolfe roared.

"Yes, your desk," Rowcliff said precisely, smirking.

The blood was rushing into Wolfe's face.

"She was killed there," Cramer said gruffly. "Did you get anything at all?"

"I don't think so," Rowcliff admitted. "Of course, the prints have to be sorted, and there'll be lab reports. How do we leave it?"

"Seal it up and we'll see tomorrow. You stay here and keep a photographer. The others can go. Tell Stebbins to send that woman in—Mrs. Irwin."

"Orwin, sir."

"Wait a minute," I objected. "Seal what up? The office?"

"Certainly," Rowcliff sneered.

I said firmly, to Cramer, not to him, "You don't mean it. We work there. We live there. All our stuff is there."

"Go ahead, Lieutenant," Cramer told Rowcliff, and he wheeled and went.

I was full of both feelings and words, but I knew they had to be held in. This was far and away the worst Cramer had ever pulled. It was up to Wolfe. I looked at him. He was white with fury, and his mouth was pressed to so tight a line that there were no lips.

"It's routine," Cramer said aggressively.

Wolfe said icily, "That's a lie. It is not routine."

"It's *my* routine—in a case like this. Your office is not just an office. It's the place where more fancy tricks have been played than any other spot in New York.

When a woman is murdered there, soon after a talk with Goodwin, for which we have no word but his—I say sealing it is routine."

Wolfe's head came forward an inch, his chin out. "No, Mr. Cramer. I'll tell you what it is. It is the malefic spite of a sullen little soul and a crabbed and envious mind. It is the childish rancor of a primacy too often challenged and offended. It is the feeble wiggle—"

The door came open to let Mrs. Orwin in.

With Mrs. Carlisle, the husband had come along. With Mrs. Orwin, it was the son. His expression and manner were so different I would hardly have known him. Upstairs his tone had been mean and his face had been mean. Now his narrow little eyes were working overtime to look frank and cordial.

He leaned across the table at Cramer, extending a hand: "Inspector Cramer? I've been hearing about you for years! I'm Eugene Orwin." He glanced at his right. "I've already had the pleasure of meeting Mr. Wolfe and Mr. Goodwin—earlier today, before this terrible thing happened. It *is* terrible."

"Yes," Cramer agreed. "Sit down."

"I will in a moment. I do better with words standing up. I would like to make a statement on behalf of my mother and myself, and I hope you'll permit it. I'm a member of the bar. My mother is not feeling well. At the request of your men she went in with me to identify the body of Miss Brown, and it was a bad shock, and we've been detained now more than two hours."

His mother's appearance corroborated him. Sitting with her head propped on a hand and her eyes closed, obviously she didn't care as much about the impression they made on the inspector as her son did.

"A statement would be welcome," Cramer told him, "if it's relevant."

"I thought so," Gene said approvingly. "So many people have an entirely wrong idea of police methods! Of course, you know that Miss Brown came here today as my mother's guest, and therefore it might be supposed that my mother knows her. But actually she doesn't."

"Go ahead."

Gene glanced at the shorthand dick. "If it's taken down I would like to go over it when convenient."

"You may."

"Then here are the facts: In January my mother was in Florida. You meet all kinds in Florida. My mother met a man who called himself Colonel Percy Brown—a British colonel in the reserve, he said. Later on, he introduced his sister Cynthia to her. My mother saw a great deal of them. My father is dead, and the estate, a rather large one, is in her control. She lent Brown some money, not much—that was just an opener."

Mrs. Orwin's head jerked up. "It was only five thousand dollars and I didn't promise him anything," she said wearily.

"All right, Mother." Gene patted her shoulder. "A week ago she returned to New York and they came along. The first time I met them I thought they were impostors. They weren't very free with family details, but from them and Mother, chiefly Mother, I got enough to inquire about, and sent a cable to London. I got a reply Saturday and another one this morning and there was more than enough to confirm my suspicion, but not nearly enough to put it up to my mother. When she likes people she can be very stubborn about them.

"I was thinking it over, what step to take next. Meanwhile, I thought it best not to let them be alone with her if I could help it. That's why I came here with them today—my mother is a member of that flower club—I'm no gardener myself—"

He turned a palm up. "That's what brought me here. My mother came to see the orchids, and she invited Brown and his sister to come, simply because she is goodhearted. But actually she knows nothing about them."

He put his hands on the table and leaned on them,

forward at Cramer. "I'm going to be quite frank, Inspector. Under the circumstances, I can't see that it would serve any useful purpose to let it be published that that woman came here with my mother. I want to make it perfectly clear that we have no desire to evade our responsibility as citizens. But how would it help to get my mother's name in the headlines?"

"Names in headlines aren't what I'm after," Cramer told him, "but I don't run the newspapers. If they've already got it I can't stop them. I'd like to say I appreciate your frankness. So you only met Miss Brown a week ago?"

Cramer had plenty of questions for both mother and son. It was in the middle of them that Wolfe passed me a slip of paper on which he had scribbled:

"Tell Fritz to bring sandwiches and coffee for you and me. Also for those left in the front room. No one else. Of course, Saul and Theodore."

I left the room, found Fritz in the kitchen, delivered the message, and returned.

Gene stayed cooperative to the end, and Mrs. Orwin tried, though it was an effort. They said they had been together all the time, which I happened to know wasn't so, having seen them separated at least twice during the afternoon, and Cramer did too, since I had told him.

They said a lot of other things, among them that they hadn't left the plant-rooms between their arrival and their departure with Wolfe; that they had stayed until most of the others were gone because Mrs. Orwin wanted to persuade Wolfe to sell her some plants; that Colonel Brown had wandered off by himself once or twice; that they had been only mildly concerned about Cynthia's absence, because of assurances from Colonel Brown and me; and so on.

Before they left, Gene made another try for a commitment to keep his mother's name out of it, and Cramer promised to do his best.

Fritz had brought trays for Wolfe and me, and we were making headway with them. In the silence that followed the departure of the Orwins, Wolfe could plainly be heard chewing a mouthful of mixed salad.

Cramer sat frowning at us. He turned his head: "Levy! Get that Colonel Brown in."

"Yes, sir. That man you wanted—Vedder—he's here."

"Then I'll take him first."

Up in the plant-room, Malcolm Vedder had caught my eye by the way he picked up a flowerpot and held it. As he took a chair across the dining table from Cramer and me, I still thought he was worth another good look, but after his answer to Cramer's third question I relaxed and concentrated on my sandwiches. He was an actor and had had parts in three Broadway plays. Of course, that explained it. No actor would pick up a flowerpot just normally, like you or me. He would have to dramatize it some way, and Vedder had happened to choose a way that looked to me like fingers closing around a throat.

Now he was dramatizing this by being wrought-up and indignant.

"Typical!" he told Cramer, his eyes flashing and his voice throaty with feeling. "Typical of police clumsiness! Pulling *me* into this!"

"Yeah," Cramer said sympathetically. "It'll be tough for an actor, having your picture in the paper. You a member of this flower club?"

No, Vedder said, he wasn't. He had come with a friend, a Mrs. Beauchamp, and when she had left to keep an appointment he had remained to look at more orchids. They had arrived about three-thirty and he had remained in the plant-rooms continuously until leaving.

Cramer went through all the regulation questions, and got all the expected negatives, until he suddenly asked, "Did you know Doris Hatten?"

Vedder frowned. "Who?"

"Doris Hatten. She was also—"

"Ah!" Vedder cried. "She was also strangled! I remember!"

"Right."

Vedder made fists of his hands, rested them on the table, and leaned forward. "You know," he said tensely, "that's the worst of all strangling—especially a woman."

"Did you know Doris Hatten?"

"Othello," Vedder said in a deep, resonant tone. His eyes lifted to Cramer and his voice lifted, too: "No, I didn't know her; I only read about her." He shuddered all over, and then, abruptly, he was out of his chair and on his feet. "I only came here to look at orchids!"

He ran his fingers through his hair, turned, and made for the door.

Levy looked at Cramer with his brows raised, and Cramer shook his head.

The next one in was Bill McNab, garden editor of the *Gazette*.

"I can't tell you how much I regret this, Mr. Wolfe," he said miserably.

"Don't try," Wolfe growled.

"What a terrible thing! I wouldn't have dreamed such a thing could happen—the Manhattan Flower Club! Of course, she wasn't a member, but that only makes it worse, in a way." McNab turned to Cramer: "I'm responsible for this."

"You are?"

"Yes, it was my idea. I persuaded Mr. Wolfe to arrange it. He let me word the invitations. And I was congratulating myself on the great success! Then this! What can I do?"

"Sit down a minute," Craner invited him.

McNab varied the monotony on one detail, at least. He admitted that he had left the plant-rooms three times during the afternoon, once to accompany a departing guest down to the ground floor, and twice to go down alone to check on who had come and who hadn't.

Aside from that, he was more of the same. By now it was beginning to seem not only futile, but silly to spend time on seven or eight of them merely because they happened to be the last to go and so were at hand. Also, it was something new to me from a technical standpoint. I had never seen one stack up like that.

Any precinct dick knows that every question you ask of everybody is aimed at one of the three targets: motive, means, and opportunity. In this case there were no questions to ask, because those were already answered. Motive: the guy had followed her downstairs, knowing she had recognized him, had seen her enter Wolfe's office and thought she was doing exactly what she was doing, getting set to tell Wolfe, and had decided to prevent that the quickest and best way he knew. Means: any piece of cloth, even his handkerchief, would do. Opportunity: he was there—all of them on Saul's list were.

So, if you wanted to learn who strangled Cynthia Brown, first you had to find out who had strangled Doris Hatten.

As soon as Bill McNab had been sent on his way, Col. Percy Brown was brought in. Brown was not exactly at ease, but he had himself well in hand. You would never have picked him for a con man, and neither would I. His mouth and jaw were strong and attractive, and as he sat down he leveled his keen gray eyes at Cramer and kept them there. He wasn't interested in Wolfe or me. He said his name was Colonel Percy Brown, and Cramer asked him which army he was a colonel in.

"I think," Brown said in a cool, even tone, "it will save time if I state my position: I will answer fully and freely all questions that relate to what I saw, heard, or did since I arrived here this afternoon. Answers to any other questions will have to wait until I consult my attorney."

Cramer nodded. "I expected that. The trouble is I'm

pretty sure I don't give a hoot what you saw or heard this afternoon. We'll come back to that. I want to put something up to you. As you see, I'm not even wanting to know why you tried to break away before we got here."

"I merely wanted to phone—"

"Forget it. On information received, I think it's like this: The woman who called herself Cynthia Brown, murdered here today, was not your sister. You met her in Florida six or eight weeks ago. She went in with you on an operation of which Mrs. Orwin was the subject, and you introduced her to Mrs. Orwin as your sister. You two came to New York with Mrs. Orwin a week ago, with the operation well under way. As far as I'm concerned, that is only background. Otherwise, I'm not interested in it. My work is homicide.

"For me," Cramer went on, "the point is that for quite a period you have been closely connected with this Miss Brown, associating with her in a confidential operation. You must have had many intimate conversations with her. You were having her with you as your sister, and she wasn't, and she's been murdered. We could give you a merry time on that score alone.

"But I wanted to give you a chance first," Cramer continued. "For two months you've been on intimate terms with Cynthia Brown. She certainly must have mentioned that a friend of hers named Doris Hatten was murdered—strangled last October. Cynthia Brown had information about the murderer which she kept to herself. If she had come out with it she'd be alive now. She must have told you all about it. Now you can tell me. If you do, we can nail him for what he did here today, and it might even make things a little smoother for you. Well?"

Brown had pursed his lips. They straightened out again, and his hand came up for a finger to scratch his cheek.

"I'm sorry I can't help."

"Do you expect me to believe that during all those weeks she never mentioned the murder of her friend Doris Hatten?"

"I'm sorry I can't help." Brown's tone was firm and final.

Cramer said, "Okay. We'll move on to this afternoon. Do you remember a moment when something about Cynthia Brown's appearance—some movement she made or the expression on her face—caused Mrs. Orwin to ask her what was the matter with her?"

A crease was showing on Brown's forehead. "I'm sorry. I don't believe I do," he stated.

"I'm asking you to try. Try hard."

Silence. Brown pursed his lips and the crease in his forehead deepened. Finally he said, "I may not have been right there at the moment. In those aisles—in a crowd like that—we weren't rubbing elbows continuously."

"You do remember when she excused herself because she wasn't feeling well?"

"Yes, of course."

"Well, this moment I'm asking about came shortly before that. She exchanged looks with some man nearby, and it was her reaction to that that made Mrs. Orwin ask her what was the matter. What I'm interested in is that exchange of looks."

"I didn't see it."

Cramer banged his fist on the table so hard the trays danced. "Levy! Take him out and tell Stebbins to send him down and lock him up. Material witness. Put more men on him—he's got a record somewhere. Find it!"

As the door closed behind them, Cramer turned and said, "Gather up, Murphy. We're leaving."

Levy came back in and Cramer addressed him: "We're leaving. Tell Stebbins one man out front will be enough—No, I'll tell him—"

"There's one more, sir. His name is Nicholson Morley. He's a psychiatrist."

"Let him go. This is getting to be a joke."

Cramer looked at Wolfe. Wolfe looked back at him.

"A while ago," Cramer rasped, "you said something had occurred to you."

"Did I?" Wolfe inquired coldly.

Their eyes went on clashing until Crame broke the connection by turning to go. I restrained an impulse to knock their heads together. They were both being childish. If Wolfe really had something, anything at all, he knew Cramer would gladly trade the seals on the office door for it, sight unseen. And Cramer knew he could make the deal himself with nothing to lose. But they were both too sore and stubborn to show any horse sense.

Cramer had circled the end of the table on his way out when Levy reentered to report: "That man Morley insists on seeing you. He says it's vital."

Cramer halted, glowering. "What is he, a screwball?"

"I don't know, sir. He may be."

"Oh, bring him in."

This was my first really good look at the middle-aged male with the mop of black hair. His quick-darting eyes were fully as black as his hair.

Cramer nodded impatiently. "You have something to say, Dr. Morley?"

"I have. Something vital."

"Let's hear it."

Morley got better settled in his chair. "First, I assume that no arrest has been made. Is that correct?"

"Yes—if you mean an arrest with a charge of murder."

"Have you a definite object of suspicion, with or without evidence in support?"

"If you mean am I ready to name the murderer, no. Are you?"

"I think I may be."

Cramer's chin went up. "Well? I'm in charge here."

Dr. Morley smiled. "Not quite so fast. The suggestion
I have to offer is sound only with certain assumptions."
He placed the tip of his right forefinger on the tip of his
left little finger. "One: that you have no idea who
committed this murder, and apparently you haven't."
He moved over a finger. "Two: that this was not a commonplace crime with a commonplace discoverable motive." To the middle finger. "Three: that nothing is
known· to discredit the hypothesis that this girl was
strangled by the man who strangled Doris Hatten . . .
May I make those assumptions?"

"You can try. Why do you want to?"

Morley shook his head. "Not that I want to. That if
I am permitted to, I have a suggestion. I wish to make
it clear that I have great respect for the competence of
the police, within proper limits. If the man who murdered Doris Hatten had been vulnerable to police
techniques and resources, he would almost certainly
have been caught. But he wasn't. You failed. Why?

"Because he was out of bounds for you. Because your
exploration of motive is restricted by your preconcep-
tions." Morley's black eyes gleamed. "You're a layman,
so I won't use technical terms. The most powerful motives on earth are motives of the personality, which
cannot be exposed by any purely objective investigation. If the personality is twisted, distorted, as it is
with a psychotic, then the motives are twisted, too. As a
psychiatrist I was deeply interested in the published
reports on the murder of Doris Hatten—especially the
detail that she was strangled with her own scarf. When
your efforts to find the culprit ended in complete failure,
I would have been glad to come forward with a suggestion, but I was as helpless as you."

"Get down to it," Cramer muttered.

"Yes." Morley put his elbows on the table and paired
all his fingertips. "Now, today. On the basis of the assumptions I began with, it is a tenable theory, worthy
to be tested, that this was the same man. If so, it is no
longer a question of finding him among thousands or

millions; it's a mere hundred or so, and I am willing to contribute my services." The black eyes flashed. "I admit that for a psychiatrist this is a rare opportunity. Nothing could be more dramatic than a psychosis exploding into murder. All you have to do is to have them brought to my office, one at a time——"

"Wait a minute," Cramer put in. "Are you suggesting that we deliver everyone that was here today to your office for you to work on?"

"No, not everyone, only the men. When I have finished I may have nothing that can be used as evidence, but there's an excellent chance that I can tell you who the strangler is——"

"Excuse me," Cramer said. He was on his feet. "Sorry to cut you off, Doctor, but I must get downtown." He was on his way. "I'm afraid your suggestion wouldn't work——I'll let you know——"

He went, and Levy and Murphy with him.

Dr. Morley pivoted his head to watch them go, kept it that way a moment, and then he arose and walked out without a word.

"Twenty minutes to ten," I announced.

Wolfe muttered, "Go look at the office door."

"I just did, as I let Morley out. It's sealed. Malefic spite. But this isn't a bad room to sit in," I said brightly.

"Pfui! I want to ask you something."

"Shoot."

"I want your opinion of this. Assume that we accept without reservation the story Miss Brown told you. Assume also that the man she had recognized, knowing she had recognized him, followed her downstairs and saw her enter the office; that he surmised she intended to consult me; that he postponed joining her in the office, either because he knew you were in there with her or for some other reason; that he saw you come out and go upstairs; that he took an opportunity to enter the office unobserved, got her off guard, killed her, got out unobserved, and returned upstairs."

"I'll take it that way."

"Very well. Then we have significant indications of his character. Consider it. He has killed her and is back upstairs, knowing that she was in the office talking with you for some time. He would like to know what she said to you. Specifically, he would like to know whether she told you about him, and, if so, how much. Had she or had she not named or described him in his current guise? With that question unanswered, would a man of his character, as indicated, *leave the house?* Or would he prefer the challenge and risk of remaining until the body had been discovered, to see what you would do? And I, too, of course, after you had talked with me, and the police?"

"Yeah." I chewed my lip. There was a long silence. "So that's how your mind's working. I could offer a guess."

"I prefer a calculation to a guess. For that, a basis is needed, and we have it. We know the situation as we have assumed it, and we know something of his character."

"Okay," I conceded, "a calculation. The answer I get, he would stick around until the body was found, and if he did, then he is one of the bunch Cramer has been talking with. So that's what occurred to you, huh?"

"No. By no means. That's a different matter. This is merely a tentative calculation for a starting point. If it is sound, I *know* who the murderer is."

I gave him a look. Sometimes I can tell how much he is putting on and sometimes I can't tell. I decided to buy it.

"That's interesting," I said admiringly. "If you want me to get him on the phone I'll have to use the one in the kitchen."

"I want to test the calculation."

"So do I."

"But that's a difficulty. The best I have in mind, the only one I can contrive to my satisfaction—only you can make it. And in doing so you would have to expose yourself to great personal risk."

"For Pete's sake!" I gawked at him. "This is a brand-new one. The errands you've sent me on! Since when have you flinched or faltered in the face of danger to me?"

"This danger is extreme."

"Let's hear the test."

"Very well." He turned a hand over. "Is that old type-writer of yours in working order?"

"Fair."

"Bring it down here, and some sheets of blank paper —any kind. I'll need a blank envelope."

"I have some."

"Bring one. Also the telephone book, Manhattan, from my room."

When I returned to the dining-room and was placing the typewriter in position on the table, Wolfe spoke: "No, bring it here. I'll use it myself."

I lifted my brows at him. "A page will take you an hour."

"It won't be a page. Put a sheet of paper in it."

. I did so, got the paper squared, lifted the machine, and put it in front of him. He sat and frowned at it for a long minute, and then started pecking. I turned my back on him to make it easier to withhold remarks about his two-finger technique, and passed the time by trying to figure his rate. All at once he pulled the paper out.

"I think that will do," he said.

I took it and read what he had typed:

"She told me enough this afternoon so that I know who to send this to, and more. I have kept it to my-self because I haven't decided what is the right thing to do. I would like to have a talk with you first, and if you will phone me tomorrow, Tuesday, between nine o'clock and noon, we can make an appointment; please don't put it off or I will have to decide myself."

I read it over three times. I looked at Wolfe. He had put an envelope in the typewriter and was consulting the phone book. He began pecking, addressing the envelope.

I waited until he had finished and rolled the envelope out.

"Just like this?" I asked. "No name or initials signed?"

"No."

"I admit it's nifty," I admitted. "We could forget the calculation and send this to every guy on that list and wait to see who phoned."

"I prefer to send it only to one person—the one indicated by your report of that conversation. That will test the calculation."

"And save postage." I glanced at the paper. "The extreme danger, I suppose, is that I'll get strangled."

"I don't want to minimize the risk of this, Archie."

"Neither do I. I'll have to borrow a gun from Saul—ours are in the office. . . . May I have that envelope? I'll have to go to Times Square to mail it."

"Yes. Before you do so, copy that note. Keep Saul here in the morning. If and when the phone call comes you will have to use your wits to arrange the appointment advantageously."

"Right. The envelope, please."

He handed it to me.

That Tuesday morning I was kept busy from eight o'clock on by the phone and the doorbell. After nine, Saul was there to help, but not with the phone, because the orders were that I was to answer all calls. They were mostly from newspapers, but there were a couple from Homicide and a few scattered ones. I took them on the extension in the kitchen.

Every time I lifted the thing and told the transmitter, "Nero Wolfe's office, Archie Goodwin speaking," my pulse went up a notch, and then had to level off again. I had one argument, with a bozo in the District Attorney's office who had the strange idea that he could order me to report for an interview at eleven-thirty sharp, which ended by my agreeing to call later to fix an hour.

A little before eleven I was in the kitchen with Saul, who, at Wolfe's direction, had been briefed to date, when the phone rang.

"Nero Wolfe's office, Archie Goodwin speaking."

"Mr. Goodwin?"

"Right."

"You sent me a note."

My hand wanted to grip the phone the way Vedder had gripped the flower-pot, but I wouldn't let it.

"Did I? What about?"

"You suggested that we make an appointment. Are you in a position to discuss it?"

"Sure. I'm alone and no extensions are on. But I don't recognize your voice. Who is this?"

"I have two voices. This is the other one. Have you made a decision yet?"

"No. I was waiting to hear from you."

"That's wise, I think. I'm willing to discuss the matter. Are you free this evening?"

"I can wiggle free."

"With a car to drive?"

"Yeah, I have a car."

"Drive to a lunchroom at the north-east corner of Fifty-first Street and Eleventh Avenue. Get there at eight o'clock. Park your car on Fifty-first Street, but not at the corner. You will be alone, of course. Go in the lunchroom and order something to eat. I won't be there, but you will get a message. You'll be there at eight?"

"Yes. I still don't recognize your voice. I don't think you're the person I sent the note to."

"I am. It's good, isn't it?"

The connection went. I hung up, told Fritz he could answer calls now, and hotfooted it to the stairs and up three flights.

Wolfe was in the cool-room. When I told him about the call he merely nodded.

"That call," he said, "validates our assumption and verifies our calculation, but that's all. Has anyone come to take those seals off?"

I told him no. "I asked Stebbins about it and he said he'd ask Cramer."

"Don't ask again," he snapped. "We'll go down to my room."

If the strangler had been in Wolfe's house the rest of that day he would have felt honored—or anyway he should. Even during Wolfe's afternoon hours in the plant rooms, from four to six, his mind was on my appointment, as was proved by the crop of new slants and ideas that poured out of him when he came down to the kitchen. Except for a trip to Leonard Street to answer an hour's worth of questions by an assistant district attorney, my day was devoted to it, too. My most useful errand—though at the time it struck me as a waste of time and money—was one made to Doc Vollmer for a prescription and then to a drugstore, under instructions from Wolfe.

When I got back from the D.A.'s office Saul and I got in the sedan and went for a reconnaissance. We didn't stop at 51st Street and 11th Avenue but drove past it four times. The main idea was to find a place for Saul. He and Wolfe both insisted that he had to be there.

We finally settled for a filling station across the street from the lunchroom. Saul was to have a taxi drive in there at eight o'clock, and stay in the passenger's seat while the driver tried to get his carburetor adjusted. There were so many contingencies to be agreed on that if it had been anyone but Saul I wouldn't have expected him to remember more than half. For instance, in case I left the lunchroom and got in my car and drove off, Saul was not to follow unless I cranked my window down.

Trying to provide for contingencies was okay, in a way, but actually it was strictly up to me, since I had to let the other guy make the rules. And with the other guy making the rules no one gets very far, not even Nero Wolfe arranging for contingencies ahead of time.

Saul left before I did, to find a taxi driver that he

liked the looks of. When I went to the hall for my hat and raincoat, Wolfe came along.

"I still don't like the idea," he insisted, "of your having that thing in your pocket. I think you should slip it inside your sock."

"I don't." I was putting the raincoat on. "If I get frisked, a sock is as easy to feel as a pocket."

"You're sure that gun is loaded?"

"I never saw you so anxious. Next you'll be telling me to put on my rubbers."

He even opened the door for me.

It wasn't actually raining, merely trying to make up its mind, but after a couple of blocks I reached to switch on the windshield wiper. As I turned uptown on 10th Avenue the dash clock said 7:47; as I turned left on 51st Street it had only got to 7:51. At that time of day in that district there was plenty of space, and I rolled to the curb and stopped about twenty yards short of the corner, stopped the engine and turned the window down for a good view of the filling station across the street. There was no taxi there. At 7:59 a taxi pulled in and stopped by the pumps, and the driver got out and lifted the hood and started peering. I put my window up, locked the doors, and entered the lunchroom.

There was one hash slinger behind the counter and five customers scattered along on the stools. I picked a stool that left me elbowroom, sat, and ordered ice cream and coffee. The counterman served me and I took my time. At 8:12 the ice cream was gone and my cup empty, and I ordered a refill.

I had about got to the end of that, too, when a male entered, looked along the line, came straight to me, and asked me what my name was. I told him, and he handed me a folded piece of paper and turned to go. He was barely old enough for high school and I made no effort to hold him, thinking that the bird I had a date with was not likely to be an absolute sap. Unfolding the paper, I saw, neatly printed in pencil:

"Go to your car and get a note under the windshield wiper. Sit in the car to read it."

I paid what I owed, walked to my car and got the note as I was told, unlocked the car and got in, turned on the light, and read, in the same print:

"Make no signal of any kind. Follow instructions precisely. Turn right on 11th Ave. and go slowly to 56th St. Turn right on 56th and go to 9th Ave. Turn right on 9th Ave. Right again on 45th. Left on 11th Ave. Left on 38th. Right on 7th Ave. Right on 27th St. Park on 27th between 9th and 10th Aves. Go to No. 814 and tap five times on the door. Give the man who opens the door this note and the other one. He will tell you where to go."

I didn't like it much, but I had to admit it was a handy arrangement for seeing to it that I went to the conference unattached.

It had now decided to rain. Starting the engine, I could see dimly through the misty window that Saul's taxi driver was still monkeying with his carburetor, but of course I had to resist the impulse to crank the window down to wave so-long. Keeping the instructions in my left hand, I rolled to the corner, waited for the light to change, and turned right on 11th Avenue.

Since I had not been forbidden to keep my eyes open I did so, and as I stopped at 52nd for the red light I saw a black or dark-blue sedan pull away from the curb behind me and creep in my direction. I took it for granted that that was my chaperon.

The guy in the sedan was not the strangler, as I soon learned. On 27th Street there was space smack in front of Number 814, and I saw no reason why I shouldn't use it. The sedan went to the curb right behind me. After locking my car I stood on the sidewalk a moment, but my chaperon just sat tight, so I kept to the instructions, mounted the steps to the stoop of the rundown old brownstone, entered the vestibule, and knocked five times on the door. Through the glass panel the dimly-lit hall looked empty. As I peered in, I heard footsteps behind and turned. It was my chaperon.

"Well, we got here," I said cheerfully.

"You almost lost me at one light," he said. "Give me them notes."

I handed them to him—all the evidence I had. As he unfolded them for a look, I took him in. He was around my age and height, skinny but with muscles, with outstanding ears and a purple mole on his right jaw.

"They look like it," he said, and stuffed the notes in a pocket. From another pocket he produced a key, unlocked the door, and pushed it open. "Follow me."

As we ascended two flights, with him in front, it would have been a cinch for me to reach and take a gun off his hip if there had been one there, but there wasn't. He may have preferred a shoulder holster, like me. The stair steps were bare, worn wood, the walls had needed plaster since at least Pearl Harbor, and the smell was a mixture I wouldn't want to analyze. On the second landing he went down the hall to a door at the rear and signaled me through.

There was another man there, but still it wasn't my date—anyway, I hoped not. It would be an overstatement to say the room was furnished, but I admit there was a table, a bed, and three chairs, one of them upholstered. The man, who was lying on the bed, pushed himself up as we entered, and as he swung around to sit, his feet barely reached the floor. He had shoulders and a torso like a heavyweight wrestler, and legs like an underweight jockey. His puffed eyes blinked in the light from the unshaded bulb as if he had been asleep.

"That him?" he demanded.

Skinny said it was.

The wrestler-jockey, W-J for short, got up and went to the table, picked up a ball of thick cord. "Take off your hat and coat and sit there." He pointed to one of the straight chairs.

"Hold it," Skinny commanded him. "I haven't ex-

plained yet." He faced me: "The idea is simple. This
man that's coming to see you don't want any trouble.
He just wants to talk. So we tie you in that chair and
leave you, and he comes and you have a talk, and after
he leaves we come back and cut you loose, and out
you go. Is that plain enough?"

I grinned at him. "It sure is, brother. It's too plain.
What if I won't sit down?"

"Then he don't come and you don't have a talk."

"What if I walk out now?"

"Go ahead. We get paid anyhow. If you want to see
this guy there's only one way: We tie you in the chair."

"We get more if we tie him," W-J objected. "Let me
persuade him."

"Lay off," Skinny commanded.

"I don't want any trouble either," I stated. "How
about this? I sit in the chair and you fix the cord to
look right, but so I'm free to move in case of fire.
There's a hundred bucks in the wallet in my breast
pocket. Before you leave, you help yourselves."

"A lousy C?" W-J sneered. "Shut up and sit down."

"He had his choice," Skinny said reprovingly.

I did, indeed. It was a swell illustration of how much
good it does to try to consider contingencies in advance.
In all our discussions that day none of us had put the
question, what to do if a pair of smooks offered me
my pick of being tied in a chair or going home to bed.
As far as I could see, standing there looking them over,
that was all there was to it, and it was too early to go
home to bed.

"Okay," I told them, "but don't overdo it. I know
my way around, and I can find you if I care enough."

They unrolled the cord, cutting pieces off, and went
to work. W-J tied my left wrist to the rear left leg of the
chair, while Skinny did the right. They wanted to do my
ankles the same way, to the bottoms of the front legs of
the chair, but I claimed I would get cramps sitting like
that. It would be just as good to tie my ankles together.
They discussed it, and I had my way. Skinny made a

final inspection of the knots and then went over me. He took the gun from my shoulder holster and tossed it on the bed, made sure I didn't have another one, and left the room.

W-J picked up the gun, and scowled at it. "These things," he muttered. "They make more trouble." He went to the table and put the gun down on it. Then he crossed to the bed and stretched out on it.

"How long do we have to wait?" I asked.

"Not long. I wasn't to bed last night." He closed his eyes.

He got no nap. His barrel chest couldn't have gone up and down more than a dozen times before the door opened and Skinny came in. With him was a man in a gray pinstripe suit and a dark-gray homburg, with a gray topcoat over his arm. He had gloves on. W-J got off the bed and onto his toothpick legs. Skinny stood by the open door. The man put his hat and coat on the bed, came and took a look at my fastenings, and told Skinny, "All right; I'll come for you." The two rummies departed, shutting the door. The man stood facing me.

He smiled. "Would you have known me?"

"Not from Adam," I said, both to humor him and because it was true.

I wouldn't want to exaggerate how brave I am. It wasn't that I was too fearless to be impressed by the fact that I was thoroughly tied up and the strangler was standing there smiling at me; I was simply astounded. It was an amazing disguise. The two main changes were the eyebrows and eyelashes; these eyes had bushy brows and long, thick lashes, whereas yesterday's guest hadn't had much of either one. The real change was from the inside. I had seen no smile on the face of yesterday's guest, but if I had it wouldn't have been like this one. The hair made a difference too, of course, parted on the side and slicked down.

He pulled the other straight chair around and sat. I admired the way he moved. That in itself could have

been a dead giveaway, but the movements fitted the
get-up to a T.

"So she told you about me?" he said.

It was the voice he had used on the phone. It was
actually different, pitched lower, for one thing, but
with it, as with the face and movements, the big change
was from the inside. The voice was stretched tight,
and the palms of his gloved hands were pressed against
his kneecaps with the fingers straight out.

I said, "Yes," and added conversationally, "When
you saw her go in the office why didn't you follow her
in?"

"I had seen you leave, upstairs, and I suspected you
were in there."

"Why didn't she scream or fight?"

"I talked to her. I talked a little first." His head gave
a quick jerk, as if a fly were bothering him and his
hands were too occupied to attend to it. "What did she
tell you?"

"About that day at Doris Hatten's apartment—you
coming in and her going out. And of course her recog-
nizing you there yesterday."

"She is dead. There is no evidence. You can't prove
anything."

I grinned. "Then you're wasting a lot of time and
energy and the best disguise I ever saw. Why didn't you
just toss my note in the wastebasket? . . . Let me answer.
You didn't dare. In getting evidence, knowing exactly
what and who to look for makes all the difference. You
knew I knew."

"And you haven't told the police?"

"No."

"Nor Nero Wolfe?"

"No."

"Why not?"

I shrugged. "I may not put it very well," I said, "because this is the first time I have ever talked with my
hands and feet tied, and I find it cramps my style. But

it strikes me as the kind of coincidence that doesn't happen very often. I'm fed up with the detective business, and I'd like to quit. I have something that's worth a good deal to you—say, fifty thousand dollars. It can be arranged so that you get what you pay for. I'll go the limit on that, but it has to be closed quick. If you don't buy, I'm going to have a tough time explaining why I didn't remember sooner what she told me. Twenty-four hours from now is the absolute limit."

"It couldn't be arranged so I could get what I paid for."

"Sure, it could. If you don't want me on your neck the rest of your life, believe me, I don't want you on mine, either."

"I suppose you don't. I suppose I'll have to pay."

There was a sudden noise in his throat as if he had started to choke. He stood up. "You're working your hand loose," he said huskily, and moved toward me.

It might have been guessed from his voice, thick and husky from the blood rushing to his head, but it was plain as day in his eyes, suddenly fixed and glassy, like a blind man's eyes. Evidently he had come there fully intending to kill me, and had now worked himself up to it.

"Hold it!" I snapped at him.

He halted, muttering, "You're getting your hand loose," and moved again, passing me to get behind.

I jerked my body and the chair violently aside and around, and had him in front of me again.

"No good," I told him. "They only went down one flight. I heard 'em. It's no good, anyway. I've got another note for you—from Nero Wolfe—here in my breast pocket. Help yourself, but stay in front of me."

He was only two steps from me, but it took him four small, slow ones. His gloved hand went inside my coat to the breast pocket, and came out with a folded slip of yellow paper. From the way his eyes looked, I doubted if he would be able to read, but apparently he was. I watched his face as he took it in, in Wolfe's precise handwriting:

"If Mr. Goodwin is not home by midnight the information given him by Cynthia Brown will be communicated to the police, and I shall see that they act immediately. NERO WOLFE."

He looked at me, and slowly his eyes changed. No longer glassy, they began to let light in. Before, he had just been going to kill me. Now, he hated me.

I got voluble: "So it's no good, see? He did it this way because if you had known I had told him, you would have sat tight. He figured that you would think you could handle me, and I admit you tried your best. He wants fifty thousand dollars by tomorrow at six o'clock, no later. You say it can't be arranged so you'll get what you pay for, but we say it can and it's up to you. You say we have no evidence, but we can get it— don't think we can't. As for me, I wouldn't advise you even to pull my hair. It would make him sore at you, and he's not sore now, he just wants fifty thousand bucks."

He had started to tremble, and knew it, and was trying to stop.

"Maybe," I conceded, "you can't get that much that quick. In that case he'll take your I.O.U.—you can write it on the back of that note he sent you. My pen's here in my vest pocket. He'll be reasonable."

"I'm not such a fool," he said harshly.

"Who said you were?" I was sharp and urgent, and thought I had loosened him. "Use your head, that's all. We've either got you cornered or we haven't. If we haven't, what are you doing here? If we have, a little thing like your name signed to an I.O.U. won't make it any worse. He won't press you too hard. Here, get my pen, right here."

I still think I had loosened him. It was in his eyes and the way he stood, sagging a little. If my hands had been free, so I could have got the pen myself, and uncapped it and put it between his fingers, I would have had him. I had him to the point of writing and signing, but not to the point of taking my pen out of my pocket. But, of course, if my hands had been free I wouldn't have been bothering about an I.O.U. and a pen.

So he slipped from under. He shook his head, and his shoulders stiffened. The hate that filled his eyes was in his voice, too: "You said twenty-four hours. That gives me tomorrow. I'll have to decide. Tell Nero Wolfe I'll decide."

He crossed to the door and pulled it open. He went out, closing the door, and I heard his steps descending the stairs; but he hadn't taken his hat and coat, and I nearly cracked my temples trying to use my brain. I hadn't got far when there were steps on the stairs again, coming up, and in they came, all three of them.

My host spoke to Skinny: "What time does your watch say?"

Skinny glanced at his wrist. "Nine thirty-two."

"At half-past ten untie his left hand. Leave him like that and go. It will take him five minutes or more to get his other hand and his feet free. Have you any objection to that?"

"Nah. He's got nothing on us."

The strangler took a roll of bills from his pocket, having a little difficulty on account of his gloves, peeled off two twenties, went to the table with them, and gave them a good rub on both sides with his handkerchief.

He held the bills out to Skinny. "I've got the agreed amount, as you know. This extra is so you won't get impatient and leave before half-past ten."

"Don't take it!" I called sharply.

Skinny, the bills in his hand, turned. "What's the matter—they got germs?"

"No, but they're peanuts, you sap! He's worth ten grand to you! As is!"

"Nonsense," the strangler said scornfully, and started for the bed to get his hat and coat.

"Gimme my twenty," W-J demanded.

Skinny stood with his head cocked, regarding me. He looked faintly interested but skeptical, and I saw it would take more than words. As the strangler picked up his hat and coat and turned, I jerked my body violently to the left, and over I went, chair and all. I have no idea how I got across the floor to the door. I couldn't simply roll, on account of the chair; I couldn't crawl without hands; and I didn't even try to jump. But I made it, and not slow, and was there down on my right side, the chair against the door and me against the chair, before any of them snapped out of it enough to reach me.

"You think," I yapped at Skinny, "it's just a job? Let him go and you'll find out! Do you want his name? Mrs. Carlisle—*Mrs.* Homer N. Carlisle. Do you want her address?"

The strangler, on his way to me, stopped and froze. He—or I should say, she—stood stiff as a bar of steel, the long-lashed eyes aimed at me.

"Missus?" Skinny demanded incredulously. "Did you say 'Missus'?"

"Yes. She's a woman. I'm tied up, but you've got her. I'm helpless, so you can have her. You might give me a cut of the ten grand." The strangler made a movement. "Watch her!"

W-J, who had started for me and stopped, turned to face her. I had banged my head and it hurt. Skinny stepped up to her, jerked both sides of her double-breasted coat open, released them, and backed up a step.

"It could be a woman," he said.

"We can find that out easy enough." W-J moved. "Dumb as I am, I can tell *that.*"

"Go ahead," I urged. "That will check her and me both. Go ahead!"

W-J got to her and put out a hand.

She shrank away and screamed, "Don't touch me!"

"I'll be—" W-J said wonderingly.

"What's this gag," Skinny demanded, "about ten grand?"

"It's a long story," I told him, "but it's there if you want it. If you'll cut me in for a third, it's a cinch. If she gets out of here and gets safe home, we can't touch her. All we have to do is connect her as she is— here now, disguised—with Mrs. Homer N. Carlisle, which is what she'll be when she gets home. If we do that we've got her shirt. As she is here now, she's red-hot. As she is at home, you couldn't even get in."

"So what?" Skinny asked. "I didn't bring my camera."

"I've got something better. Get me loose and I'll show you."

Skinny didn't like that. He eyed me a moment and turned for a look at the others. Mrs. Carlisle was backed against the bed, and W-J stood studying her with his fists on his hips.

Skinny returned to me. "I'll do it. Maybe. What is it?"

I snapped, "At least, put me right side up. These cords are eating my wrists."

He came and got the back of the chair with one hand and my arm with the other, and I clamped my feet to the floor to give us leverage. He was stronger than he looked. Upright on the chair again, I was still blocking the door.

"Get a bottle," I told him, "out of my right-hand coat pocket. . . . No, here; the coat I've got on. I hope it didn't break."

He fished it out. It was intact. He held it to the light to read the label. "What is it?"

"Silver nitrate. It makes a black, indelible mark on most things, including skin. Pull up her pants leg and mark her with it."

"Then what?"

"Let her go. We'll have her. With the three of us able to explain how and when she got marked, she's sunk."

"How come you've got this stuff?"

"I was hoping for a chance to mark her myself."

"How much will it hurt her?"

"Not at all. Put some on me—anywhere you like, as long as it doesn't show."

He studied the label again. I watched his face, hoping he wouldn't ask if the mark would be permanent, because I didn't know what answer would suit him, and I had to sell him.

"A woman," he muttered. "A woman!"

"Yeah," I said sympathetically. "She sure made a monkey of you."

He swiveled his head and called, "Hey!"

W-J turned.

Skinny commanded him, "Pin her up! Don't hurt her."

W-J reached for her. But, as he did so, all of a sudden she was neither man nor woman, but a cyclone. Her first leap, away from his reaching hand, was sidewise, and by the time he had realized he didn't have her she had got to the table and grabbed the gun. He made for her, and she pulled the trigger, and down he went, tumbling right at her feet. By that time Skinny was almost to her, and she whirled and blazed away again. He kept going, and from the force of the blow on my left shoulder I might have calculated, if I had been in a mood for calculating, that the bullet had not gone through Skinny before it hit me. She pulled the trigger a third time, but by then Skinny had her wrist and was breaking her arm.

"She got me!" W-J was yelling indignantly. "She got me in the leg!"

Skinny had her down on her knees. "Come and cut me loose," I called to him, "and go find a phone."

Except for my wrists and ankles and shoulder and head, I felt fine.

"I hope you're satisfied," Inspector Cramer said sourly. "You and Goodwin have got your pictures in the paper again. You got no fee, but a lot of free publicity. I got my nose wiped."

Wolfe grunted comfortably.

The whole squad had been busy with chores: visiting W-J at the hospital; conversing with Mr. and Mrs. Carlisle at the D.A.'s office; starting to round up circumstantial evidence to show that Mr. Carlisle had furnished the necessary for Doris Hatten's rent and Mrs. Carlisle knew it; pestering Skinny; and other items. I had been glad to testify that Skinny, whose name was Herbert Marvel, was one-hundred-proof.

"What I chiefly came for," Cramer went on, "was to let you know that I realize there's nothing I can do. I know Cynthia Brown described her to Goodwin, and probably gave him her name, too, and Goodwin told you. And you wanted to hog it. I suppose you thought you could pry a fee out of somebody. Both of you suppressed evidence." He gestured. "Okay, I can't prove it. But I know it, and I want you to know I know it. And I'm not going to forget it."

"The trouble is," Wolfe murmured, "that if you can't prove you're right, and of course you can't, neither can I prove you're wrong."

"I would gladly try. How?"

Cramer leaned forward. "Like this: If she hadn't been described to Goodwin, how did you pick her for him to send that blackmail note to?"

Wolfe shrugged. "It was a calculation, as I told you. I concluded that the murderer was among those who remained until the body had been discovered. It was worth testing. If there had been no phone call in response to Mr. Goodwin's note, the calculation would have been discredited and I would—"

"Yeah, but why her?"

"There were only two women who remained. Obviously, it couldn't have been Mrs. Orwin; with her physique she would be hard put to pass as a man. Besides, she is a widow, and it was a sound presumption that Doris Hatten had been killed by a jealous wife, who—"

"But why a woman? Why not a man?"

"Oh, that." Wolfe picked up a glass of beer and drained it with more deliberation than usual. He was having a swell time. "I told you in my dining-room"— he pointed a finger—"that something had occurred to me and I wanted to consider it. Later, I would have been glad to tell you about it if you had not acted so irresponsibly and spitefully in sealing up this office. That made me doubt if you were capable of proceeding properly on any suggestion from me, so I decided to proceed, myself.

"What had occurred to me was simply this, that Miss Brown had told Mr. Goodwin that *she wouldn't have recognized 'him' if he hadn't had a hat on!* She used the masculine pronoun, naturally, throughout that conversation, because it had been a man who had called at Doris Hatten's apartment that October day, and he was fixed in her mind as a man. But it was in my plant-rooms that she had seen him that afternoon—*and no man wore his hat up there!* The men left their hats downstairs. Besides, I was there and saw them. *But nearly all the woman had hats on.*"

Wolfe upturned a palm. "So it was a woman."

Cramer eyed him. "I don't believe it," he said flatly.

"You have a record of Mr. Goodwin's report of that conversation."

"I still wouldn't believe it."

"There were other little items." Wolfe wiggled a finger. "For example: The strangler of Doris Hatten had a key to the door. But surely the provider, who had so carefully avoided revealment, would not have marched in at an unexpected hour to risk encountering strangers. And who so likely to have found an opportunity, or contrived one, to secure a duplicate key as that provider's jealous wife?"

"Talk all day. I still don't believe it."

Well, I thought to myself, observing Wolfe's smirk and for once completely approving of it, Cramer the office-sealer has his choice of believing it or not.

As for me, I had no choice.

AN OCCULT NOVEL OF
UNSURPASSED TERROR

EFFIGIES

BY **William K. Wells**

**Holland County was an oasis of peace and beauty . . .
    until beautiful Nicole Bannister got a horrible
package that triggered a nightmare,
    until little Leslie Bannister's invisible playmate
vanished and Elvida took her place,
    until Estelle Dixon's Ouija board spelled out the
message: I AM COMING—SOON.**

A menacing pall settled over the gracious houses and
rank decay took hold of the lush woodlands. Hell had
come to Holland County —to stay.

A Dell Book $2.95 (12245-7)